The Realtor's Attendant

The Caregivers, Volume 7

Rose Fresquez

Published by Rose Fresquez, 2023.

ACKNOWLEDGEMENTS

I want to thank the Lord, my Savior. Without you, Father, there's no point in trying to do anything at all. It's my prayer that I can honor you with my words. I thank you for connecting me with an amazing group of people who helped support me in accomplishing this novel.

To my husband Joel, who works so hard to provide for our family, so that I can stay home and take care of the kids. I'm so blessed that we get to journey through life together.

To my children Isaiah, Caleb, Abigail and Micah, you fill my heart with joy. Thanks for the giggles, laughter and encouragement.

To my editor, Deirdre Lockhart. You're a true blessing from God. Your insights and wisdom have helped shape this story.

And to GOD, Who makes everything possible. Without God's wisdom and creativity, this story wouldn't be in existence.

To my insider team, thanks for always suggesting the coolest ideas.

To my Street Team. Thank you from the bottom of my heart.

CHAPTER 1

Gavin Kress stretched out on a cushioned bamboo lounger on his cottage porch, the sun's afternoon warmth soaking into his skin. The bright rays danced on the shimmering surface of Lake Victoria, a view enhanced by the shelter of lush palm trees and the scent of fragrant plants surrounding him.

The rustling leaves added another relaxing element to nature's ambient music—a peaceful symphony. But despite the surrounding tranquility, the turmoil within unsettled him. Uganda, as beautiful as it was, could only offer a temporary respite from the hurt.

Each time he closed his eyes, flashes from a not-so-distant past returned.

"It's almost February, long enough to forget and start over." He spoke aloud while mentally revisiting that treacherous day. Was it four or five months ago that he'd donned his wedding tux, expecting to embark on a lifetime journey with Lucky?

He could still see her teary eyes and smudged mascara, could still hear the tremor in her voice as she'd confessed. "I can't do this. We're moving too fast."

"Too fast?" Fisting his hands now, he nearly shouted the words, and his voice broke nature's sweet reverie. Even now, his heart mimicked the plunge it had taken that day. After numerous past breakups, they'd been dating steadily for *three* years. How could that be too fast? And they'd spent a year planning their wedding.

Yet his pleas had met indifference. Now, he was thirty-two, alone in a foreign land, grappling with turmoil, and seeking comfort in solitude a world away from home.

"Why didn't I see the signs?" Tension crept into the arms he'd folded behind his neck. Ordinarily, voicing his thoughts prompted clarity and solutions, but retrospect held no power to rewrite history.

The rhythmic lapping of the water, intertwined with the whistling cries of ducks, created a soothing natural chorus. A soft, melodic humming joined the symphony, growing progressively closer until the shuffle of footsteps on the deck interrupted him.

He blinked his eyes open, and his stomach fluttered at the sight before him. There stood his server and housekeeper, holding a tray heavy with something aromatic, her radiant brown skin glowing, a warm contrast to the golden afternoon sunlight.

"Mr. Kress." Hope greeted him, her voice as warm as her smile. "I hope I'm not disturbing you."

He parted his mouth to respond, but found his throat inexplicably dry, particularly when her gaze strayed to his bare chest before darting back to the teetering tray.

"Your lunch..." Her voice wavered, and the tray wobbled, sending the plates and cups tumbling to the deck. She clutched the juice pitcher, the only remains from the tray, and set it on the table by the lounge chair.

Scrambling to his feet, he rushed to her aid at the mess. "Here." He collected the fallen plates. "Let me help you with that."

"No, that's my job." She knelt beside him to retrieve the scattered sandwiches and pastries.

He chuckled to lighten the atmosphere. "You know, it's a good thing this didn't happen on a raft. Otherwise, the guide might be shouting, 'Let's flip the raft back.' "

Confusion scrunched her delicate brows, but his laughter at his own joke coaxed her giggle. She put the collected sandwiches on the plates he held, then took the plates. Her gaze lingered on his bare chest before she looked away and stood.

"I'll be right back." He excused himself and slipped into his cottage. Since she was clearly uncomfortable, he retrieved a T-shirt from his bed and pulled it over his head. When he returned to the deck, Hope was smoothing out the fabric of her black pencil skirt, her white shirt tidily tucked in.

"There, much better," he remarked, gesturing at his clothed torso. "We don't want to violate any shirtless policies here, do we?"

His comment earned him her bashful smile. She had the most guileless brown eyes he'd ever seen.

"I'll get you some more lunch." She folded her arms over her chest and gestured to the tray at the deck step.

It was probably almost three or so. Way past lunchtime, and he'd eaten during his rafting tour of the falls. But one had to admire her diligent efforts to ensure no guest missed a meal. His curiosity piqued. "How did you know I was back?"

"Your cottage..." She gestured toward the linen curtain swaying at the hut's entrance. "It was open when I walked by earlier."

"The juice will be enough for me until dinner." He nodded toward the table where the pitcher brimmed with enough juice for four people. She'd probably squeezed the fruit herself, such was the attention to detail she gave her tasks.

Her voice wafted over him, light as the breeze. "Did you enjoy rafting today?"

The authenticity in her inquiries about his daily escapades was endearing. Plus, she'd remembered the plans he'd mentioned yesterday. Did she give each guest such consideration? "The waves were exhilarating." A rush of laughter surged free, the memory of the tumultuous water still fresh, echoing in his ears. "It was some of the best rafting I've ever done. Have you ever been rafting?"

Her ponytail swung as she shook her head, and her eyes lit. "Does reading about it count?"

His lips curled. "It's not quite the same." He shifted his weight, crossing one foot over the other. It'd be nice to have the support of the deck railing, but that meant standing closer to her.

If he was staying longer, he'd have liked to persuade her to join him for a rafting adventure, purely as friends, of course.

They rarely spoke for more than minutes, but her presence brought a pleasant respite from his lingering heartache. Now, the sunlight shimmered in the dark hair she'd gathered into a high ponytail, and her brown eyes, so overlarge in her pixie face, sparkled with unfeigned warmth.

His jaw clenched as he turned his gaze to the expansive lake, visible beyond the shrubs that enclosed what the resort called the Sunrise Cottage. He had no business noticing her eyes, her lithe form, or anything else about her. Not when he was still grappling with the pain of a broken heart.

"I'm sorry again if..." Her voice wafted into his thoughts.

"Thank you for lunch." He met her eyes, feeling a warmth stir within, at her captivating gaze, before glancing down at the plates on the deck steps. "Everything looks wonderful."

She laughed, exposing her pearly whites and shaking her head. "You're sure you don't need anything else?"

An enthralling sincerity surrounded her, her hands now modestly clasped in front of her skirt. Each movement had a measured grace and attentiveness, but had she taken a moment for her lunch? In all honesty, that should not have been his concern. Still... "When do you ever take a break?"

"When I go to bed."

"Which is around... midnight?" Or perhaps even later.

A nonchalant shrug rolled her shoulders toward her long neck. "I don't require much sleep."

Aside from keeping his cottage pristine, she ensured his mini-fridge was replenished with snacks, sodas, and bottled water. She was always tidying the main room and serving meals at the restaurant where, likely, she acted as the chef as well. Anytime he contacted the front desk past eleven pm, she attended to him, and he suspected she provided the same level of service for the guests staying in the other two cottages.

Leaning against the deck railing, he stood closer to her, close enough to smell the soft scent of vanilla wafting from her hair. He towered about seven inches above the little pixie, but he'd hear her better without competing with the nearby pelicans' squawking.

"What's your job title here?"

"I beg your pardon?" She tipped her head way up to see him, her plush lower lip that looked so fun to nibble finding its way between her teeth while her hands relocated behind her. Was she uncomfortable discussing her role during work hours, or was it something more?

"What responsibilities do you hold here at the resort?"

"Whatever my boss requires me to." A brief shadow dimmed her vibrant eyes before she forced a smile. "Gardening, provided I finish making breakfast early enough..." The more she enumerated her duties, the more apparent it became that the resort would struggle to function without her. "There are only two of us, and the chef is here part-time."

So it must be Hope and the chef since her boss only seemed proficient at delegating tasks. The expansive property boasted three thatched cottages, each built against a private pool, which she had to maintain.

Her long fingers tucked her hair back into her ponytail. Her gaze fixed on him. "What country are you from?"

Apparently, she wasn't in a hurry to leave this time.

"I'm from America." Almost compelled to reveal what led him to take the trip, he directed the conversation back to her. Her English was impeccable, laced with a faint British accent he could listen to indefinitely. "Were you born and raised in Uganda?"

"Uh. No." She folded her arms, her gaze drifting toward the path beneath the shrubbery. "I should get going."

Her reluctance to discuss her background sparked his curiosity. Perhaps he wasn't the only one here looking for an escape.

As she made to leave, he called after her, and she turned, her breath hitching. If she was here for an escape too, she could use time to think rather than working nonstop.

"You should have a word with your boss and ask for a day off sometime."

"I don't need a day off."

"Everyone needs a day off." He winked. "I've taken two weeks to recharge before I venture to a remote village." Although his friends, Brady and Ruth Sharp, had constructed volunteer accommodations, Gavin teased. "This might be the last decent shower I enjoy for a year."

Her brows pinched together before she hid her smile behind her hand. "Should we arrange to deliver jerry cans of water to you?"

Dramatically, he placed a hand over his heart and gave a mock bow. "Now that would be a grand parting gift."

"I'll keep that—"

"Hope!" The abrasive bellow cut her off and prompted them to swivel toward the stone path where a brooding figure loomed. Even the chirping birds launched from the shrubs in alarmed flight. "What's taking you so long?"

Her boss's hand landed on his hip, adding a layer of frustration over his dress pants. His eyes harbored a simmering anger, and his hint of possessiveness scraped at Gavin's calm exterior. "The day is almost gone, and you're out here dallying."

Heat zapped through his chest, and he ground his teeth to resist the urge to confront the man for the disrespectful treatment of his employee, particularly in front of a guest. It wasn't the first time Gavin had heard him yell at Hope.

Swallowing a breath, he reined in his anger to take the blame.

"I apologize…" He scrambled for the man's name, but he couldn't remember. "I kept her—"

"See you later." Hope shot Gavin a cautionary glance that urged him not to take up her cause. "Sorry about that."

The warmth of her previous demeanor evaporated, replaced by a resolute determination in her jawline as she navigated her way down the stairs, snatched the food plates, and held them firmly.

"You are not to converse with guests!" the man thundered, veins pulsating in his temples as Hope drew near. "How many times must I repeat the rules?"

The venom in his tone, particularly as he spat out a sequence of words in a different language, was palpable. Gavin's heart lurched, and his fists clenched as if to hold back the desire to intervene, to reprimand the man, or even to rough him up slightly. However, given the man's volatile temper, Hope might be better equipped to deal with it by maintaining her silence.

Gavin kept his attention on the man to ensure he didn't physically harm Hope, who seemed well acquainted with his outbursts as she strode past her boss, her chin lifted and shoulders squared. The spritely pixie's elegant poise remained undeterred. No wonder her boss's frustration only escalated as she didn't indulge him in his fit or gratify him with attention.

Perhaps she'd be just fine. As delicate as she appeared, she also seemed capable of withstanding any challenge thrown her way.

Gavin offered a silent nod of approval, a smile lifting his lips as she disappeared down the gravel trail to the main stone pathway, her boss tailing her in a much-subdued state. How strange. She was the cornerstone of the place, yet her boss treated her with stark disrespect. She deserved far better. Drawing out a breath, Gavin redirected his gaze to the serene expanse of Lake Victoria, the source of the Nile, as he contemplated the unusual bond he'd stumbled upon.

He had been acquainted with his attendant for almost two weeks. Yet, besides the sporadic group tours he'd embarked on with strangers to revel in various water sports, Hope had been the solitary figure who inquired about his day and ensured he was fed and his laundry clean. So far, she was the only semblance of friendship he'd encountered.

Something within him shifted, a primal urge to safeguard her despite her apparent self-sufficiency. He'd devote his remaining two days here to monitoring Hope and her boss from afar. He couldn't leave without ensuring she wasn't at the receiving end of any physical harm from a man who'd proven to be a verbal tormentor and outright bully.

As Gavin took his seat, he stared at the juice. He didn't feel like going back inside to fetch a glass, and he had no appetite while Hope was back to working as hard as a construction laborer. Dinner was less than two hours away, and Hope would be attending to him in the dining area. At that, an unexpected sense of anticipation stirred.

He had no business entertaining thoughts about her considering he was leaving in less than three days. He'd have to relegate these fleeting moments to the back of his mind as he plunged into his work with the House of Blessing Hospital. Gavin wasn't a doctor, but Brady assured him they had plenty of work for him to do. As much as Hope intrigued Gavin with her quiet resilience and diligent work ethic, she seemed to harbor her own set of complexities. He was here to mend his wounded heart, not to embark on another romantic endeavor that might lead him back to heartbreak's doorstep.

CHAPTER 2

Hope Njeri hovered over the dining table, the vase in the center seizing her attention. Fallen orange lantana flowers, once part of the morning's bouquet, were scattered like droplets on the white fabric. She usually delighted in these moments of gentle adjustments, setting each petal and leaf with utmost precision. Today, however, her spirit was not in tune with her task.

A storm brewed within her. Gratitude churned against discontent as she set the silverware already tucked into the black serviettes. Getting the task done earlier had helped. Otherwise, in her current state, she might have compromised her meticulousness, a thing she loathed.

A chill ran down her spine under the icy stare of her boss, Lumbe, from the front desk. His gaze reminded her that leaving this place wasn't an option. With him as an imposing gatekeeper, forming meaningful connections in this foreign land had become impossible, and isolation had become her uninvited companion.

A suffocating pressure, a combination of her past and her present, pushed against her from all sides. She scooped up the silverware from the woven basket, her fingers brushing against the folded serviette. The meticulously arranged cutlery seemed symbolic of her elusive dreams—dreams of acceptance, belonging, and self-worth.

Her hopes of finding solace by breaking free from her home had been replaced by Lumbe's authoritarian regime. His attitude rang like an unnerving echo of the disapproval and feelings of worthlessness her father and stepmother had instilled in her. She couldn't help but wonder: Was seeking to appease others just like chasing a mirage?

The gnawing question of "home" dug roots deeper into her thoughts. What was home? Where was it? With the answers as elusive as the evening mist, she moved to another table, shifted the vase, and made room for silverware meant for two. The elderly woman residing in the Shore Cottage might invite a companion from her usual explorations.

Her hands moved, executing their task despite her distracted mind. The concept of home, the definition she'd been trying to grasp, was a mystery, a riddle she couldn't solve, an echo bouncing back unanswered.

In the three months she'd worked at the resort, Lumbe made it clear she wasn't welcome to be herself. The afternoon light shone through the window as she set the six tables, even though there were only three cottages, all occupied—one by a family of three, another by Gavin, and the last by the seventy-year-old woman. If no one came for supper, she'd deliver food to their cottages an hour after supper.

She finished setting the tables and rearranged the chairs, their scraping against the bamboo floor clashing with the tribal music murmuring in the background. Normally, she would hum along, but today, even the music was annoying.

Lumbe's scoldings were nothing new, but today's embarrassment stung differently because of Gavin and her unexpected attraction to him. Him witnessing her humiliation, especially after she'd dropped his lunch while distracted by his shirtless appearance, intensified her shame. He'd been kind, though, brushing it off and even defending her. But he was leaving in two days, and she'd be alone again, as always.

After setting the tables, she moved back to the bar counter and put the spare silverware in a basket on a shelf.

"Hope!" Lumbe's voice cut through the music. Ignoring him, she reached for her black apron hung on a hook between two shelves hosting liquor bottles.

"Hope." He called more forcefully this time. "I didn't get your tip this morning."

"Did you check your desk?" she responded, not looking at him as she tied her apron. She liked to leave her tips amid the clutter on his desk, forcing him to look for it. Lumbe had several reasons to despise her, but one stood out. The one she didn't want to think about.

"Hope!" he called again.

She ignored him, pushed through the door behind the counter, and entered the kitchen. Strangely, while she so desperately needed this job, she remained defiant. But how long could she remain silent?

She'd seen greed ruin people, including her father and stepmother. If it weren't for their greed, she wouldn't have had to leave her home country in search of a new beginning.

"Hello there, Hope." Jendu greeted, standing by the sink across from the stove. "How are you on this lovely day?"

Forcing a smile, she tried to keep her tone steady. "I'm wonderful. How about you?"

"Never been better." His square chef hat added a few inches to his height, and his dark skin gleamed under the fluorescent kitchen lights.

Grateful for the three hours she shared with him most days, she appreciated the friendly chatter. With a slow stride, she headed toward the stove, the tantalizing aroma of beef and chicken stew igniting her hunger. Her last meal, a boiled egg hastily eaten during her morning housekeeping round, felt like a distant memory.

"The chapatis turned out good today, don't you think?" He lifted one of the flatbreads from the platter, the golden-brown hue attesting to its perfection.

"Hmm, it's going to be delicious." She eyed the stew bubbling under the clear lid. Saliva gathered in her mouth. She'd best grab a bite before starting the dinner service. "Do you mind if I have a chapati and some stew?"

"Why do you think I was showing you the chapati?" Jendu teased her. "I heard your stomach rumbling like a drum."

She touched her stomach and laughed. Her gaze drifted toward the charcoal stoves lining the brick wall. They were their backup for cooking during the frequent, unannounced blackouts. "It doesn't look like we'll need the charcoal stoves today."

"That's why I worked so fast before the power changed its mind."

The excessive heat the stoves generated was unbearable in an already warm kitchen.

Jendu had placed two chapatis on a blue plate, which he extended to her. "Whenever you're in this kitchen, you can eat anything, my child." His words reminded her of a father's affection, a gesture far too uncommon in her life, but precious nonetheless.

"You're so nice, Jendu." Holding the plate closer, she breathed in the aroma of freshly made chapatis, then tore a piece to savor its warmth and taste. As she chewed, the sizzle of sautéing onions and garlic drifted through the kitchen, the aroma mingling with the fragrance of the chapati in her hands.

"What stew are you making?" she asked after finishing a bite.

"It's the stir-fry for the rice pilaf." He lifted the lid off a larger saucepan, letting a puff of steam escape. "Bring your plate over. Let's add some stew to those chapatis."

When she approached, he ladled a generous spoonful of beef stew onto it, the Irish potatoes within it cooked to perfection.

"Finish that and then try some chicken and matooke." He pointed toward a covered pot in the corner, and his eyes sparkled. "So, what do you think of the stew?"

After blowing on a spoonful of beef and potato to cool it down, she tasted it, the meat tender and the potato soft in her mouth. "It's delicious!" The savory stew, tangy with a hint of spice, boasted a perfect balance of flavors. "The guests are in for a special treat at supper."

"Thank you." He resumed his work at the stove. "Let's finish up here so we can get the buffet ready before any blackouts."

As she ate and he worked, she asked about his family. His narration about juggling multiple jobs to afford a good education for his children painted the picture of a loving and dedicated father, reminding her of the father she'd wished for.

With her meal finished, she set to work preparing a dessert of mangoes and pineapples. She also cut up collard greens and helped with his tasks. Their combined efforts filled the kitchen with a warm, inviting atmosphere, the glow of the overhead lights and the soft breeze from the open windows creating a comforting ambiance. This brief escape was her solace, a rare moment of calm in a stormy life.

In the next hours, they began arranging the buffet tables near the bar area. She was feeling rejuvenated enough to craft decorative flowers out of the serviettes, placing them as centerpieces amid the stews. She scattered chopped carrots and green onions among serving dishes filled with vegetables, rice, plantains, and sweet potatoes. A pile of fresh chapatis was tucked under a clear lid, preserving their moisture and warmth. The gentle clinking of serving spoons against ceramic dishes, coupled with her humming, brewed a symphony of anticipation for the evening meal.

Despite the adversities she faced beyond the resort's confines, she couldn't suppress a tiny flame of optimism now flickering within her, particularly as the buffet started to take shape. However, only two of their five guests, the father and his son, showed up for dinner.

She busied herself by reorganizing the stack of plates, but her gaze was drawn to the glass back door for a glimpse of Gavin. "Well." She sighed, stirring in the peanut sauce to distract herself from longing for a man who was soon to leave. Her wandering gaze found its way back to the glass door just as he emerged from behind a vibrant bougainvillea shrub. The setting sun highlighted his tanned skin and accentuated his lean muscles clothed in a pair of red shorts and a black T-shirt. His hair, still glistening and tousled, gave the impression of a recent shower.

As he slid open the door, his gaze found hers, her stomach fluttered oddly, and something jolted through her. The spoon splattered peanut sauce when it fell from her grasp and jolted her back to reality. She bent to retrieve it as he reached the table.

"Good evening, Hope." The vibrations in his deep voice set her nerves on edge.

"Uh, h—hello," she stammered, rising and holding up the spoon. "I'm sorry about this."

He glanced at the buffet, his gaze fixing on the serving spoons laid out. A grin tugged up one side of his mouth. "Seems like we're in no danger of a spoon shortage."

His lighthearted remark cut through her tension, a reminder that not everyone was as harsh as Lumbe. She wiped the floor clean with some serviettes, then, excusing herself, took the spoiled spoon to the kitchen and returned with a clean one while he surveyed the food.

He spread his hands toward it, the clear blue of his eyes captivating. "What do you recommend?"

Mustering her composure, she recommended the chapati and beef stew she'd savored earlier. "It's light and delicious."

His eyebrow rose. "And you've tasted all of it?"

Under his searching gaze, she felt as if he could see straight through her. A shiver ran down her spine. "I had some."

He rubbed his hands together. "Chapati and beef stew it is."

She filled a plate for him. "You should try some pilaf. Jendu makes really good pilaf."

"I'll take a small portion in that case."

She added a modest scoop. Amid the enticing food aromas, she could smell his fancy conditioner and intoxicating fragrance.

Their fingers brushed as she handed him his plate, sending an electric shock through her body. Gavin seemed to feel the spark too, holding her gaze, his brows arched in silent inquiry before he took his food and moved away. He grabbed an orange soda from the cooler and settled at one of the empty tables.

She hadn't needed to serve him. The previous guests had served themselves from the buffet, but in his presence, she lost her usual knack for thinking clearly.

Two more guests came in, the older lady and a friend, chattering about their day. With the restaurant's calm atmosphere, Hope found herself drifting into a strange silence as if she were underwater. Sounds muffled, all focus narrowed to a single point—Gavin. She moved around, clearing dirty plates from the other table and refilling anything running low. But she'd become a robot as she executed each task.

Even as she planned to keep her distance, her gaze had a will of its own. It flitted toward Gavin, sneaking peeks. The confident way he carried himself, the firm set of his jaw, the deliberate chew of his food, and the way he sipped his drink—each gesture left a distinct imprint.

She was midway through cleaning the serving table when he strolled back, an empty plate and soda bottle in hand. Her heart skipped a beat. She moved around to him. "I'll take that."

"I've got it," he responded, his voice gentle. "Dinner was delicious."

She opened her mouth, but the words were lost as he moved to the cart with the dirty plates and placed his plate and empty bottle in the designated basins. She couldn't help but imagine Lumbe watching them, ready to criticize her for not doing her job.

Yet, Gavin didn't seem to mind doing things on his own, a gesture contrary to what she'd experienced so far. The men she'd observed rarely lifted a finger when they could have others do their work.

"Good night, Hope." His voice hung low in the air, tinged with an emotion she couldn't place. It was electrifying and unnerving all at once.

"Sleep well." She rubbed the shivers rising on her arms. Was that an appropriate response?

As the night wore on and she set up the dining room for the morning's breakfast service, her mind kept replaying Gavin's arrival at the resort almost two weeks ago. The magnetic pull she'd sensed around him hadn't faded. If anything, it had intensified. A part of her yearned for him to extend his holiday, yet such a wish came with potential repercussions. If he were unattached and feelings did blossom between them, could she handle an additional layer of complexity added to her already intricate life?

She tried to avoid such risks. Yet, later as she lay in bed past midnight, his charismatic presence invaded her mind. She closed the Book of Wisdom, the comforting words of the Proverbs unable to hold her attention. Turning to her Bantu dictionary, she sought to distract herself by looking up the unfamiliar words from Lumbe's harsh tirade earlier in the day. But even then, she couldn't escape the memory of Gavin's voice, his protective demeanor as he'd attempted to come to her aid. The echo of his words wrapped around her like a warm, secure blanket. *"I'm sorry I kept her...."*

How could someone like him be single? Good men, especially those available, always managed to slip past her. Yet, here she was, on a silent night, grappling with feelings very deep and confusing. Her heart seemed to be in turmoil, fluttering in a dance of apprehension and anticipation at the same time.

CHAPTER 3

Walking down the stone pathway, Gavin tried to breathe deeply against the heaviness in his chest. Unable to dislodge the foreign pressure, he approached the main building.

As the first slivers of sunlight began to creep over the horizon, the sky transformed into a captivating canvas of warm hues. Splashes of pink, orange, and gold gradually bathed the landscape, providing a stunning backdrop to his morning walk.

While the same sunrises and sunsets would surely grace the village he was headed to next, Hope's absence would taint their beauty. This impending separation led him to the breakfast setup ten minutes early—a first for him since he'd arrived at the resort. Today, a yearning to see her one more time turned his habitual tardiness for meals into punctuality.

As he slid open the main building's door, Lumbe's harsh voice soured Gavin's already melancholic mood. The man was standing by the kitchen entrance, and Hope must be on the receiving end of the chastising.

"How can you burn the porridge? You've been so distracted lately." Lumbe waved his thick finger toward where Hope likely stood. "You make too many mistakes."

"I was putting away the eggs." Her voice wafted out from the kitchen, her words stumbling over each other in her rush to apologize. "I'm so sorry. I'll get the mandazi out. Then I can make the porridge again."

Her distressed voice stirred a protective instinct, making Gavin clench his fists although he managed to keep his hand at his sides. He could've avoided the escalating conflict, occupying himself with the tropical fruit laid out on the breakfast table or stepping out to return later. But he chose to stay and observe how long Lumbe would continue his tirade.

"Making a new batch won't solve the problem of time! I hope you know we've lost power."

"I've already started the charcoal stove."

Early morning light streamed into the restaurant, flooding the space with a warm natural glow, so Gavin hadn't known they lost power.

Lumbe launched into a flurry of insults including phrases in a language Gavin couldn't decipher. "What am I going to tell the guests when they show up for breakfast?"

Gavin had heard enough. He strode forward. "You'd better hope they don't show up now."

Taken aback, Lumbe spun around, his eyes narrowing.

"This isn't a scene you want your guests witnessing." Gavin moved closer, positioning himself by the bar register to look Lumbe in the eye.

"This is between me and my employee," Lumbe retorted, his lips pursed.

"Not if you're screaming for everyone on the property to hear." Gavin crossed his arms. "As long as I'm a guest here, the way you treat your staff is my business."

His gaze shifted to Hope, who was shuffling pans around, distress pinching her delicate lips tight. He wanted to reassure her Lumbe wasn't going to bully her anymore. Instead, he held Lumbe's attention.

"You call Hope incompetent. Yet, she's the one making breakfast, serving guests on time, delivering meals to those who don't dine in, cleaning the rooms, doing everyone's laundry, and tending the gardens, grounds, and pools." He couldn't even list the myriad tasks she accomplished. "Did it occur to you that she does too many jobs at the same time?"

"You don't know what you're talking about." Lumbe shook his head.

Oh yes, he did. Gavin stiffened. He managed properties himself. "Without her here, you wouldn't know how to run this place."

Lumbe waved a hand, gesturing to the room as if he didn't see her intricate touches everywhere. "The place was fine before Hope showed up."

Emerging from the kitchen, Hope balanced a basket of golden doughnutlike pastries. Her gaze met Gavin's, her large eyes shimmering with a medley of emotions—notably fear.

Lumbe's smirk followed her as she set the pastries next to the fruit. "You know what, Hope? You're fired! Pack your things and leave."

Her expression hardened, disbelief flaring the edges of her eyes even as her chin lifted in indignation. "You can't fire me."

"Oh, but I just did." Lumbe chortled. "You don't think I know you give me only half of your tips?"

Her eyes sparked, a challenging glare replacing her usual calm gaze. "Are you joking with me?" Tears welled. "I could keep some tips for myself, but I give you everything. The last thing I need is to be controlled by greed. Your crookedness doesn't mean everyone else is the same."

She squared her shoulders and braced a hand on her hip, drawing out a breath. "You're going to regret firing me."

His confidence seemed unshaken. Lumbe waved toward the door. "With a written apology, maybe, I'll consider rehiring you."

How dare he act so assured Hope would be compelled to apologize? Gavin would employ her in a heartbeat to stage or decorate his investment and rental properties if given the chance.

"An apology is something you don't deserve from me." Drawing herself up to her full height, petite though she was, she stepped closer and pointed a finger at him. "I quit, and you can keep your corrupt money."

Yes! Gavin held back a fist pump. The brave pixie finally stood up to Lumbe.

As she turned to leave, Lumbe muttered something in the foreign language again. Hope, however, stopped and spun around with a sardonic laugh. "Just because I don't speak your language doesn't mean I don't own a dictionary. I know all the inappropriate names you've been calling me since I arrived here." She didn't spare Gavin a glance as she marched out through the back door.

Torn between staying to confront Lumbe and following her, Gavin chose the latter and sprinted to catch up.

The morning was just beginning to stir, the air still cool, filled with nature's symphony. The chirping birds created an intoxicating melody, a stark contrast to his rapidly thumping heartbeat. He chased after her, his breath getting caught in the misty air.

"Hope, wait." He ducked under a low-hanging bougainvillea, its dewy petals brushing against him. "Hope!"

"Please leave me alone." She didn't stop, didn't look back, just untucked her blouse from her skirt, an act of rebellion and liberation.

Quickening his pace, he caught up and grabbed her hand.

She stopped and pivoted to face him. Her eyes were glistening, and his chest constricted at the pain radiating from her. "You're better off without that man."

"You think I don't know that?" Pulling free, she wrapped her arms around herself. "But I can't afford to be choosy."

"He doesn't deserve an apology." He widened his stance, blocking the path as if she might change her mind. "You shouldn't be mistreated."

"And who are you to decide that?" Her shoulders slumped, and her shaky finger rose to rub her forehead. When she spoke next with her face tipped down, he had to bend close to hear the low-spoken words. "He was my boss. He's entitled to make demands."

"Listen, Hope..." Gavin thrust his hands into the pockets of his khaki shorts to keep from reaching for her. "You can find a better job. You deserve a better life."

"I've been telling myself the same thing for a long time." A wisp of a sigh slid loose before she resumed her stride.

He followed, his heart heavy as she yanked the rest of her blouse from her skirt. Easily, he envisioned her in a new place, with a new beginning. He'd help, but how? "Where are you going now?"

She gave a hollow laugh. "I didn't wake up this morning with a plan to lose my job." She pointed toward a wooden gate at the end of the path. "I'll go back to bed and figure out my next steps."

"Come with me to the village." His next words surprised him as much as they did her. He never made impulsive decisions.

A flicker of consideration crossed her face. She looked at the lake, its surface mirroring the lush greenery and towering trees. "And what would you tell your friends? That you're bringing a stranger along?"

"I'll be a stranger too." Raking a hand through his hair, he shared the details about Brady and Ruth's charity and House of Blessing Hospital and Ministry. "They're only going to be there for less than a month, but the organization welcomes volunteers throughout the year."

She sighed, her gaze dropping to the ground. "With my luck, it's best I don't come along. Otherwise, as soon as your friends see me, they'll end up hating you on my account."

"As long as you don't hate me and I don't hate you, then we'll have each other." Did that even make sense? Somehow, the words resonated with him, but would they with her? She bit her teeth into the side of her lower lip. She'd need more convincing, and he had no idea why he was trying so hard.

He flexed his hands in his pockets and rocked back on his heels. And something metal jiggled against his fingers. Laughing, he retrieved the silver quarter he carried in his pocket. Dad had always used this to solve an argument between Gavin and his brother.

"How about we flip a coin?"

"Uh, what?" She blinked as she peered at the coin. "What is that?"

He explained how the coin flip worked, then asked, "Heads or tails."

"Tail?" One delicate brow rose as the word wobbled out on a question.

But before she could say anything else, he stepped back and flipped the coin in the air. It twirled, catching the morning light, before it clattered on the stone path.

He ushered her down, and they squatted across from each other.

"Yes!" He let that fist pump fly free now, forgetting this wasn't a race to the top of the mountain. "It means you get to come to the village."

Hope was silent as she stood. Her face unreadable, she drew in a deep breath and released it slowly. "I shouldn't ruin things for you. You deserve better." She turned around, her last words hanging in the air before she waved over her shoulder. "It was nice knowing you."

How was she going to ruin things for him? He wanted to ask, but it seemed she didn't want anything to do with him.

Instead of convincing her she was a breath of fresh air, he picked up his quarter, dropped it back into his pocket, and slid his hand in after it. He stood there, jiggling it as his heartbeat jittered in rhythm. How many men like Lumbe had caused her to lose her confidence—her hope?

Hope walked away, shoulders drooping, but something sparked within him. His strides back toward the main house were quick and determined, scattering the critters lazing in his path.

Lumbe, acting as if nothing had happened, was setting the breakfast table. His obliviousness to the havoc he'd just wreaked was jarring. Gavin marched straight up to him.

"You're hoping for an apology letter, aren't you?"

Startled, Lumbe jerked upright. His wide eyes met Gavin's.

Gavin planted his hands on his hips, leaning into the man's personal space. "You steal her tips, and I'm sure you don't pay her enough. Is this how you trap your employees, make them feel like they can't leave?"

Lumbe ducked his head under Gavin's glare.

"If you care about your business," Gavin continued, his voice a low growl as he wagged a finger, "you'll pay Hope what you owe her." He hadn't been keeping tabs on the tips he'd given her, but he'd been generous. "And you owe her the pay for this month as well."

"I don't have all the money until—"

"Unless you want your business to be shunned," Gavin cut him off, "I'd make it a priority. I've seen the way you treat Hope. I assure you, other guests have too. I won't hesitate to spread news about your business on all the international travel sites." Gavin had no time to squander on the man, but he had to say something to make him quiver. "No one will want to support such a business."

"I'll get her the money," Lumbe grumbled, clattering the plate he held onto the table.

"I'm checking out in two hours. I want this sorted out by then," Gavin demanded, tempted to punch Lumbe, but he kept his arms folded. "And I expect a written apology to Hope as well."

Lumbe's nostrils flared.

Gavin left him there and headed back to his cottage. The woven shoulder bag he'd bought for Hope lay on the bed. He'd bought it from a persistent street vendor yesterday, intending to leave it with a tip for Hope. Now he clenched his fist, thinking of all the time Lumbe had been pocketing her money.

Everyone Gavin met in Uganda had been welcoming, except for Lumbe. Behind his professional façade, the man treated Hope with disdain. Was it only her he mistreated? If so, why?

Gazing at the heart-shaped flowers and folded napkins on the small table, Gavin admired her creativity. Even the soap by his sink was artfully sculpted.

His fingers traced the shoulder bag's woven fabric. He'd leave it at her door. But he couldn't leave without saying goodbye, so he'd have to work out a farewell strategy.

"It was nice knowing you," he repeated her words and shook his head. Maybe it was for the best that he didn't talk to her again. He scratched the stubble on his jaw, his gaze drifting through the window where a crested crane tested the edge of the water.

He'd never forgive himself if he left without making sure her boss had given her the money he owed her. If she didn't have money, how would she start anywhere? He could give her the money, of course, but he doubted she'd take well to a handout.

"I could confront Lumbe again on my way out and ask if he's given Hope her money." But Lumbe could lie and not follow through. Ugh. All the alternatives led to Gavin having to see her one more time.

But before that, there were calls to make. To Brady to let him know he was bringing company. Then to his brother, his manager, and Eric to update them on the limited phone service in the village. Perhaps he'd also have a quick swim before the driver arrived. He had a schedule to keep.

Even if Gavin wanted to believe he'd come to anyone's defense if they were in Hope's situation, he couldn't deny his growing fondness. He was starting to care for her too much—and it terrified him.

Keeping his distance was a necessity. He'd come here to heal from being jilted at the altar, not to fall in love.

And Hope? She had her own battles. She was probably the kind to walk away from him without looking back. Like she had today.

But as he emerged from the pool, there she was. His heart whooshed, and his stomach fluttered. Gone was her uniform, replaced by a pink floral dress that fit her lithe form in all the right places. He blinked and wiped water from his face. Surely, it was all his imagination. He'd been thinking about her too much, and now his mind was playing tricks on him.

But if she had come to join him on his trip, what would the year ahead hold?

CHAPTER 4

Hope's steps traced an uncertain path along the walkway, her flats whispering against the stones. Her grip tightened around her blue duffle bag, a bag containing all her worldly possessions—four changes of clothing, work shoes, and four books, two of them dictionaries. With the various Bantu languages, she'd felt an urgent need to grasp a few phrases and not feel utterly lost amid foreign tongues.

When Lumbe had appeared unannounced at her door half an hour ago, newfound possibilities had cracked open her future. The money he handed over had given her choices.

She could now venture out to find another job—and risk winding up with another boss as harsh as Lumbe.

Or she could take the other path—the one illuminated by Gavin's offer.

When he'd told her about his destination a few days ago, she'd looked up House of Blessing Hospital on Lumbe's computer while delivering money to his office. The couple, Brady and Ruth Sharp, seemed to do more than provide medical aid. They extended their hearts and hands to the community. This tantalizing opportunity beckoned now with the promise of a fresh start, a chance to make decisions rooted in her wants and needs, and the possibility to extend her hand to those who needed help.

Perhaps, through this House of Blessing Hospital, she could lay claim to a new beginning.

As she approached Gavin's hut, she lifted one foot in front of the other in a slow march against uncertainty. Each footfall seemed to echo her doubts louder. What if he'd already left?

Panic injected a newfound urgency into her steps, propelling her up the stairs to the deck. There, she let out a slow breath as Gavin emerged from the pool, the surrounding deck serving as a stage for his ascent. With him dressed only in swim shorts, his shirtless torso revealed a lean, muscular form marked by lines of physical strength. Water droplets clung to his skin, glistening in the midmorning light, while wet hair plastered itself to his face. He looked like a character straight from the pages of one of the romance novels she'd read, exuding an allure that was hard to ignore.

And he was very much a hero. How he jumped to her defense was etched deeply in her mind, and his fierce protectiveness stirred unfamiliar emotions. She'd been both moved by his gallantry and gripped by fear of the fallout once Gavin left the resort. While losing her job was not in her plan, relief flooded her once she was free from Lumbe. No one had ever stood up for her as fearlessly as Gavin had done.

"Hope." His voice rippled through her thoughts, sending her pulse fluttering. She endeavored to contain the bloom of excitement. His smile was wide and welcoming, yet his slightly raised eyebrows hinted at unspoken questions. He reached for the towel draped over a lounge chair, ruffling his damp, wavy brown hair while maintaining his intense gaze on her.

His physique was a testament to a man who scaled mountains to keep fit. "You're here."

At the touch of surprise in his voice, she responded with a silent nod and clutched her bag tighter. Heat flushed her neck. She had been caught staring—again. On impulse, she turned her back to him, giving him privacy to get dressed, but her loosening grip caused her duffle bag to slide from her hand and thud on the wooden deck.

"Glad to see you here." Gavin spoke again, his tone a warm rumble. "Did you change your mind about going to the village?"

Her throat dry, she managed to whisper. "Uh-huh."

"You can turn around now. I have a towel around me." His voice, closer than before, left her with little choice but to face him.

With a hesitant spin, she found herself locking eyes with him, and her thoughts tumbled out. "I have no reason to trust you or for you to trust me, but you're the one person I can sort of trust right now." No, not sort of. Fully trust. After the kindness he'd shown her, he was her first friend since she arrived in Uganda. "If the offer still stands, I'd like to go and help."

A smile crinkled up his eyes, and the short stubble of his beard rippled with the movement. "I'm glad to hear that." He snugged the towel tighter around his shoulders. "I think you'll find the House of—"

"Blessing," she interjected. "I looked it up."

Mischief danced in his eyes as he lifted his eyebrow. "Did you now?"

At her nod, he continued. "The people there will be more compassionate and supportive."

After her experience with Lumbe, no doubt she could weather any other person.

"And thank you so much, Mr. Kress," she intoned, bowing her head and partially kneeling, a customary gesture she rarely used, reserved for those she truly respected. As his brow scrunched, she clarified. "My boss wrote me an apology."

Although it was a brief two-word note and Lumbe likely didn't mean it, she appreciated whatever Gavin had said to prompt such a response. She gestured toward her duffle bag on the deck. "He also gave me some money and said you threatened to shut his place down."

After lifting his hands in mock surrender, Gavin waved. "I didn't say anything of the sort."

Lumbe's harsh words when he shook the envelope at her echoed in her ears—*"Your white friend better not run this resort out of business."*

Gavin found her worth defending. Warmth surged through her chest.

"You deserved your pay." He touched her hand, turning it to show the calluses on her palm and fingers. "You work hard."

Not sure why the evidence of her work embarrassed her, she slid her hand free and tucked it behind her. "What time do we leave? I can come back later when you're ready."

"I'm not sure what time it is now, but I doubt you fancy hanging around your former boss."

What an understatement. She'd avoid Lumbe as much as possible.

Gavin pointed to a lounge chair. "If you don't mind waiting here for a few minutes, I'll check the time on my phone and let you know."

With a nod, she settled herself on the chair as he disappeared inside his hut.

Why were the kind and respectful men she encountered so often unavailable? Was Gavin available? She never noticed a ring on his finger, but it didn't mean he was single.

She'd always yearned to find someone who loved her as much as she loved them. However, she'd encountered so many disappointments from those who left her for other women to those who couldn't stand up to their parents' chosen brides, leading to a broken heart each time.

Gavin, now wearing a casual gray T-shirt and dark shorts, emerged from the hut. He gestured with a tray bearing different types of soda, bags of crisps, and a package of biscuits. "I wasn't sure which soda you'd prefer, so I brought what you stocked up for me."

Hope took a deep breath, working to steady her rapid heartbeat. She glanced toward the sparkling pool and then across the green landscape at palm trees and shrubs surrounding the secluded cottage. Not another soul was in sight. So she braved asking, "Is this for me?"

"Of course."

"I should be serving you." The principle was embedded in her from her village upbringing—women were supposed to serve men, not the other way round.

"Are you okay?" His brow creased as he set the tray on the table.

"Thank you, Mr. Kress." What more could she say after the unusual kindness he'd shown? He was unlike any man she'd met.

"You can call me Gavin." He winked. "You no longer work for the resort, and I don't need to be treated as a patron."

She managed to mumble an okay, still taken aback. Was this all a dream, or was this man genuine?

"Our driver will arrive at ten thirty. He's running a bit late. Once I'm ready, we can wait for him in front of the building."

"What do you think they'll have me do when we get to the village?" From her research, it appeared their needs were medical, but she might be able to help in other ways like cooking.

Gavin shrugged. "I'm not a doctor, either."

"You're not?" Surprised, she placed her hands on her lap. She'd never asked what he did for a living.

"I'm a Realtor."

"What does a Realtor do?"

"I help people sell and buy homes, business buildings, and anything of that sort." His smile broadened as he described restoring dilapidated homes. The morning sunshine made his hair shimmer, and she had to resist the urge to reach out and touch it. She shifted her position, trying to refocus and listen without distraction. He clearly had a passion for revitalizing things. "Occasionally, I invest in some of the buildings."

So, he was not just a business owner but also a savvy one who made strategic investments. "That sounds like an exciting job."

"I enjoy it. Like anything else, it has its highs and lows, though."

"How will your business run smoothly with you being away for a long time?"

"I have managers I trust to keep things running." He then gave a summary of the flexibility of his work. However, not seeming to want to veer too far off track, he redirected their conversation to the House of Blessing Hospital, sharing all the information he knew about it.

As he described the humble village they were heading to, her initial fear and uncertainty receded, replaced by a growing sense of hope and eagerness.

"I'll go and get ready." He winked before disappearing into the hut, leaving her with an unexpected flurry of butterflies in her stomach.

Reaching for the ginger-flavored Stoney soda, she popped open the cap. The fizzing sound was comforting, and she took a sip, savoring the refreshing tanginess.

The simple and slow-paced village life was what she desired. In her home village, she'd been the linchpin of her household, the one everyone depended on. But, in this new place with strangers, what would be expected of her?

After three tough months at the resort, she doubted anything could be more challenging.

Resolution welled up within her, similar to the feeling she experienced when she left Kenya for Uganda. No matter how things turned out, she'd be ready to face it—and deeply grateful for Gavin's kind support.

CHAPTER 5

As Gavin stood next to Hope at the entrance waiting for Dongo, he remained silent, absorbing the pull of attraction between them. It was a perfect day, temperature-wise, yet the humidity draped around him like a heavy blanket.

Hope stooped and plucked a crimson bloom from the floral carpet at their feet. "I almost forgot."

"Forgot what?"

"Smell this." She brandished the flower before him.

Bending toward the vibrant bloom, he drew in a slow, deep breath and let the gentle, sweet fragrance fill his senses. "It's refreshing."

As she stood poised to speak, her lips parted in a delicate, unsaid promise. But instead, she brought the flower to her nose, her chest rising as she took in its aroma. "I'll keep this oleander for you. In case you want to remember your time at the resort."

The only keepsake he'd want from the resort would be her.

A jolt of awareness had him avert his gaze. Through his peripheral vision, he watched her retrieve a book from her duffle bag and press the flower between its pages. Needing a distraction, he dug his phone from his shorts pocket and checked the time for the third time that morning. "He's ten minutes late," he muttered, his tone sharper than he intended.

"Ever heard of African time?" She tucked her duffle bag on the flat stone lining the flower bed.

The phrase stirred a memory, Brady's cautionary note about Dongo's tardy nature in an email. "What does that mean, exactly?"

Her warm brown eyes, alight with innocent curiosity, met his. A breeze rustled through her free-flowing dark hair, releasing a hint of vanilla that had him inhaling deeply. In her floral dress scattered with soft pink blossoms, she seemed at ease—a stark contrast to the diligent resort attendant he had known over the past two weeks.

"In Africa, we often move at a slower pace." She chuckled. "Except when I worked here, of course. But now, without any immediate obligations, there's no urgency to be anywhere."

"Interesting." Come to think of it, for the first time since his arrival in Uganda he wasn't in as much of a hurry as he thought. His daily roster of water sports had kept him on a tight schedule, but today, for the first time, he was free of any immediate commitments. Maybe, just maybe, he wasn't in such a rush to reach the village.

An insistent grumble from his stomach reminded him he hadn't eaten anything yet. "Once Dongo arrives, could we stop for breakfast?"

Hope's face scrunched. "You gave me food, but you didn't eat?"

"That wasn't much of a breakfast." However, a soda and a handful of what Hope referred to as "biscuits" would have been better than nothing. "I was hoping you'd join me for a proper meal."

She patted her slender waist. "I'm not hungry anymore."

Was she being considerate, or was she not hungry after the soda and half bag of chips? He then inquired if she had any other stops in mind before they reached the village. "I was told the village shop doesn't have many supplies."

"I–I don't need to inconvenience you with extra stops."

"I don't mind. You reminded me we're not in a hurry in Africa, right?"

Her smile bloomed. Then a shy nod dipped her pointy chin.

"Just tell me where you want to stop, and I'll be right there with you."

Her eyes, questioning and uncertain, met his. "Are you sure you won't mind?"

"Absolutely."

She seemed unaccustomed to having her decisions valued, which brought to mind her earlier surprise when he had offered her a drink, so he added, "I need to stock up on a few things, anyway."

Hope glanced at her worn, brown flats. "I'll need more appropriate shoes for the village." She brushed away an intrusive bee hovering near her face. "And a few other essentials."

She must be referring to toiletries.

Then he remembered the souvenir. Presenting it now seemed a better choice than allowing any more awkward tension to build. Crouching down, he unzipped his travel bag and withdrew the shoulder bag. "I picked this up for you."

"Oh." Her soft, doe-brown eyes widened.

"I planned to leave your tip in it." He'd already stuffed the money into the bag. "I wanted to support this persistent vendor, and she only sold bags and jewelry. I didn't need any of it, but I thought of you."

"That is so kind of you." Wonder laced her voice as her long fingers slid over the woven fabric, and releasing the bag, he exhaled a breath he hadn't realized he'd been holding.

"This is the best gift anyone has ever given me." Her voice shaking, she extracted the bundle of shillings. "You didn't have to include money. The bag is more than enough."

"I didn't want to deprive you of your tip, either."

"Thank you, truly." She traced some lines on the intricate, vibrantly colored African pattern. "I didn't own a handbag, so this is wonderful. I love the colors."

Warmth spread across his cheeks, but he managed a bashful, "You're welcome."

Then an incoming silver Rav4 diverted his attention. The man behind the wheel had a deep brown complexion and a kind smile. He lowered the window. "Mr. Gavin Kress, is that you?"

"Yes, I'm Gavin. And you're Dongo?"

"Indeed, that's me." Despite the man's slightly stilted English, his confidence was evident. "Please forgive my tardiness. Brady and Ruth remind me to be punctual for the overseas guests."

"I'm glad you're here." At least, they now had transportation.

Upon stepping out of the car, Dongo extended a hand toward Gavin, his jovial manner putting Gavin at ease. "It's a pleasure to meet you."

"This is my friend, Hope," Gavin introduced after reciprocating Dongo's handshake.

Dongo dipped his head. "I got a call from Brady on my way here indicating you would be joining us."

"Nice to meet you." She also shook his hand.

"Do you speak Luganda or Lusoga?" he asked her.

"I'm learning a few words in—"

"She has a dictionary," Gavin cut in. His gaze met hers, and her warm smile ignited a similar feeling in him.

Dongo had packed the SUV to the brim. Various items were even strapped to the roof, and the trunk barely closed. Before they could carry their luggage to the car, he held up a hand. "It'll be easier if I load your bags for you." Without waiting for their response, he grabbed Hope's duffel and Gavin's suitcase and stashed them in the front passenger seat. Then he slammed the door and rubbed his hands together. "It's always crowded when I go to the village. Ruth and Brady have a long shopping list for me to complete. But don't worry, the Sharps are well-prepared."

"We're not too worried." Gavin glanced at Hope. Her gaze seemed distant, uncertain. He refocused on Dongo, who was wiping perspiration from his forehead with a handkerchief. "Thanks again for picking us up."

"This is what Mr. and Mrs. Sharp pay me for. I transport guests to the village. I'm surprised you didn't opt to stay at their lodge in Mabira."

"They were booked." For which a part of Gavin was grateful, or he might not have met Hope.

Dongo then drew out a breath, his face serious. "I have good and bad news. Which one do you want first?"

"Good."

"Bad."

Gavin and Hope spoke simultaneously. Gavin glanced at her, and she wrung her fingers together. What was she nervous about?

"I prefer bad news first," she continued. "It will save us time."

"The bad news is a nail pierced through the passenger back tire."

"We can't get too far with a flat tire." Gavin spoke under his breath. Too bad, he always relied on AAA for roadside assistance. Uganda likely didn't have such services.

Dongo's brow creased as he stepped away to inspect the tire. His tense posture and tight-lipped expression communicated his thoughts—the situation was far from ideal.

"If I hadn't come, your tire would be fine." Hope blurted out, her self-blame echoing their previous conversation about her luck. "If I leave, I can save you from future problems." She moved toward the car and opened the front passenger door to fetch her luggage, but Gavin was at her side, grasping her arm.

"You're not responsible for any problems."

Her gaze fell to his hand on her before rising, her overlarge eyes so soulful. "With my luck, next thing you know, the car will die while we're on the falls bridge, and no one could get us out."

He let her rant, conjuring up potential disaster scenarios, but when she paused for a breath, he arched a brow. His grip further gentled on her arm as his thumb stroked her smooth skin. "If I remember, you'll have an apology to write to get your job back."

She winced. "Thanks to you, I have money to look for a new place."

Somehow disappointed she wasn't coming with him, he let go and tried to keep his response light. "If you believe in luck, then your best chances lie in coming to the village with us."

Her chest rose and fell. A flicker of a smile crossed her face. "You're right. If I look for a new place and a job, I'll end up with a mean landlord and boss."

Gavin nodded. Good and bad things happened to anyone at any time and not because of luck. But there was no reason to say that now.

"After volunteering, maybe I'll have a better idea of what I need to do."

"Excuse me." Dongo interrupted their conversation, commanding their attention. "I've called a mechanic. He'll meet us here and fix the tire."

Hope peered over the shrubs shielding them from the entrance. "Maybe we can move the car down the road a bit."

"Not a problem." Dongo ushered them into the car.

Gavin understood her discomfort to linger around her former workplace. As they waited for the mechanic down the path, he updated Dongo about the stops they needed to make, then asked her if she knew any places where they made a good breakfast.

Hope shook her head, her shiny hair swishing. "You know more about this town than I do. I've never left the resort."

Dongo leaned over the front seat. "I know a place that serves breakfast until late."

Almost an hour later with the tire replaced, he dropped Gavin and Hope off at the restaurant and left them to enjoy what was now more of a brunch than a breakfast.

Tribal music pulsed low in the background, the steady whir of fans and conversation accompanying it. Dim lighting, growing duskier further in, relied on the sunlight streaming through the front windows, but revealed clean wooden tables and well-polished floors. Brightly colored posters, though harder to see on the back walls, depicted local scenes and added flavor. With the fans stirring up the appetizing scents, his stomach rumbled, but more so, curiosity gnawed at him as they settled in. "What's the story with Lumbe?"

Hope propped her elbow on the table and rested her chin on her hand. "I did something unusual. I looked up the meaning of his name." Her smile widened a touch. "Lumbe means funeral."

He choked on his water. As he recovered, she confirmed the translation with a series of nods.

"I feel bad for him." Her gaze flickered to the abundant food display spread out buffet-style before them. "Carrying such a name... Besides, he lost his father two months before I joined the resort."

Gavin winced. "That would be hard."

"It's understandable if he sought comfort after his father's death, but he was mistaken to expect it from me." Her voice held a distant tone, blending with the tribal music and thrumming fans. "I made it clear I was there for work and had no interest in becoming his girlfriend, wife, or anything more."

He let out a low breath. So, the man's resentment toward her was more personal than professional. Good thing she'd cut ties with him. Gavin picked up a plate and approached the spread of food, taking in the savory scents. Wow. Where did one even begin? The rich aroma of the mandazi, beef stew, and spices wafting from the dishes tempted him to sample everything. Using the serving spoon, he scooped rice onto his plate.

As he resettled at a table, he considered her earlier comment about not being a local. No wonder she needed a dictionary for Lumbe's remarks. "How long have you been in Uganda?"

"Three months."

"And how did you come to work at the resort?"

She fiddled with the steaming plantains on her plate. "I found the job online. They offered accommodation, which made it the perfect opportunity, despite the low pay." She blew on a forkful of plantains. "I needed a place to stay while I figured out my next move."

So, now she had another temporary place—the village. "Did you interview for the job before coming here?"

She nodded. "I may have sounded too desperate when I mentioned I was ready to leave Kenya the next day. Maybe my being a foreigner made it easier for Lumbe to assume I'd be interested in becoming his wife. I didn't know anyone in the country and didn't have anywhere else to go."

His hand tightened at her words, the metal fork pinching against his fingers. "Did he ever... touch you without your consent?"

Her eyes flashed with residual pain. "No one touches me if I don't want to be touched."

She speared a piece of plantain and chewed with uncharacteristic force. Other secrets must be tucked behind her brave façade.

He tested a bite of his rice and stew, but his appetite had lessened. Maybe the rich aromas had been enough. Now he understood why Lumbe harbored such fierce resentment. "Why did you leave your country?"

"I needed to escape my home."

"Aren't you a bit old to be running away from home?" he teased. "You're what, twenty-five?"

"Twenty-seven." She shrugged. "Jobs were hard to come by, and after I lost my last one, I had to move back in with my parents."

Hope was proving to be a fascinating character. "Why did you need to run away?"

Her thin lips flattened, and those large luminous eyes flashed. "For the same reasons I'm now running away from Lumbe—the control, greed, and other aspects I despised being imposed on me."

Despite her cryptic response, his eyes widened.

"Sadly, it was my father and stepmother. They've been controlling my life ever since I was twelve."

Gavin could relate to controlling parents. His mother, for instance, still tried to exert her influence over him and Jeremy despite their ages and separate households.

"I may be an adult, but to my father and stepmother, I'm a bargaining chip to be traded to the highest bidder." She shivered, her eyes hardening as her gaze fell upon a wedding poster on the wall. "On the day I was supposed to be married, I caught a boda boda into Nairobi. It was the strangest day. In an internet café, I found a job." She then recounted that night at the bus station, her words painting her as a true survivor.

His painful memories bubbled to the surface, almost echoing his recent heartbreak. He tried to mask his residual disappointment. "So, you left the man standing at the altar?"

"Well, it wasn't exactly an altar." She skewered a plantain with more force than necessary, and rage heated her words. "I didn't stick around to see if he was standing or sitting. My greedy father and his wife got the punishment they deserved for trying to push me into a marriage."

While Gavin could empathize, he couldn't help but wonder about her leaving the man she was supposed to marry. Did she feel any guilt over what she'd done to him? Yes, she had compelling reasons not to proceed with it. But still... Gavin's mother had played matchmaker with Lucky, but over time, he'd fallen for her. How well had Hope known the man she left behind?

He shivered, spiraling back to the rainy afternoon he'd stood under a wedding tent, awaiting a bride who never came. Opting for a change of focus, he returned to his meal. He picked up his bottle of Rwenzori water. As long as he stuck to bottled water during his stay, he could avoid falling ill due to contaminated water. His appetite had somewhat returned, or perhaps eating was just a helpful distraction.

As if sensing his turmoil, Hope refrained from saying any more. The clinking of their spoons against the porcelain and the hum of others' conversations mixed with the music to fill their silence.

When Dongo's text arrived, it was a welcome interruption. Hope insisted on footing the bill. But Gavin suggested they toss a coin for it, and luck was on his side once again. Maybe there was such a thing as luck.

Navigating a bustling sidewalk teeming with vendors, he found himself accosted by eager salespeople. "Mzungu, here!" A teenage boy sprang in front of him, dangling an array of flashy chains. "You should buy one."

Gavin raised his hand in a polite refusal, but before he could move past, a woman slipped a wide-necked shirt over his head, haggling. "Two thousand shillings."

"I'll pay for it." Hope's voice came through, laced with mirth as three vendors swarmed him, each intent on making a sale.

"I got it," he assured her, nudging them aside as he fetched his wallet and produced some money. He had no need for the patterned shirt, but it seemed the quickest way to keep things moving. After handing some money to the other two vendors, he pointed toward a woman balancing a tray of triangular pastries. "Get some samosas."

Hope was already crouching before a man displaying his wares on dried cowhide.

"This one is good for snakebites, and this over here is for bad spider bites." The man, lacking front teeth, gestured at his items.

Hope listened attentively and picked up a couple of bottles to examine. "Are you sure this works?"

"It's original and pure."

"What do you use for a snakebite?"

While Hope was engaged with the old vendor, Gavin fended off two more vendors. One held up dress shirts while the other offered a basket of fried pastries. He toyed with the idea of joining Hope, but having had his malaria and yellow fever shots, he doubted he would need the traditional medicine.

Instead, he allowed the vendor to elaborate on the different sizes of shirts available. Already having packed a few short-sleeved button-downs, he wouldn't need formal shirts in the village.

"Ready?" Hope's voice cut through the persistent sales pitches.

Meeting Dongo brought relief, and they were soon on their way to an enclosed shopping center. "Stay with Gavin and help him bargain," Hope advised Dongo outside a men's clothing shop before disappearing into a shop selling women's attire.

Gavin found Dongo's assistance invaluable as they haggled over tennis shoes, shorts, a hat, and more. "Why don't they set prices?" he asked while waiting for Hope.

"That's how they make a profit," Dongo explained, adjusting his shirt under his pants. "If no bargain, you lose, they win."

When she returned, they made a final stop for toiletries before embarking on their journey to the village where Gavin had no idea what awaited him. Would he regret committing to a year in the rural environs? Was it a mistake to bring Hope?

CHAPTER 6

"Could you refresh my memory on the village's name?" Gavin inquired of Dongo.

But Hope answered. "Kibale. Is that correct?"

Dongo chuckled. "You pronounced it better than me." To their left, fields of sugarcane extended beyond where the eye could see. Dongo shared a story about Brady's fascination with the plantation upon his first visit.

While the driver played tour guide, Hope focused out the window, absorbing every detail of the foreign landscape, and Gavin sneaked glances at her. Her skin, flawless and glowing, seemed to lure his gaze. He shook himself mentally. He hardly knew her, just that she'd left a man at the altar. He'd best focus on the shared mission—seeking refuge from personal woes while assisting those in need.

"So, Gavin and Hope," Dongo spoke, "are you both from America?"

She shifted her gaze from the window. "No. Gavin invited me to volunteer. We met at the resort."

As they neared a bridge, Dongo gestured toward the Nile's mesmerizing waves. Gavin leaned back, offering Hope a clear view, his pulse quickening with memories of a thrilling rafting experience days ago.

The journey took them through an ever-changing landscape of verdant green and rusty red soil.

They jostled over uneven roads and passed by thatched-roofed houses cradled by trees. Occasionally, locals waved at them, and the scene, while charming, revealed the villagers' daily lives. In a humbling spectacle, women and children toted jerry cans of water, with some women displaying an awe-inspiring feat of strength while balancing infants on their backs along with their water.

Gavin attempted to strike up a conversation, but Hope had succumbed to sleep, undoubtedly worn out by the past days.

Once they crossed into an area marked by brick houses and grazing cows, she stirred awake, her voice soft, yet clear. "This is beautiful."

"Good morning." He teased with a smile, and she patted her ruffled hair.

"Did you catch me sleeping?"

He just nodded, glad she'd gotten some rest.

The car halted in a gravel yard surrounding a flower-adorned house and a distant brick building, probably the hospital. The cheerful cacophony of children playing nearby offered a welcome fanfare.

"We're here." Dongo switched off the engine, and on cue, the children dashed toward them with joyous shouts.

Hope turned to Gavin, a nervous twitch in her left eye. "How do you know these people again?"

"Brady is a longtime friend. We met in New York through our shared interest in real estate. You don't need to worry. Brady and his wife are wonderful people."

Hope may not need to worry, but Gavin squirmed. He needed to maintain a safe distance to safeguard his heart, but in this strange new place, he was her only familiar connection. And her apprehension endeared her to him as she tightened her grip on her bag, and that tick accelerated by her eye. He had to prove she was not a harbinger of bad luck as she believed.

"Ready to go?" he asked, and with a nod from her, Dongo opened the car door.

As they stepped out, children swarmed them. Their cries of "mzungu" were followed by some of them tugging at Gavin's arm hair, eliciting a surprised yelp.

Dongo intervened, reprimanding the kids with a stern look and a wagging finger. "They still do that to Brady sometimes, even after all these years," he confessed, looking apologetic.

Gavin assessed his arm. His only long-sleeved shirt would have to serve as protection against such playful attacks. He couldn't help but grin. This was, indeed, going to be an adventure.

AS SOON AS GAVIN INTRODUCED his friends, Brady and Ruth, a palpable wave of comfort washed over Hope. Perhaps they had detected her initial nervousness, and in response, Brady, a darker-haired blue-eyed mirror of Gavin, wrapped her in a comforting hug.

"Volunteers like you are always a blessing," Brady commented as he released her, making way for his wife.

Ruth's gentle smile was a balm as she welcomed Hope. "Such a pleasure to meet you, Hope." Ruth's English was perfect, and after releasing her, she inquired about Hope's language proficiency in Luganda or Lusoga.

"I'm Kenyan," Hope admitted and offered a Luganda greeting she had picked up from a dictionary. "Oliotya, nyabo."

Ruth's twinkling eyes suggested Hope's attempt was not quite accurate, yet the following Swahili exchange seemed to ease the tension. "Habari."

"Mzuri," Hope replied.

"That's as far as my Swahili goes," Ruth said, her warm brown skin glowing in the early evening light, her short hair styled in chic curls. She patted her baby bump visible under a vibrant, hibiscus-print sundress. "Perhaps we can teach each other our languages during your stay."

"That sounds wonderful," Hope responded, her gaze drawn to the men's jovial interaction on the veranda. Brady's hearty laugh echoed through the air, sending Gavin into a fit of guffaws.

"Who would've thought you'd end up in Uganda?" Gavin shook a finger at his friend.

Ruth glanced at her husband, love evident in her eyes. "Gavin's visit will do Brady good. He gets homesick sometimes."

It appeared Gavin and Brady shared a deep bond, and Gavin, too, would appreciate having someone from home around.

In the distance, children's laughter rang out as they scampered across the open field, sent off by Dongo to line up for the treats he brought from the city. After they had unloaded their luggage, Dongo drove off to deliver medical supplies to the hospital.

The yard was home to free-roaming chickens, making their way through the flowering shrubs lining the front veranda. The air here was fresh, a welcome change from the city's atmosphere.

"Let's go inside for some refreshments," Ruth suggested, before calling out to her husband. "Brady, bring our guest inside for some refreshments."

"Will do, sweetheart."

Upon entering, both women shed their footwear, their sandals and flats respectfully deposited on the welcome mat. Ruth and Brady's home seemed fresh, as if it had only recently been built. Anticipation swelled in Hope's chest, hinting this could be the fresh start she yearned for.

A middle-aged woman approached in a wraparound skirt of vibrant purple patterns and a crisp white blouse. Bowing in greeting, she extended a warm welcome to Hope. In return, Hope mirrored the respectful bow, a silent communication of mutual respect.

"This is Akiki," Ruth introduced. "She looks after our house in the village when we're in the city."

Gavin had mentioned Brady and Ruth didn't live in the village full-time. Now it made sense.

"Thank you for helping with our luggage." Hope expressed her gratitude to Akiki. Although curious about where her luggage had been taken, she chose instead to take in the impressive open floor space beyond the hallway. Natural light, courtesy of the generously sized windows, flooded the brick ranch-style house. Locally made artwork in brilliant hues adorned the walls, and the tantalizing scent of home-cooked food mingled with the sweet floral fragrance from a myriad of bouquets.

Cultural cloth banners, along with family photos, added a personal touch as they moved into the living room. Having always lived in work quarters or shared spaces with roommates, Hope had never experienced the cozy familiarity of a personal home. The cool terracotta tiles pressed against her bare feet before she stepped onto the plush rug in the living room where a standing fan provided a cool respite from the heat.

"Please, take a seat." Ruth gestured, and Hope settled into an offered chair. Gavin and Brady were still out of sight.

"Your house is beautiful." Hope nodded toward the mat and scattered cushions for casual seating. Beyond the living room, she could see a dining area, complete with wooden stools and chairs. It felt like a place designed to foster connection and camaraderie. "It seems like you have a lot of gatherings here."

"We wanted to keep things simple." Ruth settled into a plush chair opposite Hope. "We aren't here much of the time."

"And where is your other home?" Hope slid her bag off her shoulder onto the sofa.

"We have one in Entebbe. I also run a clinic in the suburbs of Kampala." Her hands moving with an energetic rhythm, Ruth continued to share about her work, her numerous projects with Brady, and their shared passion for community service. Her words painted a vivid picture of their life filled with dedication and compassion.

"And how did you establish a hospital here?" Hope settled back in her seat, considering the possibilities her new life in the village could offer.

Ruth answered, sharing personal history, tales of her village upbringing, her meeting Brady, and his supportive role in establishing their hospital. Her love for her hometown struck a chord, making Hope wonder if she could ever feel such an attachment.

"Tell me how you and Gavin met," Ruth asked, likely assuming they were a couple.

"I worked at the place where he stayed." Hope then gave a condensed version of her story, detailing her decision to move and glossing over the details of her ex-boss while emphasizing her readiness for a fresh start when Gavin extended the invitation.

Ruth offered a smile. "From what I've heard, Gavin is a man of integrity."

"We're just friends." Hope clarified, keen to avoid any misconceptions.

But Ruth was quick to shrug. "Every relationship starts with friendship."

Was that true? Hope squirmed in her seat. Could she connect with Gavin the way Ruth had with Brady? Yet after her candid confession about fleeing an arranged marriage, Gavin's easygoing demeanor had shifted, his joviality replaced by a more reserved air.

Would he judge her? She couldn't blame him if he did. Somehow, it always seemed to be her fault, her actions always backfired.

"Akiki is arranging refreshments for us." Ruth's voice broke into Hope's thoughts. "They should be ready when the men come in."

"We had a substantial lunch." Hope shared, admitting she wasn't particularly thirsty. "How far along are you?"

"I'm twenty-four weeks pregnant." Ruth rested a hand on her stomach. "We're planning to leave the village in less than four weeks. I'd prefer not to have the baby here."

Hope edged closer. "But you have a hospital right here."

"Even though we've made strides, we still lack a few things. Besides, I would prefer my own doctor to deliver the baby, especially since this is my first."

First baby? Hope blinked. She often felt so behind other women who'd long since started their families. But Ruth looked older than Hope, and Brady, with his smattering of gray hair, seemed older than Gavin. Regardless of her curiosity, sincere happiness for them radiated through her.

"Our volunteer accommodations will get crowded when everyone shows up next week, so we thought you and Gavin could stay here with us, in the main house."

"O–okay." Hope let out a slow breath, caught off guard.

Seeming to pick up on her uncertainty, Ruth twiddled with a curl. "If you'd rather stay in the volunteer housing—"

"No, this is perfect," Hope interjected too quickly. She'd prefer to stay here. She'd met and liked the homeowners, and the thought of potentially sharing space with an unpleasant roommate in the volunteer quarters wasn't appealing. But sharing a roof with Gavin... She shivered, both unnerved and thrilled.

The men joined them, and her gaze slid to Gavin. Their eyes locked before she looked away, with a flutter of unease in her stomach. His proximity didn't help as he took a seat next to her on the love seat, his shorts grazing her dress.

He smelled freshly showered—clean and inviting, yet also distinctly him. The intoxicating scent stirred such a range of emotions within her, compelling her to seek distraction. She found herself scanning the room, noting the coasters on the wooden table, the flowers in the clay vase, anything to avoid meeting his eyes. How could she share a living space with him?

Akiki returned, bearing a tray with a glass pitcher filled with what appeared to be passion fruit juice. Hope sprung up to offer assistance, despite Akiki reassuring her she had everything under control. But Hope needed the distraction to keep from stealing glances at Gavin.

As Akiki placed the tray on the table, Hope picked up one of the glasses. She held it out for Akiki to pour juice into, her hand shaking. She'd better not embarrass herself by spilling anything.

Once the juice was poured, she passed the glass to Gavin. Their fingers brushed in the exchange, sparking a charge that buzzed through her. Her heartbeat quickened, but she managed to retract her hand before anyone noticed. Gavin then passed the glass to Ruth.

Hope continued the process, passing filled glasses down the line while he helped distribute them, serving her first and himself last. Brady then asked if they could pray for their refreshments. Gavin readily agreed, and everyone echoed a collective amen after the prayer. Feeling the need to cool off, Hope downed half her glass.

"You must have been thirsty," Ruth teased, likely because Hope had said otherwise earlier.

"I guess so," Hope replied, her voice barely a whisper. No reason to explain her nerves rattled her and left her dry-mouthed around Gavin.

A brief silence fell upon them until Gavin scooted forward and braced his elbows on his knees. "Hope and I were curious about what nonmedical volunteers like us will be doing?"

Hope studied the couple. The affection Brady held for his wife was palpable, his eyes alight with tenderness and love.

Brady clasped Ruth's hand. "Would you like me to tell them what you had me do when you first brought me here?"

Ruth chuckled. "You tell that story a lot better than I do."

"As for sleeping arrangements, lucky for you, you won't have to experience what I put up with," he said. "It rained the entire first night, and the water shot straight at me from the roof!" He went on to describe the tiny shared space in Ruth's parents' house where they had all stayed on the floor. Everyone laughed when he described their bike ride to get to their patients, and Hope shivered when he brought up the cobra they encountered in one of the villager's homes.

"I almost left the next day, but Ruth kept me busy wrapping gauze and bandages on the kids and, well..." He pulled her close to his side. "No way was I leaving without her. By the way, whatever you do, don't ride on a motorcycle in Kampala."

"Oh, I don't know whether that's good advice or not." With a finger to his chin, Ruth turned Brady's face toward her. "I'd never have met you if you didn't fall off a motorbike." She kissed her husband's cheek, and a longing to someday have what the two had tightened Hope's chest. To have a husband who wasn't forced on her, to marry someone she loved rather than look for an escape...

She suppressed a sigh.

"But back to your question." Ruth smiled at them. "The work will be manageable. We can provide training for the more demanding tasks if you're up for a challenge. Otherwise, there's plenty to do."

"Your primary assignment will be to assist one of the widows," Brady added.

As the evening progressed, they were given a tour of the house, shown their respective rooms, and briefed on the occasional power blackouts. Hope's excitement amplified when she discovered her bedroom was adjacent to Gavin's.

"I know you're planning to stay for almost a year." Standing in the hallway outside Gavin's designated room, Brady crossed his arms over his chest. "Akiki will take good care of you."

"And my family isn't too far away either," Ruth added. "Feel free to ask them for anything you need."

"Are you sure you don't want to stay and deliver your baby here?" Gavin asked Ruth, his tone light and teasing.

"If I were to stay, there's a good chance you and Hope would be assisting Brady with the delivery," Ruth retorted, provoking a wave of laughter.

Brady playfully raised his hands in surrender. "That's one job I'm not prepared for."

As much as Ruth's statement was intended as a joke, Gavin's headshake promised it wasn't a job he wanted to try either.

And neither did Hope. The only task she wanted to focus on was controlling her feelings for Gavin. He clearly wasn't her type. One mealtime conversation was all it took to change his friendly demeanor into one of avoidance. She'd tread carefully from now on.

CHAPTER 7

Gavin woke with a jolt at the roosters' crowing. He bolted upright, blinking sleep from his eyes. His gaze, filtered through the gauzy white mosquito netting encasing his bed, took in the unfamiliar room. Traditional artwork livened up the walls—vivid portraits of women balancing fruit baskets atop their heads. His focus lingered on a wooden plaque bearing the inscription, *As for me and my house, we will serve the Lord (Joshua 24:15)*. While his faith wasn't as profound as his friends' faith, he appreciated the sentiment.

With a second chorus from the rooster echoing through the window, morning's reality began to solidify. The warm, honeyed light of dawn seeped through thin white curtains, casting an inviting glow against the room's beige palette.

Running a hand over his face, he began piecing together fragments of the previous night. The embracing warmth of Brady and Ruth's welcome, their friendly driver ferrying him and Hope to the village. Hope. Her magnetic eyes had clung to him at dinner, her image twirling in his mind until sleep drew the curtains on the night. Her presence, so tantalizingly close in the neighboring room, was a reality he was still coming to terms with.

As he drew himself up from the bed, a wave of familiarity rippled through him. The burgeoning day beckoned, whispering promises of village exploration and chance encounters with the residents Ruth and Brady had spoken so fondly of. The distant clatter of pots and pans suggested life was already stirring within the house. His phone on the nightstand read 6:39. Despite the absence of cell service—a detail Brady had warned him about—Gavin was determined to find a way to get in touch with his brother.

Gavin had taken his shower the previous night, conscious of the solitary bathroom and its high demand. The prospect of an outdoor basin shower, as Ruth had suggested, was a lesson he'd grapple with eventually. For now, he wasn't ready to embrace that aspect of village life.

He approached his suitcase on the floor mat, unzipped it, and plucked out a navy T-shirt. The lingering heat from the previous night had urged him to sleep shirtless. As he pulled on the shirt, anticipation stirred anew.

After slipping on his rubber flip-flops, he eased his bedroom door open, mindful of any lingering sleepers. Since the bathroom door stood ajar at the end of the hall, he seized the opportunity to freshen up. Then when he left, his gaze wandered to the shut doors of Ruth and Brady's room and Hope's room.

Drawn by the symphony of pots and pans, he wandered into the kitchen. A tantalizing aroma, a fusion of fried food and exotic spices such as cinnamon and ginger, greeted him. Amid this symphony was Akiki, the conductor, engrossed in whipping eggs. She cradled the bowl against her stomach, her hand conducting a rhythm of mix and stir.

"Good morning, Akiki."

At his voice, she turned, a surprised smile broadening her face as she set the bowl on the central wooden island. She performed a half kneel in greeting, mirroring Hope's customary gesture. "Good morning, sir. I hope you slept well."

"Indeed, I did. Thank you." His gaze roamed over the table filled with diced fruits and fried triangular pastries. "Can I assist with anything for breakfast?"

She eyed him before shaking her head. "I just need to prepare the eggs, and then breakfast will be ready. Mr. Sharp went for a walk, in case you're interested in joining him."

Gavin was a fan of morning runs. However, since his arrival in Uganda, such routines had fallen away. But if he planned to stay a year, he'd appreciate learning the local trails from Brady, albeit not today. Instead, he questioned Akiki about local customs, such as bowing and kneeling.

"It's a sign of respect," she explained.

He leaned against the wall by the counter, arms folded. "I already respect you, and you have mine. There's no need for you to kneel."

Her smile widened as she moved to the stone wall housing two charcoal stoves. "Mr. Sharp doesn't appreciate it either."

Glad to hear that, Gavin made a mental note to address the same with Hope later. As Akiki carried on with breakfast preparations, he probed into her life in the village.

"I was born here." Her English was far from fluent, requiring his undivided attention to grasp her words. Her adult children had ventured to the city for work, leaving her to reside in Ruth and Brady's house year-round. Apparently, several cooks catered for the visiting volunteer groups, but her primary role was as the dinner chef for longer-staying guests.

Speaking of long-term guests… "What do the locals do for transportation?"

"Bicycles fill our main needs—well, when our feet aren't enough. Mr. Sharp rides one if he needs to get somewhere quickly." Her attention returned to the eggs now transforming into a fluffy omelet in the pan. "If Dongo or the other driver isn't around, the alternative is to walk."

"And Dongo? Where did he spend the night?"

Humor glinted in her eyes as she glanced over her shoulder. "Dongo likes to stay with Ruth's family when he is in the village. They have a tradition of slaughtering a chicken for him every time he returns. He looks forward to it."

Gavin laughed, imagining Dongo's anticipation for the chicken feast. The thought sparked his own anticipation. "Well, I can't wait to see that."

"Smells great, Akiki," came Brady's cheerful voice from the hall. He strolled into the kitchen, looking well rested and energetic and sporting the contented smile that seemed ever-present since Gavin had reunited with him.

"I made all your favorites, Mr. Sharp." Akiki reached to retrieve cups from the cupboard.

Brady's face lit up even more, if that was possible. Mischief sparkled in his eyes, and his lips quirked. "Even some cockroaches?"

Gavin tensed, as he whipped his head around to stare at Brady. The moment was broken when Brady burst into laughter, his shoulders shaking. Gavin relaxed. It must just be a joke.

"Man, that's not funny." He gave Brady a playful punch on the arm and had him groaning in mock pain. "Don't try to scare me with your weird food stories."

"I'm just helping you acclimate to the local cuisine." Brady defended, rubbing his arm. He then cast a surprised glance at Gavin. "I thought you'd sleep in."

Gavin shrugged. "The power cut out early last night, and I hadn't expected to be in bed by eight." They'd chatted with their hosts beneath the living room's soft lantern light but had to call it a night earlier than Gavin was used to. "I'm not accustomed to sleeping more than six hours."

"Trust me." Brady winked. "After exploring the villages tomorrow, you'll need more than eight hours of sleep."

Gavin wasn't sure what to expect. "I look forward to keeping busy. I—I kinda need the distraction."

Brady nodded, knowing Gavin's recent breakup, but Brady couldn't know Gavin also meant to keep himself from getting too lost in admiring Hope.

"I'll go clean up." Brady made his exit, leaving Gavin in the kitchen with Akiki. Despite her insistence that he was a guest and she didn't need assistance, he was more than happy to help arrange the food and set the table.

As the morning unfurled, the dining room served up warmth and energy. Brady and Ruth joined them, their cheerful conversation setting the tone for the day. "It's going to be a long day for you and Hope." Ruth glanced at the living room in search of Hope. "I'm glad she got some extra rest."

Gavin nodded. "She needed it. She's been tirelessly working back at the cottages without much of a break."

"We'll have Akiki warm up Hope's breakfast whenever she wakes up." Brady reached for Ruth's hand. She accepted it with a gentle smile, then extended her other hand to Gavin. "Is it okay if we pray?"

Before Gavin could respond, a subtle change in the room's atmosphere alerted him to Hope's arrival. His skin prickled with a sudden warmth coursing through him.

"Right on time." Ruth focused somewhere above Gavin.

The long table offered several empty seats, but they'd all sat at the head of the table. Now, Hope slid into the seat beside him, looking sheepish. "I'm sorry I slept in."

He faced her, his lips curling. "About time you woke up."

Her vibrantly patterned, sunrise-colored skirt and matching headband, combined with a soft-pink top, radiated a lively energy. He smiled, drawn to the aura she exuded, the joy she found in the smallest things, like the shoulder bag she had over her shoulder. His heart swelled over how she appreciated the gift he'd chosen.

Ruth then initiated the morning prayer, and Hope slid her hand into his. The sensation of her soft touch and the scent of her floral soap captured him. Their amens echoed simultaneously.

As they began their breakfast, Brady and Ruth outlined their itinerary, which involved a hospital tour and a visit to the temporary clinic.

"With the village spread out so far"—Brady stirred his coffee—"the stations help people not to walk very far to receive treatment."

Ruth elaborated on some tasks like cleaning and wrapping wounds. "We already notified the villagers of your arrival." She set her steaming teacup on the table. The smell of cinnamon and spices mingled with the fried samosas and pancakes. They didn't look like the pancakes he was used to, but with so many food options, he wouldn't try a new dish this morning.

Gavin held his coffee mug toward Brady. "I can't believe you made this without a coffee pot."

"All thanks to Ruth's dad," Brady boasted.

"Well, it's a treat. I had to adapt to tea at the resort."

"So did I when I was first in the country. But I wasn't going to make it a habit, so I brought coffee to the village. The coffee-making process isn't nearly as convenient as using a coffee maker, believe me."

Their conversation turned to the roles they'd partake in the village, and Gavin sensed Hope's apprehension, though Ruth was quick to assure them their tasks wouldn't be overwhelming.

"But, haircuts?" he asked, puzzled.

"Some of these kids, even adults, are so busy working on the farms that they forget to set time aside for grooming themselves. Plus, they have no money to buy the supplies."

"I'm excited about the haircuts," Hope chimed in, a glint in her eyes. "Ever tried giving one, Gavin?"

He chuckled. "Only to myself once, and it didn't end well. I had to wear a hat for a month."

The table erupted into laughter before Brady added, "Well, good thing it's sunny here, then. A hat will be perfect."

As their laughter subsided, Hope fixed Gavin with a sincere expression. "It's amazing to get to be a part of this."

Her enthusiasm fueled his excitement. "I couldn't agree more."

Ruth sat back and rubbed her belly. "The more we can get done, the more opportunities we'll have to tackle the bigger projects when the next volunteer group comes. But we're done with breakfast now, so are you two ready for a tour of the hospital?"

"That will be lovely." Hope stood, her bag brushed against his arm, and he glanced at her.

"I'm looking forward to it," he added, struggling to peel his gaze away from her. He had no idea what was going on in his mind, but the logical part of him warned: *"She'll only leave you with a broken heart."*

She'd literally left a man standing at the altar and had no remorse about it. His shoulders stiffened, and he tore his gaze away. His mind told him one thing, but his heart seemed to say something else.

GAVIN AND HOPE STOOD on opposite sides of the room, trays of medical supplies in their hands. Around them, a mixture of adults and children sat on wooden benches, their faces displaying their anticipation and apprehension as they waited for their malaria vaccine.

Shared glances and smiles served as a wordless communication between him and Hope, a reassurance amid the unfamiliar tasks. Ruth was a constant presence, speaking to each patient in their native language, injecting each with the vaccine, and moving them to the next stage. Her training as an RN was evident in her confidence.

Meanwhile, Brady was putting bandages over the injection site. His high fives and warm interaction, especially with the children, elicited bright smiles, and his attempts at the local language were met with understanding grins from the adults.

"How long did it take Brady to learn the local language?" Gavin asked, intrigued by his friend's perseverance.

"He's still learning." Ruth chuckled. "It's not easy, but it's worth it."

A man with salt-and-pepper hair approached, smirking at Gavin. "You brought another mzungu."

"Actually, two." Ruth gestured toward Hope. "These are our friends, Gavin and Hope."

Gavin offered a salute in greeting, his heart warmed by the man's friendly demeanor.

"I'm glad you're getting the vaccine this year." Ruth spoke to the older man, her voice carrying a note of genuine relief.

"I almost died of malaria last year."

As the man started to share his story, Gavin became aware of the disease's severity, especially among infants and children. This was crucial work here, so he'd do his best.

"Is it okay if Gavin gives you this injection?" Ruth asked the elderly man, who nodded.

Gavin blinked, taken aback. "You want me to—"

"Immunize." Ruth set the needle on the tray and switched places with him. "This is a training moment. I'll walk you through it."

Gavin glanced at Hope for support. Her grimace and headshake did little to reassure him.

"Are you sure this is allowed? I'm not qualified."

Ruth shrugged. "These are people who give birth in their homes and deliver their own babies. And this gentleman just said it's better than him trying to figure it out himself." She explained what the man had said in his language, then handed Gavin a wipe. "Start by cleaning the injection site."

Following her directions, he cleaned the man's arm and disposed of the wipe. He then picked up the needle, slightly tilting it as Ruth instructed. He found himself holding his breath when he pushed the needle into the man's upper arm. Relief washed over him as he pulled out the now-empty syringe.

"That wasn't too bad, right?" Ruth encouraged.

"You did well." The man thanked him.

And Gavin found himself smiling. "Thank you for letting me practice on you."

Feeling Hope's focus on him, he looked up to meet her gaze. Her thumbs-up and Brady's loud applause made him chuckle, so he quipped, "I just earned a medical science diploma, and you're treating me like it's preschool graduation?"

When Ruth offered Hope the same opportunity, she declined, insisting she was content with her current job. Gavin found himself wondering why she had such a strong aversion to needles.

As the next patient took his seat, Gavin smiled. "Hi there."

The young boy's response was to reach out and touch Gavin's arm, clearly fascinated by his arm hair. Gavin tried not to flinch at memories of yesterday's hair-pulling incident.

While Ruth reminded the child about the appropriate response, Gavin couldn't help but smile at the boy's innocent gaze and pearly white teeth.

"Ready for your vaccine?" Gavin asked, rolling up the boy's sleeve. The boy nodded but grimaced as Gavin injected him. Gavin winced. "Am I hurting you?"

"You're doing fine," Ruth assured him. "Not everyone likes injections."

Then Mutesi, one of the nurses, arrived with a fresh tray of pre-filled needles, and that signaled the end of their training.

"Thanks, Mutesi." Ruth swapped out the trays, and, having likely noticed his slow pace, she confirmed his hopes. "We'll let the nurses take over soon."

Earlier she and Brady had given them the tour of the hospital and introduced them to the two doctors and three nurses on staff.

"We need to show you where you'll be set up this week, and then introduce you to Komo."

Ruth had been right. The work wasn't overwhelming, and a sense of satisfaction lifted his chest. He could do this for the year he'd planned. But then his gaze fell on Hope, and as she smiled back, a different sensation welled up in his chest, fluttering in his belly. Could he work alongside her every day for a year and keep his heart intact?

CHAPTER 8

Seated on a low, round stool next to Brady, Gavin appreciated not having to negotiate sitting on the woven mat. The room, lit by the light seeping in through the single window and the warm glow of a nearby fire, felt cozy. The scent of burning wood mixed with the earthy smell of the clay walls and the grass-thatched ceiling, adding a smoky, rustic aroma to the musty dampness.

Taking her seat on the mat, Ruth spoke. "Everyone, this is Komo."

The woman, hunched with age, knelt on the mat and shook Gavin's hand. In her floor-length dress patterned in earthy tones, with a similar cloth covering her head, the older woman looked like she stepped from a photo on his bedroom wall. "We are so happy for your arrival."

"We're grateful to be here," he replied, trying to focus on her halting English, but stealing a glance at Hope, who settled next to Ruth.

Komo moved to greet Hope and Ruth with the same warmth, taking their hands in hers.

"Komo, we wanted to introduce you to Hope and Gavin." Ruth's voice drew his attention back to the conversation. "They'll be helping out around here. If they work late at the clinic, they might need to stay here for the night."

"My grandson and I would be honored to host you." Komo's eyes held kindness as she gestured toward the mats folded against the wall. "Ali and I sleep on those when we have visitors. You and Hope can take the bed."

"We're not, um..." Hope faltered, her gaze flicking between him and the bed.

Heat crept up his neck as he took in the modest wooden bed, its frame adorned with woven mats and a thin blanket.

Brady leaned in, his voice barely a whisper. "I'll fill you in on my first sleepover at Ruth's parents' place."

"I'm sure there won't be any emergency," Ruth cut in, her gaze soft as she looked at Brady and her hand went to her pregnant belly. "Shall we show them to the clinic?"

"Yes..." Gavin stood, eager for a change of scenery. As he moved, he had to duck to avoid a low-hanging section of the roof, the grass poking him playfully. The room's simplicity was part of its charm.

"First, eat something." Komo hurried to a steaming pot. "The water is ready."

"We just ate," Gavin protested, his stomach still full from their generous breakfast three hours earlier.

"But you didn't have millet porridge." The widow reached for a plastic bowl, poured flour into the clay pot, and began stirring with a wooden spoon. "Ali and I can't eat all this porridge alone."

"Maybe next time," Gavin said, but none of his companions made a move to rise. When Brady tugged at Gavin's hand, signaling him to sit, Gavin complied, though a puzzled frown creased his forehead.

Brady leaned in, whispering. "In every home you visit, they'll want to feed you. Some people get offended if you don't eat."

Well, Gavin didn't want to upset anyone on his first day. So he accepted the warm bowl of millet porridge offered, the smooth, brown concoction seeming innocuous enough. But then Komo presented what looked like insects on a small platter.

"Thank you, Komo," Brady chimed in. "I can't believe you still have November's grasshoppers."

Grasshoppers? Gavin's gaze darted to Brady, searching for a hint of jest, but his friend seemed serious.

"I hope this year we get as lucky with the hoppers as we did last." Uh-oh. Komo also sounded earnest.

"Gavin and Hope might still be here," Brady added, his shoulder pat adding to Gavin's mounting confusion. "They can help you gather them."

Disconcerted, Gavin couldn't picture himself eating grasshoppers, let alone hunting for them. Even as Ruth and Hope discussed the delicacy with evident interest, he clutched his porridge bowl with a sudden wariness. Just what else could it contain?

After Brady had blessed the food, everyone started eating—except Gavin. He needed a moment to accept he might be consuming insects for the first time.

"This is so good." Brady's enthusiastic comment broke Gavin's spiraling thoughts. A quick look at his friend confirmed he wasn't kidding. Brady was wolfing down his share of porridge. The women, including Komo, were also eating as Hope asked about Komo's grandson.

"He took the milk to the market," Komo replied, her mouth full of porridge.

Gavin took a deep breath and tested his first bite. "This is, um—" he began, his taste buds recoiling from the bland grainy substance. He tried to swallow to escape the taste but ended up choking and coughing. "Go–od," he managed to splutter between hacking coughs.

Concerned voices chorused, asking if he was okay.

So, he nodded, placed the bowl on the floor by his feet, and clutched his chest as the coughing fit subsided.

"Komo, do you have any boiled water?" Ruth asked, looking concerned.

"I have a Rwenzori bottle in my bag," Hope retrieved a water bottle. "Are you all right?"

Eager to lighten the situation, he winked at her. "I just needed some attention."

A radiant smile spread out her delicate lips and rounded up her smooth cheeks beneath those too-big, too-bright eyes.

"That's what I thought," Brady teased. "I'll have your porridge, then." He scooped up Gavin's bowl, unbothered by his friend's struggle with the unfamiliar food. As he bent to grab it, he spoke for Gavin's ears alone. "As far as the grasshoppers go, you're on your own, buddy."

Gavin managed a glance at the full plate of fried insects. It didn't seem like Brady ate the hoppers either, so maybe Gavin didn't have to feel guilty after all.

Minutes later, they stepped outside, greeted by the pungent smell of manure and farm animals. The distant mooing of cattle echoed from an open field.

Then Komo screeched. "A black cat!" Making hissing sounds, she shooed away the skinny feline sauntering across the dirt yard.

"But it's a sweet cat." Gavin bent with an impulse to pet the feline's soft fur. "Come here," he coaxed, clapping his hands. The cat glanced at him, seemingly unimpressed, before disappearing into the nearby bushes.

"Black cats are bad luck." Komo scowled.

"Komo... Komo," Ruth chided, shaking her head. "How many times have you said 'bad luck' and nothing happened?"

"Why do you think black cats are bad luck?" Hope touched the older woman's arm, clearly intrigued by the superstition.

Komo launched into a series of unfortunate events that had happened to her, always on days she'd seen a black cat early in the morning. When she wrapped up her narrative, Brady chuckled, but Gavin found Hope's evident interest captivating as she nodded, engrossed in Komo's story.

"I hope you know that's not true." Ruth intervened with a reassuring hand on Hope's shoulder.

Then, on the left, wheels chewed against a gravel road through the dense forest, and a lean man on a bicycle approached, stopping to offer a respectful bow and wave. He then spoke rapidly to Ruth in the local dialect. Ruth's face tightened, worry creasing her brow.

Feeling the shift in her demeanor, Brady moved closer, took her hand, and kissed it. "Everything okay?"

"That black cat. Told you," Komo muttered under her breath.

"Viva is in labor," Ruth announced, turning first to Brady, then addressing the group. "If it's okay, Brady will show you around."

"I'm coming with you." Brady scooped an arm around her waist, and protectiveness resonated in his voice as his gaze flickered to her extended belly.

"We both can't fit on his bicycle," Ruth protested, indicating the modest size of the man's bicycle seat.

Brady scanned the area, then nodded to a bicycle leaning against a smaller thatched hut. "Komo, may we borrow your bicycle?"

"Of course! You're always welcome to anything of mine."

Brady then leaned to Gavin, his voice lowering so only Gavin could hear. "I need to be there to make sure Ruth doesn't overexert herself."

"You should go." Gavin nodded. If their roles were reversed, he'd feel the same. "Hope and I will manage."

"I can spot the clinic." Hope pointed to the opening of the forest and the narrow path leading out.

"If you climb that tree, you'll see it even better." Komo waved to a towering tree with a wide trunk and low, inviting branches.

Grinning now, Hope tipped her head to one side. "I'll go check it out."

"Dongo should be back to fetch you in less than thirty minutes," Brady promised before mounting the bicycle.

"Be safe," Gavin called out, saluting Brady, then Ruth. "Make sure he doesn't throw you off the bike."

Brady laughed. "I can't wait to see you drive one of these!"

Gavin watched, impressed by his friend's easy confidence navigating the winding trail as he pedaled off after the messenger.

"I can see the clinic from here!" Hope called out.

Turning to the tree, Gavin found her three branches up, her pink shirt contrasting against the lush green leaves. She'd managed some amazing agility, considering she was climbing in a skirt and sandals—correction, no sandals. She must've kicked them off. He grinned at the sight before he spun to Komo. "I'm going to join Hope."

"I'll alert you when Dongo arrives." She waved him off, then retreated into her hut.

He set off toward the tree, his heart thudding. Was the thrill of climbing the massive tree driving him, or was it the enticing prospect of time alone with Hope?

CHAPTER 9

Sitting on the sycamore's smooth broad branch, Hope arranged her skirt to maintain her modesty. The last thing she needed was an unintended peep show as Gavin ascended the tree.

"What kind of tree is this?" His voice sounded below. Peering down, she sighted him agilely making his way up the tree, his arm muscles straining against his navy T-shirt.

"It's a sycamore tree," she answered, slightly breathless.

"It's hardy." He swung onto a higher branch opposite hers. "I like it."

By hardy, he must be referring to the tree's robustness. "I didn't think Americans climbed trees." Her mental image of gleaming urban streets hadn't included mature trees.

"Well, not all Americans can, but I used to when I was younger, especially when we visited my grandparents' house." His voice grew fond at the mention of his grandparents, but before she could ask about his family, he nodded to something behind her. "I see the pergola. Is that the temporary clinic?"

"Yep, that's the one." She'd lost her initial vantage point and hesitated to shift her position for fear of revealing too much leg. "Can you see the path through the forest?"

He stood, gripping the branch above him and scanning the landscape. "I see a dirt road in there."

"We could walk if you'd like." She tipped her face to the breeze, her skin heating with her anticipation for more one-on-one time.

"Or..." He settled back down. "We could sit here a bit longer. It's not every day I encounter a massive tree like this I can climb."

His gaze met hers, and her heart fluttered. She distracted herself by swinging her bare feet, having discarded her sandals at the tree's base.

"Thanks for the water back there."

She snickered over his near-choking incident.

And he shook a finger at her, his blue eyes shining. "I can't believe you're laughing at my near-death-by-porridge experience."

"I noticed you didn't eat your grasshoppers." She stifled her laughter. "I gather the millet porridge didn't sit well with you."

A sheepish smile curled his lips. "It was rather... plain, but—"

"It could have used some sugar and milk," she finished, not wanting him to write off millet porridge. "Prepared correctly, it could be quite tasty."

"I'm glad you had that water handy."

During her time at the resort, she'd learned most tourists needed bottled water to avoid potential stomach upsets, so she'd come prepared with him in mind.

"Me too." She patted her chest for her bag. Upon finding it missing, she looked around.

"You left it down with your sandals," he clarified, apparently having noticed her search. "It's nice to see you barefoot. It shows you're comfortable with your surroundings."

His comment left her flustered, and she swung her feet more energetically as she tried to regain her composure. Even as she enjoyed the warmth of his company, she couldn't shake off the fear he might think less of her after her unguarded confession about her past. "I'm sorry I told you about my family," she blurted out. "I sensed you avoiding me after that. I won't bring it up again."

"No, Hope, you should." He rubbed the back of his neck, then raised his chin, and met her eyes earnestly. "It didn't change the way I see you. I was just... upset."

She didn't doubt his sincerity. "I don't blame you." She twisted her fingers in her lap. Even though she'd acted in good faith, guilt had an uncanny way of finding her.

"I'm not upset with you." A pained expression broke through as he spoke, so he was upset. "It... reminded me of my own story."

"What kind of story?" Did he, too, have a troubled family past? Greedy parents?

His hands tightened around the branch, his frame tensing. After a heavy breath, he released his grip and rolled his neck side to side, his deliberate actions failing to loosen those taut, well-defined muscles. "My bride left me at the altar."

Oh! No wonder he'd been upset. She reached to touch him, but the distance was too great. So she whispered, "I'm so sorry. Was it an arranged marriage?"

He shook his head, his lips pressed into a thin, white line, and the glint in his eyes stirred her. Who could abandon a man like him?

"Maybe she didn't know you well? I've only known you for a short time, but I already know you're one of the nicest people I've ever met."

His lips relaxed, and their color returned as he released the tight pressure on them. His cheeks reddened, and he ducked his head, running a hand through his hair. "That's kind of you to say. But I guess you haven't met many nice people if I rank among the nicest."

Undoubtedly, there was truth in his words, but that didn't change how tragic it was that someone as kindhearted as Gavin had been left hurt. As the midafternoon sun filtered through the leafy canopy, curiosity nudged her again.

"Tell me about this woman. How long were you together? Why did she leave you?" She expected a frown, but a twinkle lit his eyes.

"You don't have to answer," she added, lifting a hand to stop him from talking if he didn't want to. But to her surprise, he exhaled deeply and sank back against the tree trunk, his legs dangling loosely.

"We knew each other prior, but we officially dated for three years." He frowned at the leaf-littered forest floor. "Our parents were initially involved in our relationship. And with time, we found our footing. My mom, in particular, likes to orchestrate things."

The breeze carried away his mournful voice as he shared his wedding day, waiting for his bride who never showed up. This vulnerable side, so different from his usual self-assured demeanor, pained her. "When I confronted her, she said we were rushing things."

"Rushing?" Hope gasped. Someone had a good man, and they trampled over him. "Three years isn't rushing." Grateful for the distance between them, she resisted the urge to reach out and comfort him, instead clenching her fists in her lap.

"That's what I thought too. But as you said, I guess we didn't truly know each other." His shoulders rolled in a resigned shrug. "Our wedding was supposed to be last summer."

"Is that why you came to Uganda? To escape?" As her inquisitive nature turned into concern, she prayed she wasn't prying too much.

"I didn't know you were so curious." Gavin chuckled, heat burned her cheeks, and her hands further tightened in her lap.

"How about fair play, runaway bride?" He shook a finger at her, his face warming up with a gentle grin. "So, I assume you're here escaping as well. It's my turn to ask."

Hope couldn't suppress a giggle. It was only fair. "All right, ask away."

"Did you know this man before your parents arranged your marriage?"

"He visited our home two weeks prior to the supposed ceremony. I assumed he was one of my father's friends. Father didn't mention anything about him being a prospective husband." Memories came rushing back. Father had summoned her to the shade of their old jackfruit tree. As she spoke, her voice soured like that overripened fruit. "He told me he'd found a suitable man for me to marry, even gave me the date to be prepared. At first, I thought having my own home wouldn't be such a bad idea. Then I wouldn't have to sleep with the chickens or be anyone's burden."

She rubbed at the knot in her chest. "Long story short, my experience at the altar wasn't quite like yours." No need to share her parents' behind-the-scenes negotiations. Some stories were better left untold.

Gavin leaned closer, his blue eyes narrowing as if they couldn't see anything but her. "You mentioned your experience at the altar was different?"

She nodded, then recounted the peculiarities of traditional Kenyan weddings. "We weren't going to have a church wedding. My father, who'd already negotiated the bride price, wanted the ceremony to take place immediately." Silas, the intended groom, had paid an advance, and her father had invested in his bike parts business.

"So, what made you run away? Was he almost as old as your father?" Gavin asked, his gentle tone void of judgment.

Strangely comforted, she opened up more. "His age wasn't as much a factor." She shuddered over their awkward encounter. "But it wasn't just that. He already had two wives and eight daughters, but he wanted another wife to bear him sons."

His expression hardening, Gavin jerked back as if slugged. "Good grief! I'm glad you didn't go through with it."

"I can't blame Father." She rubbed the rising goose bumps that now pebbled her arms. "In my village, most girls get married by eighteen if they're not going to school or working. I'm too old to be living with my parents." She dipped her chin, letting her hair slide around her cheeks to hide the embarrassment such a confession cost her.

"You're not old, Hope. But, even if you were, your age wouldn't justify them marrying you off against your will."

Her stepmother labeled her as "spoiled" for refusing the marriage. Her father, too, had expressed his disappointment, citing the financial benefits their family stood to gain from the union.

During their prolonged silence, only the rustling intruded as Gavin seemed to be processing the information. "Have you lived in your childhood home your entire life?"

"No."

At her short response, he swung his foot out, his tennis shoe nudging her knee in a silent request for more detail.

"I worked at a school before I moved back home, but I lost my job after breaking up with my boss's son." She clamped her tongue down on the darker details. "A year later, I met a wonderful man. I thought we were in love... until I brought him home."

"What happened then?" Gavin was a natural interrogator, his inquiries prompting her to reveal more than she usually would as an earnestness about him invited trust.

"My father and stepmother thought I shouldn't get married before my older half sister. She was more beautiful, they said. They convinced my boyfriend to marry her instead."

"That guy didn't deserve you," Gavin reassured her, his foot nudging her again. The gesture elicited a tentative smile.

"I tell myself the same." Still, a sense of loss crept up on her. Somehow, every good thing slipped from her grasp. "A person should get to choose who they want to marry, but sometimes... families have a way of interfering."

He nodded. "I can see why you would feel that way. But sometimes, the darkest nights produce the brightest stars."

She chuckled at his attempt to lighten the mood, but the weight of her past was still too heavy to shake off. She rubbed her arms again, then hugged them around herself as if to hold herself up for the incoming memories. "I was only allowed to attend the local school for a year after my mother passed. Then my stepmother kept me at home for household chores."

So many strenuous tasks, so many long walks to the well to fetch water multiple times a day.

Gavin listened as she detailed the challenges during her adolescence. "I was fourteen when I got a chance to attend a good school sponsored by missionaries in my village. But my father decided my half sister was more deserving of the opportunity." Heat burned the back of her eyes as the memory still stung, her dream slipping away so easily.

A tear slid free. Gavin stretched across the distance between their branches, his comforting grip closing around her hand. "I'm sorry, Hope."

Embarrassed, she wiped away the tear. "I didn't mean to cry."

"It's okay," he reassured her, his gaze soft but probing. "Why didn't you fight for your rights?"

How privileged he was. Some people just believed everyone had rights. What would that feel like? She shook her head, easing her hand free. "I didn't feel I had the right to."

She then spoke of the grueling work at home, the arguments with her stepmother, the man she'd met on the plantation, and her unsuccessful attempt to marry him.

"That man didn't deserve you," Gavin reiterated with full sincerity.

Her heart fluttered. "You're too good, Gavin. Kinder words have never been spoken to me."

He nudged her knee with his foot again, encouraging her to continue. "What happened after your attempt to marry failed?"

"I left home again." Why was the memory of her stepfamily's harsh treatment still so raw? "I found work at the elementary school where my mother used to work, then later at a secondary school as a matron. I loved being around books... I didn't get a proper education, but I always yearned to learn."

Gavin sank back against the tree trunk, resting his head against it and tipping his face to gaze through the leaves above them. "What kind of books did you read?"

"Mostly geography and history, anything to help me better understand the world."

Gavin tilted his gaze back to her, his expression serious. "You're one of the most resilient women I've ever met. So, why did you quit your job and return home? Didn't you know you'd be forced into a marriage?"

As his question nudged at her painful past, she sighed. Dare she reveal the next agonizing chapter? "The headmaster's son at the school where I worked... We were involved. He was kind, respectful." She swallowed hard, seeking the courage to continue. "One evening, his father, the headmaster, summoned me for a meeting with him and two other teachers. However, I was the only one who showed up."

A shiver ran down her spine. The headmaster had cornered her, his breath reeking of onions. She had fought back, kicked him in the crotch, and confronted him about his disrespectful behavior.

"The next thing I knew, my boyfriend and I were over, and I was out of a job." Careful to keep her balance on the branch, she covered her face with her hands, her heart aching from the old wounds.

"So that's what led to your father trying to marry you off?"

Nodding, she felt exposed, vulnerable, having shared such trauma.

"That headmaster deserved to be fired, at the very least. Did you tell anyone about this incident?"

Stiffening at his obvious anger, she lowered her hands and jerked up her chin, but the man gazed at her with such concern that his anger couldn't be toward her. So she gathered enough courage to shake her head. "You're the only one who knows why I lost my job."

"Why didn't you report him to the police?"

She gave him a wry smile. "With my luck, I would've been the one behind bars."

But she'd unveiled too much of herself. "You can see why I'm always anticipating the worst."

"I can." His voice was soft, and a pause stretched before he added, "Did you know, Hope, that the components of our lives shape us?"

She blinked at him. "I don't understand."

His gaze held hers. "Everything that has happened to you in the past is shaping your reality today. But the past doesn't have the power to define you now. You're a different person now because of your experiences."

His words made her pause, contemplating their depth. She'd always felt chained by her past. Now, the idea that it could also shape her, make her stronger, struck her. Yes, her past may have been difficult, but it shaped her into the woman she was. And through that, she found strength. As this new understanding blossomed within her, a genuine smile curved her lips. When she looked at Gavin, he was smiling too.

"What do you say we get down from this tree?"

"It's a good plan."

They walked back to Komo's compound, side by side, in comfortable silence. He gave her a sideways glance and then broke the silence, his voice thoughtful. "You know, Hope, we should both promise ourselves that, no matter what happens in life, we'll never stop looking for the good in people and the beauty in the world."

Her heart warmed at his words, and a gentle flame sparked within her. "That's a wonderful idea." Her voice carried her thrill, her anticipation for a future she was willing to embrace.

CHAPTER 10

Laughter and light conversation permeated Ruth's parents' house as the natural evening light streamed through the windows. The aroma of home-cooked food added to the comfort around the table. Men and women sat on either side, and occasionally, Hope caught Gavin's gaze. Her heart skipped a beat every time, but she knew better than to read into it. After all, he'd mentioned that his mother had a controlling streak. Likely, she'd influence his choice of a spouse as well.

"Gavin." Ruth's father raised his glass toward him. "Is this your first time leaving America?"

Gavin finished his bite and took a sip of his water. "I've traveled to other countries, but this is my first time in Africa."

Their discussion flowed as Ruth's grandmother asked about his impressions of Uganda. His reply brought a warm flush to Hope's cheeks. "It's the people," he said, gazing at Hope. Then he went on to share stories of his adventures at the Bujagali Falls and the source of the Nile.

As the evening continued, Ruth's mother spooned some rice onto her plate and faced Hope, asking about her origins. "Is your whole family still in Kenya?"

"Yes." Hope then changed the topic, expressing her admiration for their house. Its blue walls and cool cement floors were much more luxurious than the traditional huts common in the village.

"Thanks to Brady and Ruth." Ruth's grandmother, whom everyone affectionately called "Jajja," replied as she licked the delicious groundnut sauce off her fingers.

Ruth slipped an arm around Jajja's shoulders. "Brady wanted to give my parents a house as part of my bride wealth."

Brady shrugged, his smile displaying his modest spirit. "Your parents and grandparents wanted to live together, so…"

Ruth's grandfather chimed in. "And he still bought the cows and goats too, on top of the house we didn't ask of him. Brady has been a blessing to our family."

Hearing this, Hope eyed Brady. As a mzungu, how had he reacted to the African tradition of bride wealth? She'd have to ask Ruth about it later. Ruth and Brady showed such love and admiration for each other and brought joy to their family. In some quiet corner of her heart, Hope still, well, *hoped*, to find such happiness one day.

The sudden thump of drums and boisterous chants from outside caused her to pause midchew. The others exchanged knowing looks.

"It must be the imbalu circumcision ceremony." Ruth's grandmother rose to her feet. "They're collecting gifts for the ceremony. I have some eggs."

"Jajja, they'll want money from this house." Ruth nodded toward her purse. "Especially since we have two 'bazungus' here today."

The term *bazungus* referred to anyone with white skin.

"I have some money." Hope patted the bag on her lap. Thanks to Gavin's generous tips and his insistence Lumbe paid her what she was owed, she had enough to spare.

Gavin, who'd been observing the exchange, turned to Brady. "What is this ceremony?"

Brady scratched his chin. "It's a sort of circumcision ritual for boys between the ages of ten and eighteen." He glanced at Ruth, silently asking her to elaborate.

"A tribe from the east settled here in the village," Ruth began. "Brady is right about the age. The boys have to be circumcised publicly to prove their bravery."

"The rite of passage marks a boy's transition into manhood," Ruth's mother chimed in, covering their half-eaten food with empty plates. "I can't remember how often they hold this event—"

"Every two years," Jajja interjected, fetching shillings from a decorative clay pot atop a tall stool in the corner.

Excitement rumbled outside, the wave of uproarious celebration infectious in its intensity. Jajja jittered on her feet, her eyes sparkling with an energy that belied her age as she clapped with a gleeful cackle. "Let's go join the dance!"

Brady was the first to stand, followed by a grinning Gavin. "Let's do it," he echoed, matching the old woman's enthusiasm.

Unsure of what to expect, Hope found herself swept up in the excitement as they moved toward the door. Outside, Gavin stepped closer, his arm brushing against hers. The warm evening air felt electrifying, making her skin tingle where they had made contact.

The lively crowd was dancing and chanting in traditional attire. Two boys, not older than thirteen, stood at the center wearing sorghum paste on their faces, crowns on their heads, and bangles on their ankles.

Then cries of "mzungu!" rang out. Gavin and Brady, now familiar with the term, raised their hands in response. As Ruth's grandmother had mentioned, they were collecting gifts for the boys' upcoming ceremony.

"I didn't bring my wallet." Gavin patted his jeans pockets with a wince.

"I have enough to cover for all of us," Hope reassured him, withdrew a handful of shillings, and passed them to the group leader. Ruth and her grandmother did the same, the latter also offering a basket of eggs.

The group chanted and lifted their sticks high in thanks. Then the celebration resumed, the pounding of drums and the rhythmic shaking of maracas enlivening the air. Jajja joined in, dancing with wild abandon. The group beckoned the newcomers, and Ruth and her family joined with ease.

Gavin shrugged and offered Hope his hand. "It's all about hitting our feet on the ground as hard as we can, right?"

Following his lead, she pounded her feet on the ground in time to the rhythm. The celebration's infectious energy took over, leading her to dance with abandon. The setting sun, radiant as it peeked through the banana plantation beyond the compound, painted the scene in a warm, golden glow to accentuate the joyous celebration.

Golden rays glinted on Gavin's equally golden hair. Gleeful glints sparkled in his sky-blue eyes. Surrounded by the vibrant energy, she lost herself in pure delight. An unspoken connection was growing stronger between them, a bond forged in the heart of the celebration and new experiences.

THE NEXT MORNING, HOPE sat on the porch to read Proverbs from the small book she'd clung to for years. Now, the tattered cover barely held its frail pages together. She moved the flower, almost dry and already flat since she'd tucked it there when she left the resort.

" 'Commit to the Lord whatever you do and your plans will succeed,' " She read the line aloud, then glanced from the book to the shrubs, meditating on its meaning.

The morning breeze blew the pages just the way she hoped her life was turning over to a new place. The white natal plum shrubs rustled and danced with the vibrant red bougainvillea bushes surrounding the house. Below, the herb stalks of lemongrass wafted a citrus scent, filling the air with freshness.

Gavin intruded in her mind, his smile so clear and almost ingrained in her. Patient and kind, he treated her like an equal and even told her never to kneel for him because they were equals. So unusual from the men she encountered! Well, except for Brady. However, not only was Brady taken but also it was only Gavin who made her heart beat faster.

Birds chirped in the trees, and she shook her head. So much for meditating on her reading. She'd hoped today was a good day to focus and read either the wisdom book or the survival-and-life skills book.

Brady and Gavin had left for a morning run as they'd mentioned when making plans last night. Ruth was sleeping in, which she needed since she was carrying a child. Hope had offered to help Akiki with breakfast, but Akiki already had everything cooked when Hope showed up.

The back door jerked open, and her heartbeat skittered at the sight of Gavin.

"Morning." He closed the door and flopped in the wicker chair across the table. "You look lovely."

He threw out compliments so easily.

She rubbed a hand down her navy shorts skirt and then smoothed the blue flowered blouse that matched the flowers in the skirt.

"Thanks." Warming at his compliment, she raised her gaze. His forehead glistened in evidence of a good run. "How did the run go?"

"You should come next time."

She wouldn't interfere with his time with his friend. Still, she nodded, trying not to stare at his toned and muscular arms. His sleeveless shirt revealed the outline of his muscles, and the veins in his arms. "Maybe sometime."

"What are you reading?"

He'd caught her again, staring at him. Not good. Her hands shaking, she closed the book carefully to protect the cover and handed it to him. "Just simple guidelines to get me through my uncertain days." They'd helped her hold her tongue and put up with her ex-boss as long as she'd managed.

"Wisdom for life." Gavin nodded as he read the title before he flipped the yellow book open to the red oleander. A smile curled the corners of his lips as he lifted the flower and kept the book page open with his other hand. "For the memories, huh?"

She nodded.

"You use flowers to store memories?"

"Not often. But... well, the day you came to the resort..." She crossed her ankles. The flower choice would probably give away how she felt for him, but it was too late to twist the sentence. "Those were the flowers I had in the vase."

"Huh." He stared at her before lifting the flower to his nose and taking a whiff. Then he tucked the flower back in. "Memories. I like that."

Hope wasn't sure what she'd expected him to say, but he returned his focus to the book and read aloud.

" 'Guard your heart above all else, for it is the source of life.' " He nodded, probably finding the quote applicable given his broken heart. Of all the lines he could read in the whole book, really?

He then flipped a few pages and read Proverbs 16:9. " 'A person's heart plans his way, but the Lord determines his steps.' "

He read a few more lines, nodding in approval as if the words resonated with him just as they often did for her. After closing the book, he placed it on the table and picked up another that had been lying there.

"*Survival and Life Skills*," he read the title, smiling. "Now, I'm intrigued to borrow your books sometime."

"If you wake up early enough, I'll let you borrow them."

"I wake up before you every day." His brows shot up in challenge. "At least since we got here in the village."

She'd only been joking, but at his challenge, she took it back. "I've been lazier ever since we got here."

"You're the opposite definition of lazy." He stood and stacked her books on the table. "Speaking of which, I hear you're going to immunize kids today."

"No way." Shaking a finger at his teasing, she snickered. No doubt, he'd remembered how she'd been determined to avoid immunizations when Ruth brought it up yesterday.

"I'm gonna go wash up. Meet you for breakfast in a bit?"

"Sure."

"Maybe sometime today you'll tell me why you're terrified of shots." He winked and left. He must have seen her through the kitchen window and sought her out so he could talk to her rather than going straight to clean up after his run. It wasn't like he'd had a volunteer-related matter to discuss. Instead, he'd come as a friend. Perhaps he enjoyed her company.

She'd better not overthink *that*. Shaking her head to dislodge the thought, she went inside and helped Akiki set up the table. Hope utilized the herbs Akiki had in the cupboard to sprinkle over the tablecloth before they arranged the food dishes on the table.

"The table looks very fancy," Ruth commented as she joined everyone.

"Hope added the decorations," Akiki said.

Gavin winked at her, his chest high as if proud of her. "You should give her some napkins and see the intricate flowers she makes with them."

"Maybe she can teach a class to the women sometime," Ruth said. Then she spoke about the women who made crafts and sold them in the gift shop at the resort she and Brady ran in Mabira.

Hope held up both hands before they could plan on her giving a serious lesson that wouldn't even benefit anyone. "My crafts are not good."

Brady prayed for their breakfast and thanked God for Hope and Gavin coming to help the poor village. Honestly, Hope was considered poor too, but she was better off now than some of the villagers who didn't have the money she had.

"Amen." Ruth's response pulled her back to the present, and Akiki poured their tea releasing the comforting aroma of cinnamon, ginger, and lemongrass — Hope's favorite blend.

Was God upset with her for not knowing much about prayer? She'd been to church a few times when Mother took her. But after Mother's death, her life had been a constant climb of one mountain after another, and it was hard to set time aside for God.

After breakfast, Brady spread his hands out. "Okay, guys. Today, Dongo is loading up some gospel pamphlets you can share with people who need them."

"And"—Ruth reached over and squeezed Hope's hand—"you'll be assisting one of the nurses, who will join us. Giya speaks English, Luganda, and Lusoga, so she should be helpful."

"Ali will be your interpreter." Brady scratched his jaw. "Komo will feed you lunch as well as supper in case you work late."

Gavin winced. "Will she be making millet porridge and grasshoppers again?"

Catching his gaze, Hope covered her mouth, fighting a laugh.

"Don't worry." Brady chuckled. "It won't be porridge for lunch, but possibly frogs."

Gavin's gaze flitted across to Ruth, who smiled broadly to prove Brady was messing with him again. Gavin rolled his eyes. "How do you put up with him, Ruth?"

Then he and Brady bantered until Ruth cut in. "Please don't worry about obscure meals. I can't guarantee what she made today, but it's *not* going to be grasshoppers."

"What can be more unusual than eating grasshoppers?" Gavin smirked. "I can handle whatever else she plates up. I hope."

Having assigned their tasks—to bandage wounds and give haircuts—Brady offered to come with them to walk them through the process. But Gavin said he could manage the bandages, and Hope assured them she'd given razor-blade and scissors haircuts before. "I used to do that when I was matron at the school."

Ruth clapped. "You're the right person for the job."

Faced with her enthusiasm, Hope pressed her lips tight. She'd better not disappoint anyone today.

"Good." Brady nodded, seeing them off. "Because you won't be able to use electric hair clippers as the hospital and our house are the only places where we have power so far."

Since the drive to the center wasn't far, when they arrived, Gavin told Dongo they'd walk next time if they didn't have to carry medical supplies.

"Or you can ride a bicycle if I'm not here." Dongo unloaded the boxes of their supplies for the day and carried them to the wooden tables under a sturdy grass-thatched tent. "I'm always leaving to buy things in town or bring guests from the city."

With three shelters on the property, including the one where they were setting up the medical supplies, Hope and Gavin helped Dongo unload the rest of the boxes of books, first aid materials, and medicine. The subtle smell of acacia poles wafted through the tent. Birds chirped in the trees beyond the red dirt compound, others flying from a banana plantation to a papaya tree.

"What are you up to today, Dongo?" Gavin carted a box to one of the sturdy wooden tables.

"I'm picking up ill patients from their homes and bringing them to the hospital."

"Didn't you say you have another driver?"

"He comes when we have big groups. He'll be driving the van when the rest of the volunteers arrive."

"How do we set up for haircuts?" Hope asked since she'd forgotten to ask how it worked.

Dongo pointed to the small tent next to the big one and a tree stump beyond the table. "You can sit on the stump, and the people getting haircuts can sit on mats."

After they bid Dongo goodbye, two women rode up on a bike. They both had kind smiles as they waved to Hope and Gavin. After dismounting and leaning their bike under the papaya tree, they walked toward the tent.

"I'm Giya." The skinny woman with short hair put out her hand. Giya's dark-brown face glistened under the morning sunshine as Hope shook her hand.

"You're the nurse Ruth and Brady told us about."

Giya greeted Gavin, then jostled the shy other helper forward with both hands on the young woman's shoulders. "Kisa also lives in the village."

Both women didn't have shoes on. Hope had become accustomed to not wearing shoes while working in the family garden, but she'd had wounds to nurture. She wiggled her toes, glad to have sandals to keep her feet from cuts and bruises.

Gavin planted his hands on his hips, bunching up the red T-shirt he'd worn with dark shorts, and surveyed their setup. "What time does everyone come?"

"Some people will show up after they garden." Giya passed around a box of gloves. "You'll need these if you're working with sores."

Hope waved her off. "I'm giving haircuts."

"You'll need gloves and a gown over your attire." Giya tsked, nudging the box into Hope's hands. "Most likely, you will encounter lice as well as sores on some peoples' heads, especially the kids. I'll get you the medicine for head sores."

Hope suppressed a shudder, and her scalp itched now. She hadn't thought about lice and sores. She scratched just above her ear, hoping she didn't get lice.

"You'll be fine." Gavin's hand hit her lower back. "Just don't use the same comb for your hair."

"Thank you," she whispered. Though his touch was brief, her whole body melted toward his palm. She tipped her face up at him and found him looking at her with a tenderness she'd never experienced with anyone.

Soon, people started emerging from different sides of the wooded area. Women hoisting children on their backs and men herding kids.

A ten-year-old introduced himself to Gavin. "My name is Ali."

"You're our translator." Gavin shook the boy's hand. "I met your grandma yesterday."

"Yeah." Ali flashed a toothy grin. "She told me when I came back from delivering milk."

Gavin nodded to Kisa standing next to him as she prepared to hand out pain medicine to villagers. "Well, Ali, since I have these two nurses to help me here, you'd better head over to the pretty lady over there." He winked at Hope. "Her name's Hope."

"Hi, madam." Ali sauntered over and shook her hand, displaying mature confidence.

She carried the plantain-woven mat to the small tent where the box of her supplies had been set up. "Why are you not in school?"

"School only goes to primary six." His chest puffed out. "*I* graduated primary six."

As the boy spoke about the books he was reading to educate himself for primary seven, she couldn't help but be transported to her own life story. "I'm so impressed and proud of you." She reached to rub his curly head. "Your parents must be proud too."

Ali's nose scrunched. "After Mama died, Papa married another woman."

Hope swallowed as tears clogged her throat.

"My stepmom didn't want me in their family." He shrugged, but his cheerful voice didn't waver. "I'm going to boarding school next year. Mr. and Mrs. Sharp are going to pay for my school fees."

Oh, wow! She dropped into her seat. At least, Ali's intelligence wasn't going to waste. No wonder Ruth was talking about expanding the school as their next community project. Before Hope could respond, the first person wanting a haircut arrived, a boy not much older than Ali.

Ali spoke to him in Luganda, then translated. "He has a sore in his head."

After thanking Ali, she adjusted her robe to touch her neck and had the boy sit on the mat. He had a thick afro. Unsure if he needed it cut off or if she was supposed to keep the shape, she beckoned Ali, who was now throwing a plantain fiber ball in the air and catching it.

"I need your skills to interpret, please." She then relayed her question.

Without bothering to do as asked, Ali shook his head. "Everyone who comes for a haircut needs all their hair cut off."

That was easy. From the basket on the ground, she retrieved the scissors. Then she trimmed the hair to a length that would enable her to use the razor blade without hurting him.

Hair dropped onto his ragged striped shirt and fell around his bare feet. Mud covered his legs, and his cracked fingers gave evidence of hard work. No doubt, he was training to take care of his own family someday. He was no different from the boys who grew up in Hope's village or the girls who never went to school as they worked hard cultivating crops and prepared to become wives someday.

Already, she sensed a familiar rhythm of this village, so like her own. The people and their children were always working, tending their farms, planning to plant, cultivate, and harvest crops, or out fetching water and wood or cooking. Was that what life was everywhere? A constant struggle focused on providing food for your family?

When the hair was short enough, Hope put the razor blade over the flat comb and started trimming the rest of the hair. Starting from the front center, she made her way to the back, careful around the sores and then moving sideways. She smeared salve on sores and then, using the small towel, brushed the hair off the boy's shirt.

Then she held up a hand mirror for him. "What do you think?"

His smile spread wide, so he must be pleased with his new appearance.

"Webale nyo, nyabo." The boy spoke, and Hope understood since *thank you* was one of the common words she'd learned.

In Luganda, she told him he looked nice, and his responding giggle promised her language skills were still a work in progress.

Next was a girl about the same age. With a stained dress and muddy feet, she must've come from the garden. Hope looked for her interpreter, but he was already in the open field kicking a ball with a few other kids. Their cheerful squeals warmed her, and a smile lifted the corners of her mouth.

She peeked in Gavin's direction. He, too, seemed busy as he wrapped gauze around a woman's arm. His lips were moving, no doubt talking to the woman and forgetting not everyone spoke English.

As if aware she was staring at him, he glanced her way.

Her stomach jittered, and she ducked her head. Then she smiled at the girl now perched on the mat.

Many women had short hair in the village. The men as well because, with all their hard work, it was easier to clean.

Over the next hours, she cut the hair of women who came and brought their infant children. The little ones cried as their parents held them. She cut men's hair and children's who didn't go to school. Every so often, she stole glances at Gavin, and the way he interacted with the people as if he were one of them warmed her heart. He didn't mind when kids touched his hair or his arm, curious about his skin color. They'd seen Brady and the white volunteers from America or English countries. But maybe some of the kids hadn't had a chance to be that close to a white person. She'd seen white guests at the resort, but she'd minded her business until Gavin caught her attention. Apparently, he had that impact on a lot of people.

She tried to refocus on shaving hair.

Some of the parents told her their kids would stop by on their way home from school that afternoon.

Smoke hung in the air, mixed with food flavors. Stretching her back, Hope peered at the tent beyond their two tents. Pots were nestled on wood. So their lunch was being prepared. She wasn't hungry yet. Besides, she still had a long line of people to tend to.

She was finishing up with an older woman when Ali reappeared.

"You ran away from me." She shook a finger at him lightheartedly.

A shy smile curved his lips. "My friend brought a ball."

"I'm glad you had a fun time." That's what kids were supposed to do.

"Grand mother said you can have your lunch break," Ali said, and when she looked at the line for the haircuts, he answered her unspoken question. "Kisa is going to take over for you, and Nurse Giya will take over for Mzungu."

So she was going to have lunch with Gavin. Just the two of them. Excitement bubbled in her stomach. After thanking Ali, she strode toward the food tent. Beneath the cluster of papaya trees next to the orange trees, a makeshift table and chairs were built into the ground.

After washing her hands with soap, she sat across from Gavin at a table, their gazes lingering on each other as steam rose from their food. She was trying to look away, really trying, but how could she when his blue eyes mesmerized her?

"So—"

"I—"

When they spoke simultaneously, he laughed a deep laugh that registered the vibrations in her skin. Then he looked at the two plates, one on his side and one on hers. "What do you think we have here?"

At the savory smell, saliva gathered in her mouth. "Matooke, meat, and eggplants."

He nodded. "This matooke looks different."

"It's not smashed like the one you ate at the cottage."

"It's different." He frowned, picking at the meat with his fork. "What kind of meat is this?"

"Intestines."

"Ew!" He squished his face in a way that made Hope laugh. She held her stomach, fighting not to laugh harder, but his facial expression over the unfamiliar food didn't make it easy.

"The only amusing thing about this is that I made you laugh."

His comment warmed her, and her laughter subsided.

"Are you serious?" He pointed his fork at her. "We eat intestines? I have to know what to expect, before we start venturing out into people's homes."

"We eat intestines in my country. I'm sure it's the same in many African countries." She waved toward their plates, then reached for the pitcher, and poured juice into the glasses. "We eat every part of the meat from the animals, including the feet."

He seemed to think about her statement, opened his mouth as if to say something, but instead lifted his juice glass. "Thank you."

"You're welcome."

He took a sip of his juice. "I'd offer to pray for the food, but I don't know how."

"I don't know either." While at Ruth and Brady's house, they'd learn. "But with you having thought about it, I think God understands."

He nodded. With her fork, she poked at her food to let out steam. "I used to pray when I was younger."

"Why did you stop?"

"After my mother died, I spent my life trying to be accepted into the family my father built with his wife." That had set the tone for her since. She'd put up with all the demands at home and did whatever was required of her, even to the extent of being her siblings' servant.

"All I ever wanted from my family all those years was for someone to see me for who I am, someone to care about my efforts and hard work, someone to be proud of me—like my mom would've been. I made so many wrong choices in my relationships just so I could find acceptance or even a place I could call home." Shaking her head, she swallowed a bitter regret. None of that earned her a happy ending. "Sometimes I wonder if there's ever enough of what I do."

"You're enough, Hope." His gaze locked on hers, and his voice was fierce and filled with care. "You don't have to go out of your way to be noticed. You're you. Just enough."

Under his gaze, she felt seen. She felt enough. For long moments, she sat there peering back at him, absorbing those words. *You're you. Just enough.*

Then he looked away, picked up his fork, and tested the matooke. "What happened, Hope? How did your mom die?"

"A snakebite." She swirled her fork through her food. Her gaze flitted to the chickens across from their clearing, and a heaviness pressed to her chest. Shifting, she gripped her shoulder bag tight against her chest. She carried antivenom on her ever since she could earn money. She had no idea whether it worked or not.

"I was twelve then, and I didn't know what to do." It was during the school holiday. "Mom used to work at a boarding school, but when school was over, we would go back to our remote village." To the tiny house Father had bought Mother to live in.

A shiver coursed through her over memories of Mama's last day. Hope wrapped her arms around herself. "I ran and left her so I could go call for help. By the time I came back with someone, she was…" She closed her eyes, reeling in tears, erasing the scene she'd tried to remove since then.

"I'm so sorry, Hope." Gavin leaned forward, his hand touching her leg. The compassion laced in his voice touched her even deeper, and she released an involuntary tear.

"It's going to be okay." He reached across the table and rubbed his thumb over her face as he wiped away the tear. "I'm sorry your dad and stepmother weren't as helpful when you were grieving."

Just thinking about them reminded her that she had no place to call home. Still, she squared her shoulders and snuffled back further tears. "I'm sure my father loved me in his own way. Otherwise, he wouldn't have come after me when Mama died."

She stared at the flies hovering over their food and waved them off. Here she was again talking about herself. Ugh, it showed how she desperately needed someone to talk to. "I'm sorry I've stopped you from eating your lunch."

He simply quirked his lips and lowered his hand to the table, his thumb still slick from her tear. "Lunch is the last thing I want right now."

Had she scared him off or not?

"I heard rumors there's a mango tree ripe with fruit not far from here." He gestured to the food now swarming with flies. "Maybe we can have this recooked and go scope out some mangoes?"

Glad to have the subject changed, she let his light tone buoy her. "Mangoes sound good."

Maybe she hadn't scared him off.

But how long would it be before he slipped from her fingers like every other good thing she'd almost grasped?

CHAPTER 11

Rays of morning sunlight shot through the trees around the hospital as Gavin shook Brady's hand. Brady and Ruth were taking two patients to a hospital in the city for major surgeries.

"I'm only going for moral support," Brady said. "Ruthie is the one going to be working."

"No need to convince me you can't stay away from your wife longer than five minutes." Gavin followed his gaze to Ruth and Hope, both in deep conversation close enough to hear.

"We'll be back very late tonight." Ruth pulled Hope into an embrace. "If you need anything, besides Akiki's help, have Ali take you to my parents' house."

"We'll be fine." Hope eased back, her delicate face aglow. She looked stunning with her hair wrapped with an orange cloth headband matching the top she'd tucked into dark shorts. "We've met so many wonderful people in the village, and Komo is close enough to the temporary clinic to get us anything we need."

"I take it Hope is not just a friend anymore?" Brady's hushed comment stirred Gavin from his thoughts.

"Um." Gavin scratched his stubbled jaw, heat creeping up his face. He must've been staring at Hope. He refocused on Brady. "I'm sorry, what?"

He had to act unsure of what Brady said, but his friend smiled before dropping the subject. Thank goodness!

"Are you sure you both don't need to ride bicycles to the clinic?"

"Have you forgotten I hike fourteeners in Colorado? Any hike here should be a walkover, and Hope prefers walking too." Given what Hope had been through, the woman would no doubt trek through fire. So, a ten-mile walk should be nothing, especially when she wasn't carrying water like she'd had to in her hikes back home.

"If we don't come back tonight, Akiki will take good care of you." Brady patted the pockets of his khaki pants. "I'll have my phone if you succeed in getting service."

"Quit worrying about us." Gavin had given up carrying his phone or wallet. When he glanced at the ladies, he found Hope looking at him. Her smile made his chest flutter, and he waved. After she waved back and gripped her bag tight across her shoulder, he caught Brady lifting his brows. Ignoring his friend's curiosity, Gavin addressed the inevitable. "As long as we don't have to carry any medical supplies, we'll be fine. Dongo's been great delivering the supplies the last two days, and the nurses take whatever's leftover on their bikes. So we're good."

Finally, Brady and Ruth walked to the car where Dongo and the two patients waited. Gavin strolled over to Hope, jammed his hands into his pockets, and tipped his chin to the dirt path. "Are you ready for our adventure?"

"I'm ready." She ducked her head, her smile shy as she clutched her bag. It was the most-appreciated gift he'd ever given to anyone and made him want to buy her a handbag. Had he known she didn't have a purse, he'd have bought her a quality one.

How she'd opened up about her past warmed him. She'd told him secrets she'd never told anyone.

Something had shifted in their friendship so much that he had to assure himself they were just friends. Perhaps that could set his mind straight from these unexpected feelings. It was too soon for him to pursue a new relationship.

"It's a beautiful morning." Her soft voice reeled him out of his thoughts as they started for the narrow path in the woods, a shortcut they'd explored on the way home yesterday.

"Yes, it is." As they ducked past gnarled tree branches and marino sunbirds swooped across their path, he scrambled to find a new topic. "You're skilled with your haircuts."

"So were you in dressing wounds." She walked beside him when the path widened.

"You were popular with the villagers."

"So were you." She waved a hand in the air, lighthearted compared to the heavy conversation they'd shared yesterday. He wouldn't have guessed she'd endured such hardship if she hadn't told him. "Where did you learn to wrap and bandage sores?"

"It's a skill I acquired here. Definitely going on my resume."

"It's good to have lots of skills." She gave him a sideways glance.

"Speaking of new skills... why didn't you want training on giving immunizations? What do you have against shots?"

"Ooh." She rubbed her hands up and down her arms, grimacing. "Nothing, except they terrify me. I hope I never have to get one or inject anyone."

"Bad experience with immunizations?"

"That and any sickness requiring injections." She stifled a laugh. "There was this one time I was eleven." Then she shook her head. "I was ill with malaria, and Mama took me to the doctor."

Gavin stepped ahead, took her hand, and helped her climb over the rock jutting into the path.

"As soon as the doctor pulled out the injection needle, I started running out of the clinic. Mama and the doctor had to chase after me across the road." She snickered. "I don't know how I got the energy to run, but the doctor caught me. I remember fighting out of his arms."

Gavin chuckled, picturing an eleven-year-old Hope—probably even more petite, but just as determined as the girl she was now—flailing to get out of the doctor's hold.

Her laughter rang through the field mingling into nature's lullaby as birds sang in trees and cattle mooed in the distance.

"Mama won when she promised me a sweet." Her voice dipped low when she talked about the last year and special memories of her mom. "Vanilla ice cream." Her gaze flitted to the vibrant yellow shrubs wafting a sweet scent. "That was the first and last day I had ice cream. I didn't even enjoy it since I wasn't well, yet it's one of my favorite memories of me and Mama."

Sadness engulfed Gavin. He didn't even know what to say since he'd never lost anyone close. He'd have to take her for ice cream before he left Uganda. They walked in silence approaching a narrow road, and he touched the small of her back to let her lead.

"I feel like I'm always the one doing all the talking." She spun to face him, walking backward. "Tell me more about you. About your family."

"I have a brother. Two years younger than I am, and we're best friends. He loves the city and prefers corporate work." Jeremy couldn't be more different from Gavin, but Jeremy landed his dream job with Stone Enterprises, thanks to Eric and Logan Stone. "He likes to work too much, and I like having some down time every so often."

While Jeremy tried not to stress over what Mom expected of him, he and Gavin still had to put up with her meddling. Gavin the most, since he lived closer to home.

Hope kept walking backward, her delicate face tipped up at him, her eyes alight with curiosity. "What about your parents?" She pivoted to walk forward, her voice dipping into a whisper. "Are you close?"

"We have a decent relationship." He could imagine it being a painful topic for her, but whatever problems he had with his folks were nothing compared to what she'd shared. So he kept it simple. "They live in the same town I do."

She gave him a sideways glance. She was so adorable with her teeth bit into her plush lower lip. "Besides bandaging sores, what do you do for fun?"

"What we're doing right now. Hikes." He kicked a broken tree limb on the path. "Rock climbing and anything that gets me up and going."

"By rock climbing, you mean, instead of climbing a tree you climb a giant rock?"

He scanned the dense forest. Broken tree limbs and random rocks scattered about, and the smell of rotten wood tinted the air while hammers in the distance split the silence. "So far, I haven't seen any rocks here similar to the cliffs we have back home. I also like traveling." He halted, pulling her to stop when a critter scampered in the path.

"Are there lots of beaches in America?"

"In Colorado, we don't have beaches, but there are several states by the ocean."

"I've always dreamed of going to the beach." She talked about the few resorts she'd read about in her country and Uganda. "I also find waterfalls fascinating. Do you have any in Colorado?"

"We do. But there are more fascinating waterfalls outside Colorado." His focus spiraled, waylaid by thoughts of visiting Niagara Falls with her or them standing in front of any waterfalls as he—

"Uganda has some waterfalls too." Her words brought him back to focus.

"Looks like you did some research."

"I like reading and looking at magazines with pictures of captivating places and things." Her face radiant, she adjusted her bag on her chest. "One time, I saw a magazine with decorated homes. They displayed pictures before and after the homes were decorated. I can't believe people get paid to do that. It made me dream of doing something like that."

"Like interior designing and staging?"

She turned, her eyes wide. "Is that what it's called?"

He nodded. "I have to hire interior designers to stage the homes I sell." His mind wandered to a future of them working together. "If you came to America, I'd hire you as my stager."

"Going to America? I never dreamed of something like that."

They stepped out of the dense forest and walked through an expansive field with cows grazing, the smell of soil and manure tinting the air.

"Would you ever like to come to America?"

"That would be a dream come true." She laughed. "Things don't go as I plan, but it would be nice to see what a highly-developed country looks like."

"Not just looking. You'd stay with me." His excitement mounted, his words tripping, which was the first. "I mean work. Doing something you enjoy."

But she held up a hand. "I don't know how to decorate. I just have a feeling it's something I'd enjoy doing."

"I've seen the way you arranged the restaurant tables and buffet spread and folded those napkins into flowers." How she moved the tiny bookshelf in his cottage at different angles to keep the room more open. "You're creative, and you pay attention to detail. You even folded the toilet papers into flowers." He'd said that or something similar already, hadn't he?

"I enjoyed it."

At least she didn't seem to mind his lack of expressiveness. She bent forward and plucked a flower from the grass, reminding him of the bouquets she'd arranged on every table and in every room. Then she brought the bloom to her nose. "What was life like growing up in America? Did you live in a fancy city?"

He relaxed, keeping their pace slow as the dewy grass kissed his bare shins. "I didn't play much sports, though my brother did, but we both liked going to the movies and watching TV."

"Hmm." She tipped her head to one side, swept her hair over her shoulder, then tucked the flower behind her hair. "We never saw movies and such, having no television access. But I *love* reading. I'll read just about any book anyone lets me borrow."

Sad how she'd only had limited access to books. It was incredible how she'd taught herself since she was twelve. She spoke English so fluently that he'd assumed she'd at least graduated high school.

As Komo's grass-thatched house came into view, they walked through vibrant and unique shrubs and more flowers sprinkled through the grass. Hope knew almost all the names of the plants and flowers he inquired about.

"How do you know all about those?" He took her hand in his and helped her jump over another log on their path. Her long, delicate fingers fit so perfectly in his.

"I read this book about plants. It's good to know what plants can be used for medicine in case I don't have real medicine."

As they approached the hut, dust stirred in the air from Komo sweeping.

A black cat, probably the same stray from the other day, flitted across the yard, and Hope shuddered. "I hope the cat doesn't give us bad luck."

"We'll be fine." He shrugged, not much into superstition, but little wonder she was so swayed by Komo's beliefs when she believed bad luck followed her. "Bad things can happen to everyone, even without encountering a black cat."

Once they were within hearing distance, he waved and called out his hello, so they didn't startle Komo. He slowed his pace as he approached. The smell of cow dung soured the air. Nearby, five cows lolled in a grassy area with a wooden split fence.

Komo smoothed her long floral gown. "What an early surprise." Her smile was soft as she braced the stick broom against a wall and walked toward them. "I thought Dongo was taking you to the clinic."

"Don't let us keep you from your work." Hope tipped her chin to the dense forest across the yard. "We're headed to the clinic."

Komo shaded her eyes to look up at the clear blue sky. "I can make you some tea as soon as I put out my maize in the sun."

"We just ate." Gavin spoke fast, not ready for the millet porridge and insects again, but also unwilling to hurt her feelings by turning her offer down. "You'll be making us lunch in no time."

"We'll be glad to help you put out maize before we go." Hope then glanced at him as if wondering if it was okay.

"Yes, tell us what to do, and we'll help." He smiled. He'd rather work than scarf down an exotic breakfast.

"Ali is supposed to help me, but he went to make milk deliveries."

With their insistence, they helped Komo with corn. She took them to her small storage house where corn ears formed a pile in one corner. Using metal buckets, they carried the corn and spread it out on the dirt.

"I'm going to ask Komo to make us millet porridge for lunch." Hope's breath tickled his neck as she whispered while they walked back into the hut.

"Don't you dare." He poked at her ribs, and she jumped, chuckling a sweet laugh that warmed his insides.

Working with her seemed natural and easy. A special connection was forming between them, which became clearer when he found himself stealing glances at her and caught her staring at him during their tasks at the clinic almost an hour later.

Today was slower, and the two helpers from yesterday were there today too. The children who showed up midafternoon only came to talk to Gavin and wanted to touch his hair. Oddly, they found his hair intriguing. They lingered and played in the open space, their laughter refreshing.

When he didn't have people to bandage, he moved to Hope's tent where she was finishing cutting a middle-aged woman's hair.

"You want to try haircuts today?" Hope offered over the razor, and he elbowed her.

"If I give haircuts, we will be treating head injuries." He'd nick someone's scalp with the razor for sure.

"I can teach you."

"Maybe I'll take you up on that." After all, they were in the village for almost a year, or at least, he was. Who knew how long Hope would stay? He pressed his lips tight, the thought of her leaving unsettling him.

Then a preteen girl showed up, and Hope spoke to her in English about Gavin cutting her hair. The girl's face lit up. "Haircut from a mzungu?"

Gavin felt like a celebrity, although he was just a normal guy from Peasant View. He took Hope's place on the stump, and she showed him how to position the comb and scissors onto the hair. Then he carefully moved the razor from the front center and toward the middle, asking the girl if he was hurting her.

"I'm okay." She giggled. "I'll tell everyone that Mzungu gave me a haircut."

Odd to picture her boasting about him. Knowing he was the one being privileged to help, not the other way around, Gavin concentrated to ensure he didn't hurt the sweet girl. Then he and Hope alternated between giving haircuts and bandages. After lunch, several kids showed up in their blue school uniforms, but they didn't need haircuts. They wanted him to play soccer. Others, who knew English, asked him to read them the Bible story from the pamphlet they'd given out.

Hope played football with him and the kids, falling a couple of times when the game got overly exciting. Eventually, some kids wanted to play a different game, and she led that group in the game of kwepena with two shooters throwing a soft ball at a group of dodgers between them.

While Gavin played soccer with his group, they kept correcting him.

"It is football!" they shouted, giggling. He coughed a few times when the dust stirred.

Once the clinical day ended, he and Hope walked back toward Komo's house. His arms hurt from the arm hair the kids had been tugging and from kids who sat on his arm while they all fought for his lap. But, after seeing the children's smiles and experiencing his growing friendship in this foreign land, there was no place he'd rather be.

Now, they paused, watching the sun dip below the horizon and the sky transform into a canvas of colors. As the day gave way to twilight, he savored this connection with Hope that went beyond their shared pain. They were two souls on a journey of healing and self-discovery. Would they find it alone—or together?

CHAPTER 12

As the colors faded, Gavin guided Hope to start along the path to Komo's house again.

She tugged at her shoulder bag, adjusting the strap. "You were a superstar out there."

"So were you." Stopping short of pulling her close, he thrust his hands into his shorts pockets. What was wrong with him? One moment, he was reminding himself to avoid heartbreak, but the next minute, he couldn't keep himself away from her.

"What did you think of 'football'?" she teased.

"By the end of my trip, all the kids will be calling it soccer." He eyed her sideways as they continued strolling, their dirt path illuminated by the golden sunset peeking through the dense tree canopy.

"Maybe by then I'll have improved my skills so I'm not slipping whenever the game gets exciting."

"You just didn't see me, but I had a worse tumble."

"No way!"

"Yes way." A low chuckle rumbled in his throat. "This kid yanked at my leg hair, and I staggered, tripping and trying to make sure I didn't crush the little guy when I fell."

She curled her fingers around her shoulder bag's strap, and her shoulders shook. "I wish I'd seen that."

"Yeah, well, of course, they all thought it was funny." He mocked a frown, but couldn't help laughing along with her.

As their laughter subsided, she touched his shoulder, excitement sparkling in her eyes. "Well, you missed some mischief from the kids on my team. This monkey snatched a banana from a boy's bag, and these three kids... they..." As she spoke through laughter, the sound cut off her words and rose to meet the chattering of exotic birds, and he fought to understand the story.

He nudged her arm. "You mean to tell me there was a monkey and I didn't see it?"

She nodded, gesturing to the trees around them.

The breeze rustled the surrounding foliage as if whispering tales of the day's adventures. It seemed their joy infused the very air with a special connection amid the simplicity and beauty of their shared work.

Then something black leaped from one branch to another. Gavin halted, stopping and touching Hope's shoulder to stand still. It leaped again, and another one jumped to the branch. "You see that?"

"Monkeys." She shrugged as if this happened daily.

He patted his pockets, but they were empty. "I should've brought my phone."

"You'll have plenty of time to take pictures. If I remember, you said you plan to be here for a year."

"That's right. How about you?"

"As you already know"—her voice fell to a whisper—"I don't have much of a plan. I'm happy being in the village as long as I can."

"Let's go see the monkeys." He'd never seen a monkey in its natural setting this close. Leading the way into the tall grass, he stomped his tennis shoes on it to make a path for her, his feet sinking into the soft earth. The cool grass brushed dew against his legs. Then an intense pain jabbed his left ankle. He hadn't expected a complicated trek.

"Maybe we should turn around—"

He struggled to lift his foot off the ground, clutching at his left shin where a tender soreness spread.

"What happened?" Her brows narrowing, she reached for his hand.

"Something bit me. We better go before you get..." He tried to look through the rustling grass. But his eyes felt fuzzy, and the forest seemed to be narrowing in on them.

"Gavin!" Hope called, her hand sliding to his back and around his waist. "What if it's a *snake*? Where does it hurt?"

"I..." He tried to focus as her voice rose. His heart started a rapid race. He'd never been bitten by a snake, so how could he know what it felt like?

"Let's get to the path, so I can check." She helped him, her heavy breaths indicating he was leaning his weight into her, but he was struggling to hobble. His vision remained blurred, and beads of sweat poured down his forehead.

At the path, she lowered him to sit on the dirt. His body dropped when he tipped his head back and thumped on the ground.

"Gavin!" Hope's screech became more urgent and distant. Her soft fingers touched his leg. "There's two bite marks. It's a poisonous snakebite!"

Whatever she meant, it had better not involve him walking out of here on his own.

"Oh dear God, please! I hope this medicine works."

Something pierced through his flesh. Like an injection.

"Gavin? Can you hear me? I can't be too sure this will work. We need to get you out of the forest. I can't leave you here alo..."

Her voice was fading with each word until he couldn't hear her anymore. He felt trapped in a disorienting rollercoaster ride, hurled around in the void. Where was Hope? Why couldn't he hear her soothing voice to anchor him? Was this what being on the brink of death felt like?

Through the fog, he half sensed movements and bumps. But who knew how long that lasted? When he stirred, his eyes adjusted to a dim, flickering candlelight encased in a glass holder. In its tender glow, he could make out Hope's figure curled up on a mat next to him. The wavering light caressed her pixie face, accentuating her flawless skin and the long eyelashes kissing her cheekbones. She was huddled up, shuddering breaths rocking her body. Dried tear tracks marked her cheeks. Had she been shedding tears for him?

Fragments of memories began to piece together, disjointed images of Hope in a state of panic as she urged him from the cool, dew-kissed grass to the dry path. She had spoken in a panicked voice about needing to bring him to help, insisting that she couldn't leave him alone to go get assistance.

Somehow, he summoned the strength to lift his hand, reach out, and touch her head. Her hair was caught back in a ponytail, but he yearned to see it loose, his fingers itching to sift through her tresses.

Feeling her stir, he retracted his hand. Her eyelids fluttered open, a hint of confusion creasing her face as if she was rousing from a disorienting dream.

A wave of intense emotion washed over him, his heart constricting at the sight of her. Here was a woman, a ray of sunshine and warmth, who had never felt loved by her own family. "I..." He fought for the strength to speak. "I see you, Hope."

"Gavin!" She gasped, sitting up with a start. The disbelief etched on her face gave way to a relieved smile.

And he touched her face, his shaky fingertips grazing flawless skin. "Even if you think no one sees you. Don't ever let anyone say you don't matter."

"You're alive," she breathed out, her voice barely a whisper. Her hand covered his, cupping his palm to her cheek. Tears welled in her eyes, wetting his hand and cascading down her other cheek. Then she flung her arms around him and buried her face in the crook of his neck. The warmth of her breath kissed his skin, and her whisper resonated in his ear. "I was worried you were going to die."

"You saved my life." He moved his shaky hand up and down her back, trying to still her trembling form. She was still frightened, and that stirred a wholehearted feeling of gratitude.

"I'm okay." He wasn't fully recovered, but he was alive. All thanks to her.

She moved off him. "I'm sorry for my outburst." She palmed tears away from her cheeks before lying back down next to him. "Running into that black cat this morning didn't—"

"The black cat didn't send the snake." Gavin cut her off, not wanting her to dwell on superstitions that had nothing to do with the outcome. "*I* caused what happened. *I* was foolish. *I* ventured off the path without wearing boots as Brady recommended."

Still, his heart swelled. She cared for him. That much was clear.

"Did you get help?" Uncertain of how they had made it from the forest to the house, he moved his hand toward hers resting nearby. His pinkie grazed hers.

"As soon as I got you here, Komo and Ali left on the bicycle to go find a doctor."

The ten-year-old Ali could ride his grandma on a bike like a pro. But that meant Gavin hadn't been treated yet. He tried to lift his aching leg, but he grunted at the pain. The leg felt like it was buried under a brick, too hard to move. The mat pressing against his back didn't help either.

"How come I feel better?"

She reached into her bag and pulled out a tiny, now-empty glass vial. "I had some medicine."

"Was that one of the medicines you purchased?"

She nodded. "I have an older one in the bag, but I figured using a recent one would be more successful. I wasn't sure it was going to work." She shuddered. "I–I injected the fluid into a vein with a needle I've kept for such a time."

His pinkie twitched and linked with hers. "I thought you were terrified of giving injections."

She grimaced and shuddered. "It was a matter of life or death."

The unspoken fear that had loomed over her now dissipated. Her joy for his survival stirred him, and his throat tightened. His pinkie locked tighter around hers as he battled the overwhelming sentiment.

Then he reached out and cradled her soft cheek. Her luminous eyes stared at him with an astounding warmth and tenderness.

"I prayed. For you. It worked." Her conviction and quiet strength resonated.

"Thank you," he managed to say. His thumb wiped at the lone tear now glossing her cheek, and his fingertips probed her hair. Then curiosity got the better of him. "How did you get me here?"

A breathy chuckle escaped her lips, and she rolled her eyes. "You don't want to know."

Her words further fueled his curiosity. For someone who weighed half what he did, how had she managed it?

"I carry a cloth hammock in my bag in case I get stranded and I have to use it."

Gavin couldn't help but laugh as she described hoisting him onto a large tree branch she'd put below the hammock. "Of course, the cloth ripped, but I didn't want to leave you behind."

Her voice fell to a somber whisper, her eyes clouded over, and he understood. She must be bombarded by memories of when she'd had to leave her mom to seek help. As the weight of her past hung between them, he scooted closer and drew her against him.

"I'm sorry about your mom." He pressed the words into her soft hair, hoping they'd be powerful enough to carry a world of sympathy.

She nodded against his chest, and they lapsed into a tender silence. As he lay there with her, a profound certainty grounded him. Tonight marked the beginning of a new chapter in his life. He wasn't sure where Hope fit into this newfound path, but he was sure she was etching her presence in the hidden recesses of his heart.

CHAPTER 13

After tugging the bone bead onto the black leather cord, Hope propped her chin on her hand, displeased with the necklace. She detached the bead and rummaged through a wooden tray on the table for more. As she selected two petite antique silver beads, an idea sparked. Flanking the central bone bead with these could amplify her creative side.

Low-slanting afternoon light streamed in through the posts supporting the gazebo-style church, and voices reverberated under its tin roof. Ruth had invited Hope along for a craft afternoon with the widows. With Gavin and Brady showing some new volunteers around the market, Hope found solace in making things by hand.

After visiting various crafting groups, she'd retreated to the jewelry supply table to attempt to create a necklace, a technique she'd learned from one of the local women.

"What are you making?" Ruth's hand on her shoulder made Hope jump in her woven chair.

"I..." Hope lifted the necklace. "I'm still figuring this out."

Ruth plopped into a nearby woven chair, then patted her stomach, smiling. "This little one might have some football skills." Hope didn't register what Ruth was saying until Ruth offered. "Would you like to feel the baby move?"

"Really?" Hope set the necklace down and scooted her chair to Ruth's side. "You can feel the baby?"

In answer, Ruth took Hope's hand and placed it on the side of the lower abdomen. Instantly, Hope gasped. "I can't believe it!" It was the most incredible and unique thing she'd ever felt. "I can't wait to meet her or him."

Ruth had said that they chose not to find out the gender, wanting it to be a surprise.

"Thank you for letting me feel your baby." Hope settled back in her chair, still surprised Ruth felt comfortable letting a stranger like her touch her baby. It meant a lot, like Ruth considered her as a friend.

"That looks perfect." Ruth nodded to the necklace on the table. "I think Gavin will like it."

Heat tingled up Hope's neck to warm her cheeks. "How did you know it was for him?"

Ruth exhaled, resting her hand on her stomach. "It's a man's necklace. I mean, I guess it leans more toward the unisex style, but I'm a romantic at heart. I just have a feeling."

"Do you think he'll like it?" No reason not to be honest since Ruth was onto her.

"He'll like it because you made it for him." Ruth reached for the bead tray and stirred the beads. They jingled in response. "You can never go wrong when giving a gift to someone you love."

"He and I are not—"

"Not together yet, and your heart won't keep you from fighting that attraction toward him."

That was undeniably true. "He's been so kind to me." After Ruth had considered her a friend with such an intimate moment, how could Hope not reciprocate by confiding in her? She'd already explained her reason for leaving home when Ruth had inquired. Ruth was becoming her closest friend here, besides Gavin, but Hope couldn't discuss her attraction to him *with him*.

"I'm certain he feels the same about you." Ruth smiled her reassurance. But how would she know how Gavin felt?

"He didn't need to express his feelings." Ruth continued. "It's evident in the way he looks at you when you're not looking. Much like how you look at him." Her smile widening, she shook a finger at

Hope. "I saw you fanning yourself the other day as you watched him stretch in the compound."

"No, you didn't." Hope's words came out weak. Surely, no one had seen her check Gavin out? Ducking her head, she buried her face in her hands, but her heart fluttered. Especially when Ruth added that Gavin hadn't stopped appreciating her for saving his life.

A chill crept up her spine. "His face was so pale." That evening could've changed her life for the worse. "I'm grateful I had some medicine." And that it worked.

Gavin had taken a few days to recuperate. Komo and Ali had returned with a doctor who identified the king cobra bite. He had more antivenom vials available to complete his treatment.

Upon their return, Ruth and Brady were shocked. Ruth claimed they'd never had any incidents of snakebites on that path, while Brady again advised everyone to wear boots when traversing the village's dense forests. The locals often walked barefoot without issue, so Gavin's encounter was an unfortunate outlier.

"You both will be in the village for a while. Soon, you'll come to realize you're in love." Ruth's words, laced with certainty, drew Hope back from that horrid experience and left her awash with anticipation.

She'd noticed a change in her relationship. Gavin seemed to be making an effort to spend time with her. When the new volunteers arrived and they were assigned to different clinics throughout the village, he requested to work alongside her.

"If only my past didn't keep haunting me," she whispered, unintentionally voicing her thoughts. Embarrassed, she grabbed the necklace and started to knot the end as a distraction. Gavin would return to his homeland and reunite with his ex.

"Hope." Ruth touched her shoulder. "You mentioned you're in Uganda to start new. Every day, God gives us a fresh start. Transformation defines you."

Hope pinched her brows together. "I'm afraid I don't understand what you mean by transformation."

"Your past may shape you." Ruth's gentle eyes searched Hope's, her hand warm on her shoulder. "But you have the promise of transformation to overcome your past. If you let your past hold you back, it will prevent your promise of a bright future. You must always remember the power of transformation that comes with our quest for God. When we're surrendering everything to Him, He can rewrite all the wrongs in our past and grant us a fresh start."

A fresh start. God.

Did God still care for her? Had He been with her during her challenging journeys up the mountains? Was He with her now? Even as she battled those questions, Ruth's advice not to cling to her past resonated. Yet, how could anyone forget everything all at once? It was all too much to think about in one evening. But there were many other topics she could talk about with Ruth.

Hope stilled her fingers on the knot she'd bunched up too thick. "I was wondering... You and Brady... Do cultural differences ever cause any issues in your relationship?"

Organizing the beads with a fond smile, Ruth replied, "Those were minor issues. The real struggle was when Brady was ready to return to America and I couldn't accompany him. I had people relying on me here."

Just like how Gavin would have to leave Hope behind. The thought bored a deep hole of sadness within her, and she slumped over, collapsing into it.

"Long-distance dating was challenging, but our love for each other and our faith in God carried us through those times."

Hope sat up straighter. "What does faith in God mean?"

"Faith is more than mental agreement. It's about trusting God and having confidence that He will fulfill His promises."

"Promises like?" Hope tipped her head, intrigued by these spiritual terms.

"The Bible is brimming with God's promises. Like the book of Proverbs that I often see you reading. It contains some of these promises."

Hope jerked her head up. She'd never thought of it like that, but Ruth was still speaking.

"It's important to have a personal relationship with God. Just like having a personal relationship with those around you helps you understand them—their wants, thoughts, and needs—a personal relationship with God helps you understand who He is." Ruth shrugged, holding up both hands. "I must sound confusing, but understanding spiritual things becomes easier the more you engage in them."

Hope pressed her lips together, then blurted out, "With my limited experience in nurturing healthy relationships, it takes me longer to understand how to manage personal relationships with people, let alone with, well, God." Still, she felt a sense of relief knowing there were things beyond her control, and she could only do so much.

Ruth and Hope chatted about the upcoming days, Ruth's impending motherhood, Brady's parents' visit after the baby was born, and other random topics. Then she mentioned the plans for the day after tomorrow, her eyes gleaming dreamily. "I hear you and Gavin are camping on the veranda tomorrow."

"He did mention something about camping, but I didn't realize he planned to give me the full experience." Excitement bubbled. Just what would camping on the veranda entail?

That same anticipation stayed with her as she and Ruth bicycled back home. The scent of Akiki's cooking greeted them when they entered the house. After a refreshing shower, Hope demonstrated how to craft table centerpieces using napkins.

"How did I do?" Akiki placed her tower-shaped napkin in the center next to Hope's.

"You're a quick learner," Hope complimented, then glanced at Ruth's creation that kept collapsing.

Ruth's shoulders sagged. "I'll need more detailed instructions."

"You're getting there, but let's start over." Hope then helped Ruth to unfold the napkin and start again. "Bring in the other corner and—"

"I wouldn't trust your driving skills again," a deep voice down the hallway interrupted, and Hope pivoted toward the sound.

"Like I would trust yours," Gavin's voice retorted, and her heart pounded.

"I'll get dinner ready." Akiki slipped away, and Ruth responded with something Hope didn't quite catch, too absorbed in deciding whether to look at the table or the hallway.

The men continued their banter and emerged before Hope could avert her gaze. When Gavin's gaze met and held hers, a dizzying rush of admiration left her tipsy.

GAVIN PANTED, BREATHLESS, as he pushed the bicycle over a steep incline. The weight of his passenger, Brady, added to the already demanding challenge, making the task far more rigorous than his usual mountain-biking escapades. The narrow winding road and the flimsy bicycle didn't help matters.

The sun was setting, hidden behind the trees lining the horizon, yet the sticky humidity lingered in the evening air. The chafing of bags against his back increased his discomfort as he maneuvered over broken tree limbs and swatted away persistent mosquitoes. When the front tire swerved off the path, he almost lost balance but managed to steer back on track.

"I'll assume Hope is a better cyclist than you," Brady grumbled from the back. "I'd hate to see my wife take a tumble."

"Hope is an excellent rider," Gavin interjected. The need to defend her was high. She had skillfully driven him to a remote clinic just the day before. And she'd praised him when he'd taken a turn cycling them to help a local villager with his roof. "Unlike you, Hope knows I'm a good bicyclist."

"Speaking of Hope..." Brady prodded. "Has she helped you forget, um, about...?" He cleared his throat, and predicting where the conversation was heading, Gavin focused on the last bit of the climb. "I mean... are you two—"

"It's too soon for me." Gavin cut him off. The response seemed more to convince himself not to fall for Hope, though he suspected he was already halfway there, if not entirely smitten. Lucky was becoming more of a vague memory and Hope a lively reality.

"The necklace you bought her today is all about friendship, then?" Brady snickered.

Unsure of where he stood with Hope, Gavin opted for a safe answer. "The necklace is to thank her for saving my life. And the hammock, like I already told you—"

"I doubt Hope expects you to repay her."

Of course, Hope didn't expect him to repay her, but it gave him an excuse to buy her something.

"If you want to keep things in the friend-zone, spending each moment with her is not going to help your situation."

Right. Gavin was becoming increasingly aware of the palpable chemistry between them. Every thought of Hope brought an anticipation, a thrill he struggled to deny.

"And tone down those smoldering looks."

Heat zapped his neck and ears. Apparently, he hadn't been subtle enough about his growing attraction.

"You're always ogling your wife," he retorted. "How would you know about anyone's stares?"

"Do you want my advice?"

"No." But Brady would share his thoughts regardless.

"Lucky has been in and out of your life since high school. I doubt you've dated anyone else."

Gavin tensed up. His history with her was complicated and painful. They had dated on and off, breaking up only for her to return and him to welcome her back. The past three years had been mostly steady until their wedding-day fiasco. "Can we not talk about Lucky?"

"Today is the last day I'll utter her name. But first, I have to say this. Your mother tried to orchestrate your relationship with Lucky, restricting your freedom to make decisions. She reminds me so much of Bryce's mother that I think you should have a conversation with him about it."

Wendy Solace's interference in her son's relationships was notorious. Perhaps the two women being friends had rubbed off on each other somehow. "My mom is not that extreme."

Something large and dark darted into their path, and Gavin swerved, nearly crashing into the bushes.

"Come on, bud. It's just a rat."

"A rat?" Gavin's heart pounded. Now he had to worry about potential rodent encounters too? The rest of the ride was filled with imagined rodents, forcing him to swerve and dodge on multiple occasions.

"You're going to get us killed." Brady groaned.

"Quit being such a backseat driver," Gavin retorted, relieved when they reached the safety of their brick house nestled among the shrubs. They dismounted the bike, and Gavin parked it against a tree.

"That was the most harrowing route I've ever taken." Gavin removed his helmet and welcomed the cool evening breeze. Despite the excitement, he'd enjoyed the vibrant local market and the thrill of haggling with vendors. Perhaps he could take Hope sometime.

"I'm just glad to be alive." Brady handed Gavin his bag and continued complaining about Gavin's biking skills as they entered the house.

"Let's not forget who got us lost on the way."

Gavin's sentence faded when he spotted Hope. Something inside him stirred—a breathless magnetic pull. Her infectious smile tugged at his heart and trapped him between the urge to hold back and the desire to draw her into his arms.

But before he could decide what to do, Brady's mumbled words—*"keep lying to yourself"*—seeped into his consciousness anew, an icy splash of reality. Their sting reverberated through the veil of his daydream.

With a subtle headshake, he observed his friend move toward Ruth. Brady embraced his wife with a fervent kiss as though they were the only two people in the room before he leaned down to kiss Ruth's stomach and talk to their unborn child. Then he slid out a chair to settle beside Ruth. Yearning pulsed through Gavin.

"Gavin?" Ruth's voice cut into his thoughts. "How was the trip?"

"You should have seen him every time he thought he saw a rat." Brady chuckled, and soon, the couple became engrossed in conversation.

Gavin's heart thudded in his chest as he moved, taking the seat next to Hope at the dinner table. A close proximity he could neither ignore nor deny.

"Hey, you." He swallowed to moisten his dry throat. Then he handed her what he'd bought at the market.

Her eyes widened, and a smile spread across her cheeks as she pulled out a sturdy, yet comfortable hammock. And then—a vibrant two-strand necklace from the drawstring pouch.

"Oh, Gavin... These are wonderful." She caressed the small pendant dangling from the longer beaded strand.

"May I?" He extended his hand, offering to help her put on the necklace. Which was stupid, as it was pure torture when she turned her back and swooped her hair aside, exposing her long, delicate neck. Trying to concentrate, he fumbled with the clasp. Then his fingertips grazed her flesh. An outburst of goose bumps scattered over her neck and arms where her short-sleeve top exposed her skin.

"Thank you." Her appreciative tone wrapped around him, her sweet scent mingling with the earthy aroma wafting from the kitchen.

As the intensity of his emotions hit him full force, now seemed a good time to leave the room. He needed to breathe, but he also needed to shower. His clothes felt grimy against his skin, the dust and sweat of the day seeping through.

"I, uh, I need a shower," he mumbled, not waiting for a reply before retreating to his room, gathering clean clothes, and carrying them to the bathroom.

I'm not ready for relationships. He echoed this sentiment to himself as he lathered his hair, wishing he could rinse away and refute this yearning he harbored for Hope. He'd better remind himself why he was in Uganda. He tried doing so throughout dinner. Then he insisted on doing the dishes alone. "I want to learn how to hand wash them." He sent Hope and Akiki away. He didn't need their help mastering the technique.

Thus, he succeeded in maintaining his distance that night. Today, he hoped to do the same. They now had a group of over twenty volunteers, and their daily tasks had become more enriched and demanding as an optometrist, a dentist, and several more nurses offered their services, creating an energetic buzz.

The minivan dropped his group off at the far clinic, while Hope stayed with the group at the hospital. Perhaps she'd sensed his distance.

As he worked, his stomach churned. He rubbed at the clenching sensation. He shouldn't be acting this way. He'd have to make up for it tomorrow. After all, one couldn't be aloof with friends on Sunday. So, the next day, he accompanied the others to a packed church where a collage of colorful vibrant clothes formed a living rainbow. The contrast of how fancily the people dressed when not working their farms struck him yet again. When the greeter squashed them in between people in a row of benches, Gavin sat next to Hope, their hands brushing.

The church was unlike any he'd attended, not that he'd stepped into many churches. The structure was a combination of a gazebo and a tent, the metal roof amplifying the rich sounds of drums and cymbals.

Gavin settled in, determined to forget the last twenty-four hours now that Hope was beside him. He'd missed working with her, and even though they'd shared dinner and breakfast, it felt as if he hadn't seen her in a while.

During the songs, people danced, others raised their hands, and some let out exuberant cheers. Hope clapped along, appearing much more at ease than he felt, but each time, her body brushed against his. The man to his left also kept bumping his elbow into Gavin when he clapped.

A group of women from Sweden, two rows in front of them, followed the lead, their claps synchronizing with the others.

"Never seen anything like this before," he admitted to Hope, shouting over the singing and dancing.

"I feel alive here." She laughed, her face a canvas of joy. Though he barely heard her, he got her gist.

Embracing the vibrant energy, he began to clap, a feeble attempt to blend in. He found himself nodding along to the sermon, a lyrical mix of the local language and English. The audience's jubilant responses reaffirmed the preacher's words. The air brimmed with an energy he'd never experienced. And so many showed contentment, despite their limited means.

After the service, everyone gathered under the trees to share a meal prepared over open flames. Kids' cheerful voices rang out, and their happy faces exposed toothy grins as they sat in circles eating and laughing. Women with toddlers and infants breastfed in the open, not seeming to care about privacy.

Someone tapped his hand, drawing him from his contemplation. Another group of men and women then greeted him with warm handshakes and genuine smiles, and a surprising sense of belonging in the community enveloped him.

Most people spoke to him in the local language, so he had no clue how to respond. Unlike Hope who took the time to study the dictionary and managed to greet the locals in their language.

Before the Jesus film that night, he'd have to borrow Hope's dictionary and learn a few words so he could greet the villagers in their language.

Hours later, he sought out Hope where she'd tucked her feet up beneath her on a wooden chair, engrossed in a book on the porch. The necklace he'd given her twinkled in the afternoon sunlight against her green top, and her jean skirt exuded a sense of comfort.

"Gavin." Her British accent on his name stirred something in him.

"It looks like you've got a new book." He slid onto the wooden chair next to hers. The book's brown leather cover looked crisp and new, so it probably wasn't one from her well-loved collection.

She closed it to reveal the title. "Ruth gave me a Bible when I asked for one."

"I won't disturb you, but I was hoping to borrow your dictionary. I'd like to learn a few words before the evening's Jesus film."

Instead of handing him the dictionary, she reached into her bag and produced a clear pouch. "Actually, I made something for... you."

She gulped, not offering the pouch, but holding it close to her chest, perhaps hesitant to overshadow his previous gifts to her.

"May I see it?" He held out his hand. When she surrendered the bag, he slid out an African map pendant nestled between two antique silver beads on a leather cord.

The unexpected gift sent warmth coursing through his veins. "You..." His voice cracked, his heart hammering in his chest. "You made this for me?"

"I hope you like it."

He slipped on the necklace, then turned toward her for approval. Her pixie face tipped sideways. Her smile curved up her cheeks and set her eyes aglow. "It's perfect!" She clapped, echoing the words he had yearned to say about her.

"Thank you, Hope."

A moment of tension stretched between them as he shifted to pull her into a hesitant side hug. When he withdrew, he could feel her stiffen, and his heart sank at the reminder of unspoken feelings between them. "I'll always cherish it."

Hope rummaged in her bag and offered him a small green dictionary from her bag. "You said you needed this?"

"Thanks." He riffled through the pages, then stepped back. "I'll take off with this and let you enjoy your alone time."

Her gentle touch rested on his wrist, and her kind eyes peered into his. "Stay. I could use the practice too."

He sank back in the wooden chair beside her, only too willing to do as requested. Then, together, they delved into the language lesson. But, with Hope as his teacher, he was either going to master the language or be too distracted to learn anything at all.

CHAPTER 14

Encased by a mosquito net, Gavin folded his hands behind his head, the scratchy mat he reclined on softened a tad by the blanket he'd improvised as a cushion. Hope lay parallel, her quiet presence radiating a soothing calm.

Above them, the half-moon draped a tranquil light across the landscape while stars punctuated the night sky, their shimmering glow mimicking distant flames. The mosquito hums and frog croaks from the shrubberies' unseen depths reverberated through the vibrant wilderness beyond.

"This sure beats actual camping." He broke their companionable silence, his voice threading through the nighttime serenade. "Especially after that snake encounter, I'd rather not venture to sleep in the woods." Not in Uganda anyway. In his mountain town, there were no poisonous snakes as far as he knew.

"This is amazing." Wonder carried in her voice. Her gaze locked onto the star-studded canvas above them. An intense fascination lit up her features as she voiced her musings barely above a whisper. "Ever wonder what God looks like?"

Blindsided, he inhaled a sharp breath, and his thoughts flickered to the movie they'd watched. "I've never dwelled on that." That was just the truth. "My Christian friends often perceive God as a kind and merciful father."

"Hmm." Her sigh whispered toward him, the sound a poignant reminder of her past. "It's tough to picture that if you didn't grow up with a loving father."

His chest tightened. He could only imagine her relationship with her father. His childhood recollections were warm and affectionate, though marked by the subtle undertone of his father's yielding demeanor to his mother's dominance.

"That movie..." Her voice faded into the persistent hum of mosquitoes. "The subtitles didn't capture it fully, but it reminded me of the time I watched it in my language when the missionaries visited our village."

Hope had mentioned the missionaries offered her a scholarship and her father had passed the opportunity onto her sister. As he shifted his position to face her, the wavering light of a lamp set on the corner table caught the glint in her eyes. Talking about the movie was a better topic than her painful past, so he asked, "What did you find most captivating about the movie?"

"The crucifixion."

"Brutal." His brows pinched together at her answer. Did she favor action-packed scenes?

"But forgiving." She pressed her hands to her chest, her tone rich with reflection. "The sheer brutality of it... and amid it all, Jesus asking God to forgive them... It was... overwhelming."

Ah. Her sentiment sank in deeper now. He had imagined a more wrathful response from Jesus, a fierce reprisal on His tormentors. The on-screen portrayal of forgiveness felt almost divine. "And the resurrection... the realization of His prophecy." That thought alone had moved him to the brink of tears.

" 'I am with you, always—' "

" 'Until the end of time,' " he echoed, his gaze drifting back to the celestial display beyond their meshed canopy.

What did it mean to find solace in God? To pledge one's life to Jesus as they had been urged to do with numerous villagers demonstrating their commitment through prayers and standing in unity.

He barely noticed the shift, but her arm brushed against his. His hand found hers, and their fingers wove together, the physical contact anchoring their deep reflections while night sounds kept them company.

"I said the Sinner's Prayer," Hope confessed, her fingers squeezing his. "I thought I should tell someone."

Gavin recalled the overwhelming scene when people, young and old, had cried and prayed for divine acceptance. Their entwining fingers served as a tangible symbol of the spiritual experience they'd shared. His voice softened, his words emerging husky yet heartfelt. "I'm glad you did."

As silence descended again, they lay under the cosmic canopy, hearts grappling with the echoes of the film. Regardless of whether he prayed or not, he felt an invigorated sense of hope and faith and an understanding of God's love that ran deeper than ever before.

"What's your typical camping routine?" She redirected the conversation, her eyes reengaging with the stellar expanse.

"Sadly, I don't get to camp as much as I'd prefer. But I do make sporadic ventures into the wilderness every two or three years. The highlight is always the campfire."

She chuckled. "The lamp is doing a great job impersonating a campfire, then."

"Tonight"—he pointed upward at the sprawling canvas of stars—"it's not about the tent or the gear or even the fire. It's about connecting with nature and being present in the moment."

Shifting onto her side, she tucked her hands beneath her face, her luminous eyes reflecting the lamplight—or perhaps moonlight or starlight—seemed to shimmer with an inner light that was uniquely Hope. "You mentioned camping with your dad before?"

It seemed she remembered everything he'd told her—and he'd told her more things about himself than he'd assumed.

"Yes, a couple of times with him and my brother, Jeremy. One was for a Boy Scout event, the other, a school-organized father-son trip." How he cherished those moments, recognizing the sacrifice his father made. "He wasn't the outdoorsy type, but he showed up anyway."

"Tell me more about yourself. What was it like growing up in America?"

Leaning back on the hands he'd laced behind his head, Gavin sifted through his memory and started with the first camping mishap. Man, that stuck to his memory the most. He twisted his lips up in a nostalgic grin. "The first camping trip, we were supposed to cook our dinner over the campfire—sausages and beans. Simple enough, right?"

She giggled, her anticipation palpable even without him looking her way.

"Well... Jeremy was entrusted with the sausages. In a spectacular display of culinary misadventure, he managed to lose half of them to the fire within minutes."

Hope's laugh unsettled the quiet night. The frogs silenced, while somewhere an owl answered. "I can imagine a younger, more uncoordinated version of your brother wrestling with runaway sausages."

"But instead of getting upset, my dad just laughed it off and said, 'Well, boys, I hope you like your sausages extra crispy!' We were starving. We ended up eating the most charred, crunchy sausages I've ever had, and our beans were half cooked because we forgot about them amid the fiasco. Despite everything, that night remains one of my favorite memories with my dad. It's the hardest I ever remember seeing him laugh."

She sighed. "I would've loved to see a younger Gavin eating burned sausages and half-cooked beans."

He, too, would've loved seeing a younger version of Hope and shielding her from her past traumas.

They spoke of constellations and distant galaxies, of the stars above and the earth beneath, and of their journeys that had somehow intertwined in this small village. As she recalled the constellations she'd read about in nature books, he found himself in awe of her curiosity and thirst for knowledge.

Despite her limited travel experience, their exchange revealed a shared longing for adventure, another thread weaving together their friendship.

"I'm glad we're camping today." He reached out, his hand finding hers and their fingers interlacing. It was one of their first, um, dates? Ugh... No, this was still friendship, right?

"Camping with you is a fun adventure."

Just being with her now filled his heart with comforting warmth. His grin broadened as he peered into her eyes twinkling now under the moonlit sky. "It is."

Brady was right. Gavin's heart had always been held captive by Lucky, a woman ever-present in his family circle. Now, however, with Hope, he sensed new possibilities and an urge to break free from Lucky's shadow.

Shifting the focus to Hope, he asked about her childhood. There had to be happy moments, despite the hardships. He squeezed her hand. "Besides memories of having ice cream with your mom and the hospital-visit adventure, what else comes to mind?"

"Sneaking out Mom's favorite book and reading it." She giggled. "Of course, it was so big for me to read at nine, but I always laugh when I remember taking it from her table and reading it by the candle at night."

"Do you remember the title?"

"*Gone with the Wind.* I couldn't read most of the words, but I liked the idea of reading something." Her voice trembled as she recounted an altercation with her stepmother, resulting in the latter burning that book and Hope's other keepsakes from her mother. "That was the first time I ran away."

Torn between rage and sorrow, he moved closer and slipped his arm around her shoulders. As she leaned into him, her shaky breath warm against his neck, he felt her pain and ached over the injustice done to her. They lay in silence, his hand rubbing her back. He was willing to stay awake all night if it meant comforting her.

Tomorrow would be another day of reading to the children in the hospital, but perhaps afterward, they'd have some time for a nap.

The silence enveloped them, and soon her breathing grew shallow, her head relaxing against his chest. He closed his eyes and let his mind wander to the unknown future rather than the heartbreaking past. Taking her on new adventures, like skiing, mountain biking, and other activities he enjoyed in his mountain town. Perhaps Hope could help him explore the exotic dishes he hesitated to try. A future with those possibilities appealed to him. Yet he'd be lying if he didn't fear that Hope would break his heart like Lucky had.

The lure of sleep was strong, and he succumbed, despite the discomfort of the thin mat.

Then a distant rooster crowing awakened him. Hope was nestled against him, her rhythmic breaths warming his chest, her face snuggled into his shoulder. Her innocence stirred his protective instincts. His gaze roamed her sleeping form, taking in the gentle rise and fall of her chest, the sweep of her lashes against her cheekbones, the pointy tip of her chin, and the pouty form of her lips... A thought made his heart pound. What would it feel like to kiss her?

His body thrummed with exhilaration and anxiety. This was moving faster than he'd anticipated, and yet he craved more. His movement stirred Hope. Her eyelids fluttered open, and she sat up, the little pixie looking bewildered and adorable with her tousled hair.

"Sorry, I fell asleep." She tried to smooth her hair, her face scrunching.

Gavin shrugged, a grin stretching out his mouth. "You slept well?"

She rubbed her eyes before covering her mouth to stifle a yawn. "I must look like a mad person."

"I stopped worrying about my appearance when we got here." He scratched at his burgeoning beard, overdue for a trim.

"You always look good." Her gaze now drifted to the sun rising over the distant banana plantation. "Without even trying."

Unable to resist, he reached out to tuck loose strands of hair behind her ear. "You're naturally beautiful. That makes you perfect."

She hitched a breath and darted a glance at him before looking away.

New understanding charged the morning air. Then the rooster crowed again, bringing him back to reality. "Should we head back?"

She nodded. "Maybe catch another hour of sleep in a proper bed before starting the day?"

Sleep was the furthest thing from his mind while his heart was still racing from the night and the unknown possibilities of the day ahead.

CHAPTER 15

"Jambo, jambo bwana…" Gavin's voice trailed from behind, the melody dancing around Hope as she dug holes in the freshly turned earth. His singing threaded into the rhythm of their work. She dug the holes, he dropped the maize seeds, and Ali tucked them into the soil. Meanwhile, across the garden, Komo trimmed the imposing banana plants, her agile fingers working around the leafy abundance.

"What comes again after 'habari gani'?" Ali asked as Hope paused, her hands cradling the worn handle of her hoe. Her boots sank into the moist earth, the effects of yesterday's rain.

"Perhaps if we unite our voices, the words will find us easier," she suggested.

The glint in Gavin's eyes hinted at mischief as he lifted his seed-filled metal pail. Just his presence made each nerve in her body spring to life. "Our duet might need a leading lady, don't you think, Ali? Maybe that's why the lyrics elude us."

Ali bobbed his head, his toothless grin painting a playful picture as he nudged a clod of earth with his bare foot.

A mischievous grin lit Gavin's face as he stared at her. "Will you lead the chorus?"

He appeared at ease in this setting, wearing loose pants tucked into his boots. Aside from the necklace he'd been wearing since she gave it to him, he'd adopted this attire following Ruth's persistent warnings about the danger of snakes in the garden. Komo and Ali, however, seemed unconcerned, preferring to go barefoot like most of the villagers.

As Hope's knees weakened, she turned around to continue her task, plunged her hoe back into the earth, and resumed her pattern of neat rows. But a song would be a good distraction and motivation. "Just remember, it's a working song."

"Lucky for us, we're working." Infused with his lighthearted laugh, his words held the warmth that always seemed to touch her.

The familiar chorus rose in the garden once more. "Jambo, jambo bwana."

Now, the words flowed while they sang in unison. Yesterday, she'd told Gavin how singing energized her work, so he'd asked about the song. Then, alongside him, Ali had learned the melody while they cleared the garden for today's planting.

As the rains began in mid-March, Komo had worried about missing the planting season. With the abundance of volunteers at the clinics, Hope and Gavin could help Komo. They peeled dry corn from the cob and beat millet grain from the husks, getting both ready for grinding at the mill. And they'd cultivated the soil with oxen before Komo dug through for planting corn. This work, familiar to Hope, was unusual for Gavin, whose hands had become blistered, although he never complained.

"They'll get calluses soon and be fine. But we're in the village to lend a helping hand after all." Was his response wherever Hope voiced concern about his hands.

As the end of their song hung in the air, Gavin jammed his hands on his hips. "Why are we planting more maize when Komo's granary is full?"

"Maize is a staple," Hope explained, absently wiping the sweat off her forehead.

Ali chimed in. "And the stored maize is bound for the mill. We need more posho."

Hope understood the process. The maize needed to be fully dried before milling, a task she and Gavin had attended to earlier that morning.

The garden work, already second nature to Hope, became even more enjoyable with Gavin and Ali's playful banter. Gavin's interest in Ali's animal husbandry skills was endearing.

Ali took pride in his roles, sharing the names of their cows and chickens. "I sell milk and eggs too."

"You are a remarkable young man." Gavin clamped a hand on the boy's shoulder. Indeed, Ali's diligence was refreshing, particularly when compared to her siblings.

After their hard work, they retreated under the shade of clustered mango trees. They stood since Gavin was afraid to let them sit where snakes might creep up, and they savored the sweetness of ripe mangoes and guavas, their juicy delight a well-deserved refreshment. The tranquility seemed undisturbed, even when Ali decided to educate Hope and Gavin in the craft of slingshot creation.

"Perhaps we could learn after we've finished eating," Hope suggested, although Ali was already tearing a piece from his tattered T-shirt, displaying his bare stomach without a second thought.

"I've gathered some good sticks already." He gestured toward a pile of Y-shaped branches he'd extracted from a nearby shrub. "We should hunt some birds for a late afternoon snack."

"What!" Gavin nearly choked on his mango. The fruit, half-eaten and slick with juice, tumbled from his grip to the leaf-strewn ground.

Hope managed to swallow her guava just in time to let out a laugh.

Gavin held up a sticky hand, still wet with mango juice. "Let's save bird hunting for next year."

Hope selected a large, soft leaf from the surrounding vegetation and handed it to him as a makeshift serviette for his sticky hands. Then she winked at Ali. "Gavin might not be here next year."

Gavin shot her a daring look. The corners of her mouth twitched into a smile, and she couldn't suppress her laughter, even as she clamped her hand over her mouth. Amid the sweet aroma of ripe mangoes and the gentle whispers of the cooling breeze, a tantalizing promise lingered in the air.

A DANCE OF TWO STEPS forward and one step back. That was how Hope perceived her relationship with Gavin. He was a riddle she couldn't solve, an equation she struggled to balance. And, in his heart, she sensed she'd been caught between the blossoming of new affection and the lingering of old hurt, a space he hadn't cleared yet.

Since the wedding they'd attended two days ago, a humble traditional ceremony where the groom had paid the bride wealth by laboring on his in-laws' land for two years—things had felt different. In preparation for the ceremony, Gavin had helped build the tent, while Hope had the privilege of decorating it with the other women. He'd kept to himself after the ceremony, so perhaps it triggered memories or regrets of his own almost-wedding.

An invisible barrier shielded him during breakfast and supper. It manifested in his fleeting glances and the way he averted his gaze when she tried to engage him in conversation. The noticeable avoidance created an unwelcome gap she could neither understand nor bridge.

His detachment grew worse when he decided, at the last minute, to join the roofers instead of accompanying her to fetch water for another villager. Their shared chore had become a sort of cherished ritual for her. Now, Gavin seemed intent on disrupting it.

The following morning, she found herself asking him, "Aren't you coming to Komo's house today?"

"Not today." He gripped the back of his neck. His gaze wouldn't meet hers, and the discomfort radiating from him pushed her away. So she accepted his response and left him to whatever plans he had.

At Komo's house, she lost herself in organizing Komo's staples, plates, and cups in one of the cupboards Gavin had made when Hope had wondered how she could create more space in the widow's house. She also ground groundnuts, peeled maize from the cobs, and laid out kernels to dry in the sun. She embraced the rhythm of her chores, each task serving as a diversion from her confusion.

The following day, weary of his elusiveness, she didn't ask Gavin to accompany her. As she trudged along the path, her hands brushed against the dew-kissed shrubs, the slight chill a reminder of her brewing sadness.

But then a familiar voice behind her called out. "Hope, wait."

A flutter of anticipation welled up in her as she turned around. Gavin was there, smiling. "What are we doing at Komo's today?"

His inquiry made her heart dance, and his smile, along with the genuine interest in his eyes, stirred emotions she hadn't anticipated. Instead of delving into her confusion, she chose to embrace the moment, push her questions aside, and respond with renewed optimism. This dance they were in—confusing as it was—wasn't over yet.

Until its final steps, she'd appreciate each moment with Gavin, knowing the sweet music would end soon. Things never went the way she wanted, and her desire for Gavin didn't mean he belonged to her.

Several minutes later, they made it to Komo's house, and Gavin lightened the mood with jokes as they laid out corn that morning. They then planted nuts in the small garden behind the hut. With the sky getting dark, he suggested they return the corn to the storage hut.

They found Komo skittering across the compound with Ali on her heels, her tethered skirt swaying. For a woman with a hunched back, she moved fast. "Ali and I need to get the pregnant cow under the tree."

Gavin gave them a salute. "I hope that works out smoothly."

Then, as he and Hope gathered corn into the buckets, he belted out the work song. His voice confident, he sang, stopping short of throwing corn in the pail. With a hand, he urged her to sing along, then moved his hand as if conducting the music. "Jambo, jambo bwana..."

A smile curled around her lips as she shook her head, then continued, "Habari gani." She crouched to shove the full bucket aside, the song flowing as Gavin's deep voice made it sound wonderful.

"Your song seems to work." He stretched open an empty sack after they filled the pails. "We're almost done."

She glanced up at the cloudy sky and raised her hand. "We may not beat the rain."

He winked. "All the more reason we need the song."

She'd never enjoyed music as much as she did now, singing with him.

Then he grabbed her wrist, stopping her motions as she reached for another ear of corn to husk. "We've got ten ears left. Let's do a countdown in Swahili. You know? Backward like a rocket launch."

She had no idea how a rocket launched, but she could count. So she let him pick the corn while she counted.

"Kumi."

He tossed the maize into the wide-open sack.

"Tisa... moja." She counted from ten to one.

"We did it!"

When he raised his hand to high-five her, she was so willing to lift her hand to his. He did everything with fun. He was so carefree.

"Mzungu... Hope." They turned to Ali, plodding across the compound. The boy panted as he ushered them to come. "Grandmother needs help."

"What kind of help?" Gavin and Hope sprang to their feet simultaneously.

"The cow."

"Let's put this corn away first," he insisted.

With him hoisting two full pails, she tried carrying two, but she groaned and had to leave one. Once he'd stored the grain and seed, they hurried after Ali toward the field.

"The cow is ready to give birth, and Grandmother doesn't know how to do it."

Gavin jerked to a stop so fast, he nearly tripped Hope. "You think *I* can do better than your grandma?" His eyes widened, and he pulled Hope back with him as if needing confirmation that she had heard what he thought Ali had said. His voice climbed to a higher pitch, his panic setting her nerves on edge. Gavin knew more about medical-related things than she did, yet even he seemed nervous. "I've never been around cows, let alone helped birth a calf."

Of course, he'd never been around cows. Cows didn't exist in the streets of gold.

Hope touched his bare forearm, the hair soft beneath her fingertips. "I'm sure between the four of us..." After all, Komo surely had an idea and would guide them through the process. "Maybe she wants us to hold a leg or something."

Gavin jammed his hands on his hips and shook his head. "Unless you want me to take pictures, I'm going to be useless. Besides, I didn't bring my phone." His blue eyes bulged. "Ali, who usually delivers your calves?"

"I usually get help." The boy shrugged. "But the calf is already starting to come out."

"Afraid you have the wrong people for the job." Gavin shivered and resumed walking.

His protests had her fears vanish, replaced by her stifling a laugh.

"You think that's funny?" He waved both hands in the air. Then, taking a deep breath and seeming to calm, he reached for her hand and threaded his fingers in hers.

Holding his hand seemed like such a natural thing. His fingers felt like a lightning rod, zapping energy through her entire body. As if that alone wasn't enough to set her on fire, he lifted their entwined hands and kissed the back of hers. He then flashed a brief smile that warmed her clear through.

Frazzled by this simple gesture, she swallowed and tried not to imagine how his lips would feel if they kissed hers someday. It wasn't going to happen anytime soon. Not only was he out of her bracket but also he still had feelings for his ex.

She set aside her crazy thoughts and slipped through the split fence. The humidity thick and the air muggy, they neared a gully, and the situation became real when they arrived and Komo let out a relieved sigh.

"Glad you're here." She patted the cow's stomach, her upturned face hopeful that Hope and Gavin had the situation under control.

Odd for someone so terrified, but he went straight to the back of the cow. His horrified look seemed like something that would forever be etched in Hope's mind. "I see the legs!" he shouted, almost gagging before he stumbled two steps backward and ran his hands through his hair.

"Are you okay?" She nudged him aside to take a close look.

"I just need a moment." He spoke through rapid breaths, and it took all her strength not to laugh. But she focused on the cow.

This was incredible. The black feet kept moving in and out from behind the cow. Hope touched Komo's shoulder, needing to be honest. "The problem is we've never delivered a calf before."

"I've seen how." Komo nodded, bobbing her head again and again. "I'll walk you through." She then sent Ali to fill the water basin for the cow to drink.

"Okay." Gavin's breath was warm against Hope's neck. He must've walked back to join her. "Let's do this."

She pivoted to him, taking in his overly pallid features. "Are you sure?"

He nodded, and his brow remained scrunched. Then he touched her shoulder. "The job has to be done."

Under Komo's guidance, Gavin and Hope worked together to assist the cow. She could feel his hands trembling as much as her own while the cow's desperate cries tugged at her heart.

Komo patted the cow's stomach, Gavin spoke soothingly to the animal, and Hope tried to focus. No amount of singing would make her speed up the process.

"It's going to be okay." His fear seemed to have vanished as if he, too, were now empathizing with the animal. "We're almost there."

He wiped the sweat from his brow using his clean forearm. "We better be careful not to hurt the calf or its mother."

"You two are doing well," Komo said, no doubt to encourage them and prevent them from panicking.

"We won't hurt the animals." Hope smeared the grime on her hands as she touched the cow. The calf and its mother's well-being depended on their efforts.

Finally, after what felt like an eternity, they managed to free the calf. It took its first wobbly steps, and the cow nuzzled her newborn. Just like the little one, Hope wobbled, relief loosening her knees and warmth flooding her heart. Gavin wobbled, too, watching the mother and calf bond.

Komo threw her arms around them in a joint hug, tears streaming down her cheeks. "Thank you, Mzungu and Hope. You saved them both."

As they stood in the pasture, the clouds threatened to explode, and Gavin glanced at Hope, his smile holding a special fondness and pride. Then he lifted his grimy hand that looked the same as hers. "We make a great team."

"Yes, we do." She smiled, tears blurring her eyes. They'd had a part in bringing new life to earth. Through their teamwork, they were making a difference for the villagers, one day at a time.

"Here, Mzungu and Hope." Ali showed them the other basin. "You can wash your hands."

"Wait. Here is the final part." Komo lifted the sac bag she'd pulled out of the cow.

"Ew!" Gavin winced and walked toward the basin. "I'm literally going to throw up."

"You'll be fine." Hope fell in step with him.

They washed their hands using the bar soap Ali had prepared.

"You should go back to the house before the rain starts." Komo spoke without facing them as she watched the cow drinking water.

Hope wiped her hands on her skirt. "You should all go too."

"Ali and I will stay here until the mama cow and her baby settle."

As they strolled through the grass, Hope bumped Gavin's arm with her shoulder. "Your reaction when you saw the calf's feet... I'm inspired to start writing a diary today."

He elbowed her rib cage, his tone light. "Don't you dare write about my fears in your journal." He shook a finger at her. "I still can't believe we birthed a calf."

Their boots crunched in the grass, and something wet struck her arm. Then another raindrop.

"We'd better hurry." He clasped her hand, probably to help her catch up to his pace.

Soon, a torrential downpour pounded around them. Her hair slicked to her face, and the weight of her water-filled boots slowed her steps. By the time they reached the compound, several yards from the house, Gavin seemed to have the same problem. He stopped walking, so she stopped too.

His shoulders shook with laughter, his wet T-shirt clinging to him and accentuating the rise and fall of his chest muscles. Leaning toward her, he asked, "And why are we running?"

She could barely hear him through the downpour, but she laughed as the water ran over his hair and down to his mouth. She looked down at her skirt and blouse, all wet and pasted to her body, before she looked at him.

Gavin's smile vanished, replaced by an intensity that washed warm anticipation over her. His gaze dropped to her mouth, and the focus in his eyes ignited a longing within her. He touched her lips with one hand, sending a sensation like sizzling coals through her, even in the pouring rain.

He unclasped their joined hands and threaded his fingers into her hair. Hope froze, afraid that if she moved, this moment might slip away. If he didn't kiss her, she felt as though she wouldn't be able to breathe.

Slowly, he lowered his mouth to hers but paused just before their lips met. His hands cupped her face, holding her in place, his finger-tips trembling. Then his mouth found hers, his tongue grazing her lips, eliciting a sigh that whispered past them.

She pulled back to look at him, but he leaned in to kiss her again, sweeping her into the best kiss she had ever experienced. Every part of her body felt as though it was on fire. As she caught her breath and slowly eased away, he seemed unwilling to let her go.

His hands slid from her face, down her back, his arms wrapping around her waist and pulling her closer. Cradled against him, she could imagine them moving as one entity, their hearts beating in unison. She reached up to touch his chest, feeling solid muscle beneath her fingers, and looked into his eyes. The deep blue held a new intensity that weakened her knees, and the connection they shared in that moment felt as profound as it was overpowering.

"You're incredible, Hope," he whispered, his voice husky. "I've never met a woman so strong and compassionate."

More heat crept up her cheeks, reaching her eyes, and she grinned. "We did this together, Gavin. You're just as amazing." He made her feel special in a way no one ever made her feel. "You're the nicest person I've ever met." Besides, her mom.

"That's because you haven't met many people."

Maybe, but he was the first in her world. Could he be hers and only hers? He was a dream come true, but dreams didn't come true for her—ever.

As the words hung between them, she became aware of their proximity, their breaths mingling. The world seemed to fall away, leaving only them and this connection they shared.

He reached out and tucked a stray strand of hair behind her ear. "I never expected to find someone like you, here in this country or anywhere else in this world. But now that I have, I can't imagine my life without you."

Her heart swelled, her eyes burning with unspoken emotion. The thought of separating from him terrified her. "I feel the same way."

In that tender moment, as if drawn by an unseen force, he cupped her face in his secure palm and leaned in. Their lips met in a gentle, yet passionate, embrace. The kiss deepened, fueled by the love and admiration growing between them. Warm and tender, it was the most sincere kiss she'd ever had.

She'd expected a brush on the lips. Those were the kind of kisses she'd had before, but the way Gavin kissed her was different. New. The massage of his fingers in her hair left her dizzy. As did how he seemed to enjoy kissing her. And the heat of their bodies together and the thundering of their hearts against each other outmatched the rain.

Each kiss, marked by the rasp of his stubble against her chin, created a memory she'd always cherish. They held on, lost in each other, until they were both gasping for air, kissing and swallowing rainwater between breaths.

When they finally broke apart, they exchanged a warm, loving smile, their hands woven together. Their connection had deepened, blossoming into something more meaningful and lasting.

Together, standing under the relentless downpour, they were starting a new journey—one filled with love, strengthened by their shared commitment to making a difference in the lives of those around them.

CHAPTER 16

Throughout the week, Gavin felt an undeniable and magnetic pull toward Hope. Falling in love so quickly after his breakup hadn't been part of his plan, but there he was, unable to deny the attraction any longer, and determined to stop pretending otherwise.

Saying good night and parting from Hope felt more difficult each time. The exhilarating sensation within him was akin to the rush of first love he'd experienced in his teenage years.

But back then, family expectations overshadowed his previous love story. With how their parents almost predestined them together, he could scarcely pinpoint when their friendship had transitioned into something more. Now, with Lucky far away, she was becoming a dark memory and Hope the constant ray of sunshine in his life.

She stood just a few feet away with a stewpot separating them. They were dishing out the last meals at the medical clinic, bringing to a close their shared responsibilities with the current group of volunteers who had been working in the village for the past two weeks.

Around them, the villagers and volunteers bustled, the air rich with the scent of food and recent rain. Children's laughter added a musical lilt to the contented chatter of the elderly creating a comforting hum in the background.

His hands brushed against Hope's now and then as they ladled out servings. The fleeting contact sent a thrill down his spine. He stole a glance at her. The joyful spark in her eyes seemed brighter here than when they had been back at the cottages in Jinja.

"The last two weeks have gone by so fast. I can't believe it's April already." He broke the silence, handing a bowl to a young child. Time seemed to move faster now that he was having too much fun.

Her eyes met his. "I'm looking forward to our first holiday together."

"Brady and Ruth's idea," he admitted. "But after that, I want to take you somewhere you'd love to visit. Somewhere with waterfalls, maybe?"

Her face lit up, and he couldn't help but smile.

"You're planning to come back here, right?" she asked, turning to the villagers trickling in her line.

He winced at her palpable concern. Unlike him, she had no pressing need to return to her home country.

"I'll be here for another nine months." But his mind was already racing ahead. What would it take to bring her with him to Colorado for Christmas? As she served the villagers, a smile curving up her pixie face, he wanted to explore that possibility.

Later that afternoon, Mairu, the village elder, demanded attention. His commanding presence silenced the chatter and laughter as the villagers turned their attention to him.

"We thank our volunteers for their hard work." Unanimous agreement rang out in his pause. "Ruth and Brady have always shown us kindness. As they prepare to welcome their first child, we pray for God's blessings to fill their home."

The chickens, baskets of fruit, yucca root, and crops, and other gifts the villagers had given Ruth and Brady overflowed under the nearby papaya trees. Clearly, this couple meant a lot to them. And Mairu's message, spoken in heartfelt broken English, reminded Gavin of the kindness and warmth he'd found in this community.

Then Mairu called out, "Gavin and Hope, we look forward to the months to come of your visit."

Gavin took Hope's hand and raised it, his voice echoing Mairu's sentiment. "We're looking forward to it too."

Hope caught her lower lip between her teeth as she looked at him with so much love in her luminous eyes. His heart swelled. An urge overcame him, the desire to kiss her under the jackfruit tree far from the watchful crowd. But he restrained himself when Mairu announced the commencement of the dance.

The drummers' rhythm and the dancers' sway added to the excitement palpitating in the air. Gavin joined the rhythm of the claps, taking in the spectacle.

As the dancing concluded, the villagers began their goodbyes, bestowing gifts of fruits, chickens, and handcrafted items upon the departing volunteers. A couple handed Gavin and Hope a rabbit, and he reminded them of their plan to build a kitchen together. The lingering looks and shared moments between him and Hope, as they'd built the couple's shed, seemed to have given them an impression they were a couple.

Hope, engaging in the lighthearted banter, promised to take good care of the rabbits. The woman then handed her a beautiful handwoven shawl, and the gesture seemed to catch her off guard.

"For me?" Her voice wavered, and her hand pressed to her chest as if unwilling to reach for it, so he drew her closer, providing silent support as she accepted the gift.

"This shawl is a symbol of the kindness you impressed on our hearts."

"Thank you." Gavin offered his gratitude on their behalf, and Hope nodded her agreement, resting her head against his shoulder.

"We have something else," the woman's husband interjected before his wife presented them with a beautifully crafted wooden elephant.

Astonished, Gavin responded, "You guys are so talented."

"Ruth and Brady, they let all the villagers sell their carvings in their gift shop in Mabira." The man's words made Gavin even more eager to visit their resort. The handcrafted elephant was more than a memento but also a testament to the villagers' skill and artistry, a talent fostered and supported by their friends.

Long after dinner, when Ruth and Brady had retreated for the night, Gavin and Hope walked into the house. Akiki was busy tidying the kitchen, the soft clink of utensils filling the space as they bid her good night. Holding hands, they strolled down the dimly lit corridor toward their separate rooms.

At her closed door, he guided her to the wall, placing her back against the door. His eyes searched hers as he leaned closer, his intended "good night" morphing into a whispered thank you. He felt her surprise, her heartbeat echoing his rapid pulse, her breath dancing on his lips.

"What for?" she whispered back, her voice barely audible beneath the thrum of their heartbeats.

"For being you," he answered, his voice hoarse. His lips grazed hers, and she drew in a sharp breath. "For making this trip unforgettable."

"You're so good to me," she murmured before initiating a searing kiss. His hands found their way to her hair, the thick damp curls resisting his fingers, but he didn't care. His heart pounded in his chest, the desire for her nearly overwhelming. This heat between them was like a wildfire, threatening to consume them both. But he was no teenager. He had control. So, with a valiant effort, he broke off the kiss and cradled her in a tender embrace, their breathing heavy, their bodies pressed together.

"Good night, Hope," he whispered, pressing a soft kiss to the top of her head. Then, somehow, he stepped back, creating space between them. In the dim light, he saw her confusion, her mouth opening and closing as she struggled to form words. She raised a hand to cover her mouth, while her other hand reached to touch his shoulder. Then she pushed open her door and slipped inside, leaving him alone in the hallway with the lingering sensation of her touch.

A BREAK IN THE VILLAGE routine had Gavin and Hope accepting Brady and Ruth's invitation to their resort for a few days. Despite it being early April and not the prime season for water activities in Jinja, Gavin and Brady managed to squeeze in some zip-lining in Mabira Forest, the resort's serene location. Ruth and Hope, not as eager to zip line, had stayed back to engage in craft activities with the lodge guests.

Walking back after their exhilarating adventure, the clouds above darkening and the air heavy with the promise of rain, Brady turned to Gavin. "You know, you don't have to stay for another nine months in the village."

Gavin didn't have any urgency to go back home. Still, he nodded to agree with Brady. "Surprisingly, it's been a better adventure than I anticipated."

"Especially with Hope being around." Brady winked, ducking under a canopy of shrubs.

Gavin followed. Just the mention of her name brought a smile to his lips. Her influence was undeniable, but he also recognized the deeper impact the village lifestyle had on him.

"Not just Hope." He exhaled, reflecting on the village. The simplicity of life, the unwavering faith, all despite having so little, had stirred something within him. "I've learned to appreciate what I have."

Brady nodded, and they shared a moment of understanding. The conversation drifted to faith, love, relationships, racial differences, and even immigration, with Gavin absorbing Brady's wisdom. The man's deep faith and commitment to Ruth was inspiring. Perhaps Gavin and Hope could have that strong a relationship someday, but they had to start somewhere.

"For paperwork to process faster, Hope might have to return to her home country to apply for the visa."

Gavin shook his head. "She won't be keen on that." But that was something to consider later. "But thanks for the tips about the visa application process—and recommending the best waterfalls. I'm looking forward to taking her there."

As the rain ceased the next day, Gavin found himself diving into cool water alongside Hope. Nestled amid lush greenery, the pool provided them with a private sanctuary, their only audience being the monkeys leaping from tree to tree. They laughed, splashed, and stole kisses under the open sky, warmth spreading through them.

Her cheerfulness rang out as she leaped into the pool and he caught her in his arms. He pulled her close, brushing away the wet strands of hair sticking to her face. As those luminous eyes blinked up at him, the lashes around them dewy, he sucked in a breath, aching to give her some of the joy her very presence gave him. "I'm taking you on a surprise trip to a waterfall resort. You'll have to decide between two locations—Rwenzori or Mount Elgon."

"Mount Elgon?" Her face fell, and she stiffened in his arms, a shiver coursing over her. Mount Elgon was close to her home.

"Never mind. We'll scratch that one off the list," he hurried to promise, not wanting to upset her. "Rwenzori will be great."

"I miss my dad, sometimes," she confessed, her grip around his waist tightening. "But I've always wanted to see Elgon."

"Maybe your dad misses you too." He kept his arms looped loosely around her. Take your time deciding on the national park. And just so you know, you could use my phone any time you want to call home."

She scowled, quick to shake her head. "I'll let you know when I need to call home."

Then she eased back to look at him. "You know what I'd like to do? I want to see some of the homes you own. You know, while we have the internet and a computer here." Her soft smile replaced the hint of sadness in her eyes. "Maybe you could show me after dinner."

"Sounds like a plan." Anything to spend more time with her.

Seated in his hut before dinner, he brought out his phone to catch up with his brother. With it just after five p.m. in Uganda, it should be seven a.m. in San Francisco. Jeremy, an early bird, would already be in his office.

"Hello?" Jeremy picked up on the second ring, a note of surprise in his voice.

"Were you debating whether to answer?"

"Are you kidding me?" Jeremy laughed. "I've been worried you had vanished in that remote village."

Gavin couldn't help but chuckle. "We've got such limited service, and I can't always make it to the market to call you. Besides, don't you have a life over there?"

"Well, unlike some people, I'm not on an extended vacation."

"Now, Jeremy." Gavin relaxed into their playful banter. "Don't forget your own 'escape' from our small hometown to avoid Mom's endless matchmaking attempts."

Ever the pragmatist, Jeremy justified his move to San Francisco for a job at Stone Enterprises.

Soon, the banter gave way to serious catch-up. When Gavin mentioned Hope, Jeremy didn't know who she was, so Gavin recounted how she came along after leaving the resort. "And that turned into a huge blessing because she saved me from a snakebite. I can't picture being here without her as we've shared so many experiences, including helping a cow give birth."

"No way!" Jeremy guffawed on the other end. "*You* delivered a calf?"

"You won't believe it then when I tell you ants and crickets are part of my diet."

"I'd like to see you eat a cricket." Jeremy dared, obviously not sold on Gavin's new diet.

So Gavin had to come clean. "I *almost* ate the grasshoppers when Brady dared me, but I ended up losing."

"Do people really eat those insects?" Jeremy sounded as surprised as Gavin had been when Komo served them grasshoppers.

After being around the villagers and seeing what they ate, it didn't surprise Gavin anymore. "Let's just say they eat most things with meat of some sort." Including the birds Ali had roasted over open flames and eaten.

"Yuck. Let's just talk about Hope, then." Jeremy seemed to need the topic change. "What's she like?"

"She's nice." Far from dramatic. "Different." Gavin touched the necklace she'd made him. It had become part of his daily attire, a comforting reminder of their shared experiences.

"I can't wait to meet her," Jeremy enthused. "Are you bringing her home for Christmas?"

"I hope so." Although he wasn't sure how Hope would feel. "What about you? Can we expect you to bring anyone home this Christmas? Or are you still sadly lacking a romantic partner?"

"I gave it a shot!" Jeremy retorted, his laughter good-natured. "Right now, I have a life."

The call ended on a high note, with promises of regular check-ins. Feeling light and cheerful, Gavin headed into the lodge to join his friends for dinner. The meal was both swift and scrumptious. Once they finished, Gavin and Hope found a quiet spot in the computer room adjacent to the gift shop.

He leaned back in his chair, hands laced in his lap, waiting for the computer to boot up. "Would you consider coming with me to America when the year ends?"

Her mouth slid open as she gaped at him. "You'd want me to come with you?"

"Why the doubt?" He slid his hand over her shoulder, giving it a reassuring squeeze.

And that mouth curved into a soft smile. "I'd be honored."

"Then let's do some research. After we've looked at my company website, we'll check out the US immigration site to see what we'll need to do." After all, Hope needed to feel involved in the process.

With a flurry of keystrokes, he had multiple tabs open—one for his real estate website, another for his email, and a third for the US immigration services site. When his website loaded, he showed his property portfolio.

"These are some of the properties I own, but I rent them out." He stood. "Slide into this seat for a better view."

"No." She nudged him back into his seat. "I'd prefer to stand and let you drive. I'm not proficient with computers."

So he navigated the site, her hand resting on his shoulder as she leaned in to browse the images. With the moment companionable and intimate, he let his mind wander to the possibilities of a future together. Her fascination with the colors and designs of his homes warmed him. She'd be great at helping with renos.

He was switching to his email when he noticed a slew of messages from Lucky. His heart seemed to skip a beat as he skimmed the subject lines. What could she want now?

"Are you all right?" Hope asked, her voice warm on his neck, her grip tighter on his shoulder.

"Yes." He managed to keep his voice steady. "Let's look at the immigration site."

As she began to massage his tense shoulders, she said, "You must miss her."

It took him a moment to realize she was talking about Lucky. He hadn't mentioned Lucky's name before, so she was quick to connect things.

Anger and humiliation flared up, but he didn't want to add to Hope's worries. So he pulled her closer and placed a gentle kiss on her head.

"I'm glad I met you." He tried to occupy his mind with images of a life with Hope. But fear of another unexpected breakup nagged at him. "I do wish she'd explained why she did what she did."

Hope whispered, "I like you so much."

He looked at her, seeing her sincerity. "I like you too."

With his arm around her waist and her warm form curved against him, he brought up the immigration website, and a new possibility unfolded before him—a future with Hope, far removed from the pain of his past.

CHAPTER 17

Hope was accustomed to long walks, but this path leading to a series of three majestic waterfalls cascading down the lower slopes of Mount Elgon was far from easy. It was also a good distraction from thinking about Gavin's reaction to those emails from his ex. While he said he was over Lucky, that he held any kind of emotion toward her was unsettling. He shouldn't be angry with Lucky. He should be happy enough with Hope not to stress over what he'd lost. Was Lucky beautiful? Of course, she was smart and had better qualities than Hope. Hope let her shoulders sag, and no wonder she lost her footing.

"Oh no!" She halted as her foot slipped through a rung of the rickety ladder they were navigating. Her grip tightened on his hand.

"You're doing great, angel." He assured her, gesturing along the narrow trail. "We must be close to the first waterfall by now."

Focusing on the beauty, she kept the unwelcome thoughts away. After all, Gavin just called her angel.

"I didn't anticipate this to be challenging." She wasn't sure whether she referred to the walk or their romance.

"Good things require hard work," he replied cheerfully, unaware of her internal fear. "You just have to take each step carefully."

As he encouraged her to take another step on the unstable ladder, she wondered if the same could be said of their relationship.

They had seen the main drop of Sipi Falls from the lodge where they were staying, witnessing the falls from numerous vantage points. Unfortunately, the journey to see all three waterfalls turned out to be a demanding seven-kilometer loop hike, filled with steep ascents and descents, precarious ladders and catwalks, numerous farms, and plenty of mud.

"The morning rain hasn't helped our cause," she remarked as they completed their first ladder challenge and moved onto a steep path.

"On the bright side, we're not battling crowds." He adjusted his backpack straps. They'd been just as optimistic that morning when a hotel employee had shown them the map of the waterfalls and explained how they could reach each one. Gavin was good at reading maps, so Hope was following his lead.

Their first day at Mount Elgon had begun last night at eight. After they'd said goodbye to Brady and Ruth, who'd become dear friends, they'd taken the bus to Mbale and were staying at one of the lodges close to Mount Elgon. Although they hadn't decided how long they would stay, they were both eager to explore different parts of the mountain each day.

Now, the air was cool and smelled clean. Trees towered overhead, birds chirped, and lush greenery seemed to absorb them in a world all its own, taking them in as the only two people in the world, cocooned in natural beauty.

She let out a wistful sigh. "I love this place."

His hand rested on her lower back. "I love it even more with you here."

Wow. His resounding words warmed her heart. "The feeling is mutual," she promised, lifting her muddy shoe. Her breaths were labored now, the mud weighing her down. But they pressed on, hiking through the verdant forest, pausing to marvel at the scenic vistas. He moved with ease, never once complaining about the rigorous climb, and his determination inspired her to keep pace. With their ladder challenges behind them, ahead lay the promise of breathtaking waterfalls—once they'd trudged this slippery trail.

She stumbled, and he moved to catch her. But he, too, lost his balance, and they tumbled onto the muddy ground. His protective arm served as a cushion, preventing her from getting hurt.

"You're all covered in mud." She giggled, giddy and delighted in his strong arms. Mud had splashed into his hair, so she began to brush it away.

He lifted a muddy hand to her cheek and smeared it along her jaw, grinning.

"That is not a nice thing to do." She tried to scowl, but she cared less how she looked when his touch had the rest of her body breaking out in goose bumps. He smelled so good, a fancy smell she could get lost in forever.

Regardless, this mud could turn into a playful game.

Smiling, she scooped up a handful and smeared it on his cheek in the shape of a heart.

"My turn to draw a heart on you."

She arched an eyebrow. "How did you know I drew a heart on you?"

"I just knew." His cool fingertip traced a path along her cheek. The sensation made her close her eyes and draw in a sharp breath. His breath was warm on her face, and his heart drummed as loud as hers, a steady backdrop to the chirping birds.

Next, his warm lips whispered a breathy kiss against hers, and she returned his touch with equal tenderness. They were both breathless when he separated their lips and stood, helping her to her feet.

"We need a swim," he declared, examining his mud-covered black shirt and shorts.

She glanced down at her attire, a skirted pair of shorts and a yellow blouse, now turned brown. They needed a good wash-off.

"The man at the hotel said we could swim in the waterfall. It will be cold, though."

"Which makes it even more fun." Gavin winked, his eyes twin-kling before he tipped his head to urge them forward. They followed the rushing whir of water until the waterfall tumbled into view.

"We made it!" Relief crashed over her as in a cascade like the falls. If her cheeks hurting were any indication, a smile stretched out her face.

Gavin wiped his muddy fingers on his shirt, then eased his back-pack off and set it on a boulder. He gestured toward the base of the waterfall, one of the few waterfalls people could swim in. "We need to get closer to that pool."

Then he took her hand, and with their fingers interlaced, they picked their way down the slope. Her heart pounded at the sight of the real waterfall she'd read so much about.

"This is beau—"

"*You're* beautiful." He cut her off and tugged her into his arms. As they embraced in front of the powerful waterfall with the rush of the water crashing into the pool below creating a romantic backdrop, a wave of happiness washed over her.

"I forgot about the new camera." He released her to retrieve it from his backpack.

She laughed. "We were having too much fun to remember to take photos."

"The fun has just begun." He positioned the camera lens in front of them for a selfie. She pressed her muddy cheek against his and mir-rored his broad smile, the hearts on their cheeks meeting.

"I prefer using a phone for selfies, but someone talked me out of bringing it." He squeezed her waist with his other arm.

"Considering how muddy we are, 'someone' made a wise sugges-tion." She had worried it might rain during their climb up the steep hill.

After snapping photos, he returned the camera to the backpack, and she refocused on the waterfall. It was as powerful as she'd imagined. Faint colors lined the water from the partial sunlight breaking through the overcast skies. "Look." She pointed. "Rainbows!"

"They are there just for us." He stepped next to her and tucked loose strands of her hair behind her ear. "Remember the story you were telling me about the rainbow the other day?"

"From the Bible?" She snuggled into him, impressed he paid attention to everything she said. "God sent it as a covenant that He'll never flood the earth again."

"In this case, it's a symbol that we have a new beginning... together."

Contentment, almost too intense, expanded her chest, and she slid her hand around his waist and sighed out the words, "A new beginning."

They stood there, taking in the view before he stooped to remove his shoes.

"Would you care to join me for a swim?" He extended his hand, bowing slightly. The mud on his palm seemed dry, probably from him wiping them on his pants earlier, and the spots of mud on his face made him look so sweet and carefree.

She glanced down at her muddy clothes. Walking back in muddy clothes seemed more practical than in wet ones, but the prospect of spending time in the cold water with him was far more appealing. "I'd love nothing more."

She knelt to remove her shoes and socks. Then he took her hand and led her toward the pool the waterfall plunged into.

They yelped as the chilly water engulfed them, and goose bumps erupted on her skin. The cold water felt cleansing, washing away the grime and fatigue from the challenging hike. It became more than just a swim, though, when he shivered, laughing. "It's cold."

He then wrapped his arms around her—an intimate moment between them. She hadn't felt this safe with anyone in as long as she could remember.

Rather than swim, she wrapped her arms around him, and they clung to each other in the water, sharing tender kisses, their laughter echoing off the surrounding cliffs. Now and then, they broke away to admire the waterfall, its power and beauty serving as the perfect backdrop for their romantic getaway. With his strong arms around her, the water crashing into the pool, and the mist creating prisms in the afternoon sun, it was a moment she'd always cherish.

After seemingly forever, they left the water. Her body felt numb, and she already missed his warmth close to hers.

"How do we dry off?" She waved at her dripping outfit, then his pants and T-shirt.

"I've got this." He moved to her, gathered the edge of her blouse, and wrung out the water. She laughed at his unexpected creativity. He made her laugh so much! Had she ever laughed this much in anyone's presence?

"We have to improvise." Chuckling, he crouched and gathered the edge of her skirt to wring out the water.

She hadn't felt so spoiled and taken care of since her mom died. Her throat tingled with so much appreciation she could barely speak. "You're something else, Gavin Kress."

"So are you, Hope Njeri." He squeezed water from his T-shirt hem.

As they made their way back, hand in hand, she savored the moment—the sound of their footsteps on the trail, the lingering chill on her skin, and the warmth of Gavin's hand in hers.

TWO DAYS LATER, HOPE was seated on the patio, engrossed in *Gone with the Wind*. Gavin had surprised her with the book as soon as they arrived at the lodge. Not only was it her favorite book but she also cherished the fact that he'd snuck away while they were in Jinja to take the time to buy her something she held dear. She probably loved the book due to its memory of Mama.

She breathed in the fragrance of the lush flowers hanging from the balcony. They'd spent the past two days exploring the area, and today, they had taken a guided tour. Now, with lunch done, Gavin was indoors, making calls to his family and friends.

The breeze rustled the book's pages. Even though she should be focusing on Scarlett's tangled love affairs, Gavin's laughter as he spoke with his family made her yearn to call home. Or at least call her friend, Hawi. They hadn't kept in touch often, and Hope never knew when Hawi's husband would be home if she called.

Perhaps being at the border of her home country, Kenya, made Hope long for home.

Father. Her heart ached as she thought of his kind smile when he'd visit her and Mama. Mama would wear her nicest dress and make sure Hope wore her nicest dress too. Mama's face would light up whenever Father was around, her love for him evident.

For Mama's sake, perhaps he missed Hope now that she'd been gone for a while. Had her stepmom's heart softened toward Hope? Would Shani and Father love and accept her now that she was sort of independent? She couldn't know all the answers while she was away from home. When Gavin presented the options for visiting waterfalls, Hope's first choice was Mount Elgon. She had always wanted to see it, but it hadn't crossed her mind that being this close to home would be unsettling.

The door to the right opened and closed. Gavin poked his head around the divider separating their balconies. "How's the book coming?"

"How did you know I was out here?"

He grinned, a look that always made butterflies flutter in her stomach. "I had a feeling you'd be here."

He gripped the balcony post and swung his legs over to her balcony with ease.

"You weren't joking when you said you used to climb mountains back home." A mix of admiration and affection warmed her. She closed her book, no longer pretending to read. "How's Jeremy?"

"He says hello." Gavin sat in the woven chair next to her.

"Your brother knows about me?"

"I tell my brother everything."

If only she had someone to tell everything to. Well, she used to tell Hawi almost everything, but Hope hadn't called her since she landed in Uganda.

"Jeremy thinks I should call home. Mom and Dad are worried about me." Gavin scratched his jaw. He seemed to be dreading talking to his parents, which made no sense while he had a healthy relationship with his family.

"When are you going to call them?"

"I tried calling Mom, but her phone went to voice mail." And he sounded relieved. "I'll try again tomorrow."

His words stirred her guilt. She should call her family.

"What's wrong?" He leaned in, his eyes searching hers.

She exhaled, wringing her hands together. "Is it odd that, despite everything that's happened, I feel I should call home?"

"It's okay to miss home." He took her hand in his and rubbed his thumb over hers. "Do you want to call?"

"Not really, but it wouldn't hurt to make a reconciliation." The Jesus movie's scene rang in her mind. As Jesus was in pain, He begged God to forgive His tormentors. She wasn't ready to forgive Shani. What would she say when she called anyway?

"Do you know your dad's or stepmom's phone number?" Gavin's voice pulled her through her thoughts.

She nodded. "I'll just call Father." Or Hawi? "Maybe I'll call my friend instead."

"That's a good start." He slid his phone from his shorts pocket and handed it to her. "I'll give you some privacy. If you need anything, holler for me, okay?"

After a gentle kiss on her lips, he leaped back to his balcony, leaving her with a decision.

Hope placed the book on the small table to her left and throttled the phone as if holding back a snake from biting her. After a deep sigh, she dialed Hawi's husband's number. On the second ring, a female voice answered with a hesitant hello.

"It's Hope. Hawi?"

"Oh my, Hope! Where are you calling from? Where have you been?" Hawi then bombarded her with such a flurry of questions that Hope struggled to answer them all.

With Hope from the Kikuyu clan and Hawi from the Luo clan, they couldn't speak each other's language, so they usually spoke English.

"I'm in Uganda. Remember, I mentioned wanting to go away to another country someday?" Even before the forced marriage, Hope disclosed her desire to travel. She filled Hawi in on how she'd ended up working at a resort in Jinja, her time in Uganda, and her current visit to Mount Elgon.

"You have to come and visit me before you go back. I had a baby!" Hawi squealed. She mustn't have known she was pregnant last time Hope had talked to her.

Hope congratulated Hawi. "I'd love to come, but it's complicated." If she left Gavin to return to Uganda, she might never see him again. "I'm here with someone, and we're just visiting Mount Elgon."

"Hope?" Hawi's tone dipped. "Does your family know your whereabouts?"

"I didn't feel like telling them. They were forcing me into a marriage." Hope shared the sudden arranged marriage and how her father had agreed to the bride wealth before talking to Hope.

"That's terrible." Hawi sighed. "This is not the early century anymore where they force you to marry someone."

"I know." Hope squeezed her forehead with her other hand, feeling an onset of a headache. "I've been feeling like I should call Father, though."

"It wouldn't be bad to call him if you feel like doing so."

Not wanting to make a definite decision, Hope switched the subject. "Why did you answer your husband's phone?"

"He has a work phone now, so he lets me use his phone often. You should call me. Can I reach you on the number you're calling from?"

"I'll call you." After all, phone service in the village was scarce, and Gavin kept his cell phone off since he said it was no use without reliable service.

After catching up with Hawi and promising to consider a visit, Hope ended the call, not wanting to use all of Gavin's airtime. Then, taking a deep breath, she started a new call. Each punch of the numbers for her father's phone felt like an eternity. As the phone rang, her hands trembled. On the fourth ring, she was about to end the call, relieved to have tried, when a feminine voice sounded.

"Hello?"

Her stepmother's voice pierced through her, bringing back unwanted memories.

Hope should've known Shani would answer, making sure Father wasn't engaging with other women outside their marriage. Not that that had stopped him from engaging with Mama.

The urge to hang up was high.

"Can..." Hope stood, needing to pace, then sought the railing's support to brace herself. "Can I talk to Father?"

"Do you really care about your father?" Shani's accusatory voice didn't surprise Hope, but her next words sucked the air out of Hope's lungs. "Your father is ill. He might not make it through the next two days."

Hope's legs started trembling. Her heart dropping, she moved back to sit. "Oh no! What happened?"

"You need to come home." Shani's voice remained void of emotion. Perhaps it was her way of grieving her husband's illness. "The sooner you come the better."

Panicked and rattled, Hope sucked in a shaky breath and pushed out even shakier words. "I'll be there no later than one o'clock tomorrow."

Once Hope said it, Shani hung up, and the line fell dead, leaving Hope reeling, her mind spinning with regret and scenarios of what she could do to make Father feel better. But she couldn't control his health, whatever illness he had. Setting the phone on the book, she wrung her hands together, not seeming fast enough.

"Hope, what's wrong?" Gavin spoke before flinging his legs over the divider and leaping to her balcony.

"It's my dad." She couldn't look at him as tears welled up. "I need to go home."

"I'm coming with you." He knelt on the wood floor in front of her and cupped her chin. The concern etched in the deep blue eyes searching hers tore at her heart.

Still, she lurched back from his touch. "I couldn't ask that of you. My family situation is complicated, and if my father is dying, I don't know how long I'll be gone. It could involve a funeral—"

"I don't care how long it takes," he interrupted with the serious look of someone who wanted to be helpful. "Family is not just blood relatives, Hope. It includes people who love and care about you."

Was he considering himself her family? That would be nice if he'd accepted her and loved her regardless of her crooked past.

But once he met Shani and she fed him lies about Hope, he'd flee.

As his penetrating gaze held hers, he seemed to see through her mind and doubts. "You're a part of my life now, my family if you don't mind it being that way."

Overwhelmed, she opened her mouth to say she didn't deserve him, but the words lodged in her throat.

"I'm coming with you. If you end up not wanting me there, then I'll leave. But you shouldn't travel alone, especially not like this."

She nodded, swallowing the lump in her throat.

"We're in this together." He leaned in and kissed her lips tenderly. She kissed him back. It was a simple kiss, but it held the world and meant everything to her.

All her life since Mama died, Hope had always done things alone. Could she trust that she had support now?

CHAPTER 18

When Hope approached her father's home, nostalgia swept over her. Each memory flashed as vivid as the one before it—the grueling days spent sweeping the dirt compound, the rhythmic ebb and flow of planting and reaping crops, the tiresome treks to the well under the scorching midday sun, and the relentless succession of the seasons.

She allowed her gaze to roam, taking in the nearby garden, her former source of pride. Once lush and vibrant, it now lay shrouded in weeds, and tall grass encroached on the compound. Despite this, she managed a smile. There, amid the overgrowth, the resilient flowers she had tended to were blooming, a testament to her past care.

She'd always felt a strong connection to this garden, yet the rest of the homestead felt alien, an unsettling sensation that manifested in the tension coiling in her shoulders. The home she should have been ecstatic to revisit now seemed unfamiliar, foreign.

"Are you okay?" Gavin's hand moved to her lower back, comforting her.

But her emotions were too intense to articulate. "I'm so glad you're here." She fought to steady her voice, hoping it didn't betray her inner turmoil. A double-edged sword, having him here was comforting but also risked their wonderful bond.

They had journeyed to the village in a rented taxi, now hidden away in the shrubs down the road, as per Hope's request. She didn't want to seem like they were showing off. Gavin, still shaken by Brady's harrowing tale of a disastrous motorcycle ride, had insisted on the taxi.

The simple brick house held a myriad of memories. A duo of goats grazed, tethered in the shade of a sprawling tree. The chicken house, once her sleep quarters, now looked abandoned with one part of the roof broken. She'd acquired the remains of the metal roof from a neighbor when their house had been built. She had then hammered nails into the roof of the clay house to make it secure.

An echo of anxiety reverberated within her. The yard was too quiet, the familiar faces missing. Where was everyone? Was her father still holding onto life?

An almost tangible heaviness hung in the air, not laden with the familiar scent of rain she had grown accustomed to in Kibale and Mount Elgon, but infused with the raw, earthy scent of the goats, a symbol of the rain's scarcity here. Her fingers danced over the necklace Gavin had gifted her, the soft rustle of her skirt against her knees a comforting background melody to her anxious thoughts.

Then, like a ray of sunlight breaking through storm clouds, a familiar face erupted from the confines of the brick house. Deere, her younger half sister, the embodiment of youthful exuberance, charged toward her, with an infectious grin.

"Hope!" Deere's voice sang through the heavy air, a sweet balm to Hope's anxious heart. As if on cue, Hope's arms swung open to embrace the girl. Deere had always treated Hope with kindness and respect.

"You've grown so much." Hope marveled, touching Deere's short braids.

"I've missed you." Deere's simple sentence tugged at Hope's heartstrings.

"I've missed you too."

Seeing her sister again, Hope felt a pang of regret for letting their connection fade. Deere glanced to Hope's right, at Gavin, then back to Hope. "You brought a mzungu."

"This is my friend, Gavin." Hope introduced him, uncertain of how else to define their relationship.

Gavin shook Deere's hand with a warm smile. "Nice to meet you."

"How is Father doing?" Hope asked, her worry gnawing at her again.

Deere lowered her gaze and started guiding them toward the house. "I don't think you're going to like it. Things have changed a lot. You'll see. Mama won't like it if I tell you everything now."

"What do you mean?" Hope stopped her, her gaze darting between the wooden door and her sister. "Is Father all right?"

"You'll find out soon," Deere muttered, her voice barely audible as she spoke to the ground, refusing to look up.

Foreboding seized Hope's throat, each breath becoming a struggle as they approached the house. It was as if a thick blanket of unease had been thrown over the homestead. The only sounds were their hesitant footsteps against the well-trodden dirt pathway.

Standing in the doorway, staring at her with eyes more weary and bitter than Hope remembered, was her stepmother. "I see you've brought us a mzungu," Shani said, her voice edgy. "Is he your husband?"

"No, Mama." Hope slid her gaze to the floor. She didn't need anything from Shani, but she still felt small in the woman's presence. "He's my—"

"Boyfriend." Gavin's firm response cut through her fear, gaining Hope a semblance of confidence to make introductions.

A noticeable change swept over her stepmother's demeanor. Her curt expression softened, and she motioned them to follow her to the sitting room.

Once inside, Hope was thrown back to her past. The window in the nearby sitting room allowed dim light into the corridor. The well-worn wooden chair at the end of the corridor she'd spent hours oiling was covered in dust. The threadbare curtains shielding the doorway to the sitting area were overdue for a wash. Clearly, she'd been the only one up-keeping the house.

When they entered the sitting room, her father was in deep discussion with a man she recognized all too well—a man they'd wanted her to marry before she'd escaped. "Silas."

Tension gripped her chest, and she fought to breathe. This was not a mere visit—this was a setup, a reunion she hadn't agreed to.

"Hope, my child." Father stood, smiling and seeming far from ill when he moved to shake her hand.

She was supposed to kneel and greet him, but her knees were too tight, matching the rest of her stiff body. Father was okay, but she'd been lied to. The room was closing in on her, and only Gavin's gentle hand on her back supported her. So she turned to him, and he was staring at her with unspoken questions.

"This is my father." She introduced him as her boyfriend and ignored Silas with so many vague things happening.

"Please take a seat." Shani addressed Gavin to sit in the recliner across from Silas, and Gavin lowered himself into it. Shani then sent Deere to fetch her other sisters. "You don't need to return, but tell your sisters to take charge of serving chapati and juice."

"You're... not sick." Hope spoke through gritted teeth, keeping her anger in check, not merely to be respectful but also because he may not have known his wife lied.

"You, um..." Father pinched the bridge of his nose, clearly guilty. More gray had invaded the black hair cropped close to his head.

"Take a seat, Hope." Shani took charge, her voice high, probably irritated by Hope's confusion. She then tugged at Hope's hand, almost forcing her to sit on the mat. Hope snatched her hand from Shani and glared at her, but her stepmom's leer still made Hope cower, especially when she rolled her eyes. "How else were we going to get you back here?"

Hope lowered herself to the mat, her heart heavy. She wanted to flee, but with Gavin's presence, she'd still have to explain the dowry her family had already consumed.

She folded her hands like a defiant teenager, her gaze on Silas's shiny black shoes. He was dressed in a white robe and black jacket as if ready to claim his bride.

The room fell silent, and she struggled not to squirm with the focus on her, the tension in the air thickening. If only she was seated right next to Gavin so he could comfort her with his gentle hand. It would help ease her stiff shoulders.

"Gavin," Father started, and Hope felt like closing her ears, not wanting to hear whatever Gavin was to be told. "I don't know if Hope told you, but she's already been spoken for."

"I'm not!" She flung up her chin, her fierce gaze directed to Silas, who was probably innocent. This debacle was all Father and Shani's fault.

"You're not to speak to your husband like that," Shani chided.

"Husband?" Gavin's whole body jerked.

"I'm not his wife." Hope tilted her head to look at Gavin. "I didn't—"

"Silas paid Hope's dowry," Father cut off her words, leaving her mouth hanging as she waited to defend herself.

"She pretended to like Silas and then..." When her stepmother started feeding them lies, Hope could only shake her head. It was even hard for her to look at Gavin. The room grew three times hotter, and she was suffocating from the lies threatening to smother her. "She will do the same to you," Shani continued as if aware of Gavin's weak spot.

He'd been left at the altar. He'd assumed Hope was a runaway bride who would crush his heart. She managed a glance at him, a line etching deep between his brows as he was fed one lie after another.

The woman had a degree in smooth talking and convincing any-one. Even Hope had been convinced Father was dying.

Silas only nodded, clueless that they'd taken his money and dowry without her consent.

"I didn't use any of your—"

"Hope!" Shani shrieked in her ear, silencing her from protesting. "You made a mess, and you're not embarrassed at all?"

Hope blew out bubbles from her mouth, helpless and defeated.

"If you don't marry Silas"—Father's voice was firm, his face seri-ous as if Hope was one of his business transactions—"you'll need to pay back the money and animals he paid for you."

"I'm not going to marry him." She ground her teeth, wringing her hands over her lap. The mat straw bit into her legs, but she could tolerate that pain. She'd never tolerate marrying someone she was forced to.

"Unless you have that kind of money." Shani smirked.

Whoever said life was fair hadn't lived in Hope's shoes.

Her twin sisters she hadn't seen since she arrived emerged, carry-ing drinks, and the smell of chapati wafted through the room. They were only a few years younger than Hope, but they didn't acknowl-edge her presence, too busy giggling as they set the drinks on the table, their eyes never wavering from Gavin.

Jealousy stung as they introduced themselves to him, but she pushed it aside. This wasn't the time for such feelings. Her family was treating her as a bargaining chip, a means to an end. Silas was wealthy by their standard and influential, and Father was trying to secure his favor through marriage.

And her whole world was falling apart.

Shani rose and spoke to Father. "I'll take Gavin and the girls out-side, so you and Hope and Silas can continue this discussion."

Gavin whispered something in Hope's ear as he brushed his hand on her shoulder, but she didn't hear. She could only see her two sisters following Gavin with their mom in tow. No doubt, this was the end of her and Gavin.

Between Shani's lies and her sisters' flirtatiousness, she could feel her past catching up to her and closing in. She tried not to think of the man she'd almost married before her parents had talked him out of marrying her and into marrying her sister.

Was her relationship with Gavin strong enough to withstand her family drama?

"Here's the deal, Hope." Father's chilled voice sluiced over her. "As we agreed to sell the cows for school fees…"

Her eyes blurred as Father lined out the lies he'd told Silas, saying Hope had agreed on how her dowry was to be spent. "The goats are the only ones we have left."

While she didn't want to marry Silas, she had no money to pay him, but she knew how to run. If Gavin was still on her side, perhaps she could convince him they leave while their taxi was still waiting.

She drew her shoulders back to stand. "Let me say goodbye to Gavin, and I'll be back."

Father nodded. "I know you'll do the right thing this time."

She should feel guilty about lying, but marrying someone out of obligation was an even bigger lie she wasn't going to be a part of.

Her heart sank when she stepped outside. Gavin stood with Shani under the jackfruit tree—right where Hope sat with Father when he wanted to marry her off. It seemed like the bargaining tree in this family.

Since the twins were out of sight, their mother was probably convincing Gavin to choose one of them.

"He's mine." She spoke to herself as she strode in their direction. She never fought for anything in the past, but Gavin was worth proving she still wanted him, if he could run away with her.

They both turned when she approached.

She felt out of breath. "Gavin." His smile didn't meet his eyes. But it was a smile, and that was all she could ask for. "Can I please talk to you?"

Shani lifted a brow, crossing her arms like she wasn't leaving, but Hope faced her firmly. "I'd like to talk to Gavin alone."

"Sure." Gavin stood, then glanced at Shani, his eyes asking her to leave, which she did. But not before giving Hope that look, the one that said Hope had lost again.

Beneath the afternoon shade the jackfruit tree offered, Hope hated the smell of ripe jackfruit mixed with goat poop. Not a romantic scene as they stood close to the golden grass that stretched further on the property.

Gavin was pacing, clenching his jaw. From its hard set, he was mad. Then he paused, and his troubled gaze met hers. "Hope." He raked his fingers through his hair, his chest rising and falling beneath the blue polo shirt. "Did you promise Sa—whatever his name is." His words lingered in the stagnant air as he cut a hand through that air as if swatting his hesitation away. "Did you agree to marry him?"

"No. I was being forced to." Like she'd told him already.

"Why didn't you say something before he paid for you?"

"I didn't know until after Father made the bargain." She fiddled with her necklace. She didn't even feel like explaining if he'd already bought into the lies.

Pain throbbed in her heart, the hurt washing over her in an unexpected wave. His doubt was a wound. Didn't he know her by now? Her eyes searched his.

"Gavin, do you question my integrity?" Her voice, barely above a whisper, may not have reached him. "Or do you believe the deceptions of a woman who trapped me with the news of my father's health to force my return?"

He stared at her, his eyes narrowing, but something—doubt or confusion?—clouded their blues.

Hope turned to leave, but his touch on her shoulder halted her. When she faced him, his eyes held a familiar, softer glow. "I ask these questions not out of suspicion, Hope." He closed his eyes, then opened them. "But to hear the truth from you. My last relationship..."

She gave a gentle nod to imply she understood why he'd have doubts. Inhaling a deep, steadying breath, she pressed a hand to the heart hammering against her chest. "I dreaded being forced into marrying Silas. I almost married him until I learned my father had already accepted his money and used it for his business." She again told him the events of that afternoon and her escape. "I still had some money from my last job." If she'd stayed, she would be married by now to someone she didn't love, someone who had other wives, and she would've missed out on meeting Gavin. "I don't regret leaving."

A certain level of softness replaced his hardened look. "I'm sorry," he murmured, moving closer and trailing his tender hands on her cheeks, causing her to inhale a sharp breath. "I'm so sorry that the very people who should've been your safe haven have let you down. I've been deceived before by someone I thought I was destined to spend my life with. So, I know how it feels to be betrayed."

His raw honesty tugged at her heartstrings. If only he could perceive the depth of her emotions for him! She lifted her hand to his heart, which was beating against her palm, and she spoke her thoughts. "You're the first man who treated me with respect and worthiness. You've made me think that maybe—just maybe—I'm not as unlucky as I thought." Lately, she'd even let herself envision a future with him, assuming he wasn't as out of her reach as she'd thought.

His lips curled into a soft smile, and the tenderness in his eyes filled her with a burst of hope.

"So, what's your next move?"

The tension disappeared as she spoke lightly. "What I do best—run."

"Running may be a bit challenging with me in tow."

"We still have our taxi." She motioned toward the road and through the shrubs, though she couldn't see it. She wouldn't have trusted leaving their bags in the car if she hadn't asked to keep the man's driver's license, which Gavin had shoved in his jeans pockets.

"I don't want you to run anymore, Hope." Determination jutted out his jaw as if he had a solution. He cupped her face in his hands again, and she dropped her hand from his chest. "I want you to confront your problems."

She didn't have the money, and the debacle her family was in wasn't her fault. She raised her chin as well, though she kept her voice low. "My father took Silas's dowry, not me. I never gained anything from it."

Gavin's forehead creased. "I want to pay for your freedom."

She blinked, trying to grasp his statement. Something flickered in her mind. Something she'd heard the pastor teach in one of the messages. Something about Jesus paying the price for our freedom. Was Gavin trying to do something Jesus would do? "I don't understand."

"I want to pay Silas whatever your family owes him. And I also want to cover your dowry so you won't be forced into another unwanted marriage. I want you to be free to visit your home without fear, and I don't want you to feel indebted to anyone."

Was this even her home if she wasn't welcome? His thoughtfulness and care for her squeezed her chest. But did he know what he was getting into?

"Do you know what dowry is?"

"Your stepmom told me while she tried to marry me off to one of your half sisters." He rubbed the back of his neck. "Your parents didn't raise you in the way you deserved. But bride wealth seems important to them, and even though they'll keep what Silas paid them, I want to know they won't try again."

Her throat closed up. He said all the right things. Yes, the dowry was a present to the parents for all the work in raising their daughter. They'd given Hope a place to stay, and she'd paid back by being the maid. They didn't deserve anything, and if she left today, no way would she come back. They could still run instead of him feeling obligated to clean up her family's mess.

She met his gaze. "I can only accept your offer if it's a gesture of love, not pity."

Nodding, he held her gaze, trailing his finger along her jaw. "I offer this out of love, Hope. Even if you weren't caught in this dilemma and it came down to me paying a dowry for you, I wouldn't hesitate. I love you, and I want you to be free. But I also want you to know you're not bound to me. I don't want you to feel trapped because I paid your dowry. I want you to be with me out of your own free will, not obligation."

Tears trickled down her cheeks, her heart drumming a sweet rhythm. "Gavin," she whispered, her throat too clogged to form a true sound. "I've never loved a man the way I love you. If I'm ever deserving of you, be certain you're the one I'd choose in this entire world." She didn't want to impose and assume he was now trapped since he'd paid her debts. They were not getting married after all. While traditional marriages counted in her culture, that wasn't the case in his.

He leaned in, and their lips met in a passionate kiss. Then his right hand curled around her waist, and he tugged her against him.

Her breath hitched in her throat as a deep longing for him unraveled inside her. He kissed her with confidence, and she kissed him with relief. This kiss felt like hope, comfort, and stability, and she was so happy she could burst out in tears.

As they separated, her stepmother and Silas on the veranda caught her eye.

"We seem to have attracted an audience," Gavin quipped, his arm snaking around her waist.

Hope remained unfazed. Gavin had been right. Her relatives, her father the most, though bound by blood, didn't have to be her only family.

"Let's go talk to your dad." He took her hand, and she felt so relieved not to have to do this alone. "I'll need to get to a bank and withdraw some money. Maybe you can come with me?"

Hope nodded, having no desire to stay behind. She could stay for Deere's sake, but Deere was surrounded by people who loved her. Plus—Hope sneaked a glance at the chicken house—she didn't feel like staying with the chickens tonight.

"When we're in town, today or possibly tomorrow, can we make a stop somewhere?"

"Of course."

"I'd like you to meet my friend Hawi. Tomorrow will be best actually. Not too short a notice."

A smile crinkled up Gavin's face. He lifted their entwined hands and kissed the back of her fingertips. "Any friend of yours is a friend of mine too."

When they approached the veranda, Shani walked back to the house, and Father stood next to Silas. Gavin kept hold of Hope's hand. "How much money and how many cows does Hope owe?"

Silas gave a polite nod. "Two cows, four goats, and..." He also voiced the sum of money.

"Is it okay if we pay you for the animals, instead of going all over town to shop for them?"

Silas nodded, and Gavin asked how much it would cost in total and didn't argue when Silas voiced his demand.

"Mr. Njeri." Gavin inclined his head toward Hope's father, his voice gentle and respectful. "I've fallen in love with your daughter."

His words left Hope breathless, her legs weak.

"I would humbly request your permission to marry her, not right now because we're on a mission in Uganda and have responsibilities there but after our commitment to the villagers." Gavin squeezed her hand, keeping his focus on Father. "I'd like to thank you for raising her into the wonderful woman she's become, and I'll be honored to pay for whatever you request."

"You can marry her." Father's voice emerged gruffly, his features softening and chest puffing, no doubt from Gavin's kind words of him raising her. Hope wanted to roll her eyes. Father would be convinced over any sum of money, let alone with Gavin offering to pay whatever sum he wanted.

The dusty curtain by the front window swayed, and a few heads peeked out. Mother and the twins had to be watching the exchange. Whether they were hearing anything, Hope had no idea.

"We still need to have a dowry payment celebration." Father pointed to the jackfruit tree. "I'd like to speak to you privately, young man. To discuss Hope's bride price."

"Yes, sir." Gavin followed Father toward the tree Hope now despised.

Hope stood there, awkward with Silas as they waited. She didn't know the man besides the two times she'd met him when he'd exchanged greetings as a houseguest. What else was she supposed to say?

Bronze-winged mannikin birds chirped in the tall sorghum by the house. And she scuffled her feet. She still felt bad over how her family deceived him. She swallowed. "I'm sorry you had to deal with my family mishaps."

Silas cleared his throat and adjusted his jacket over the long robe. He half smiled his understanding. "You're going with Mzungu, I see."

"Yes." She glanced back at Gavin and Father, relieved when they started walking back toward them. Father was beaming like he and Gavin were the best of friends. Gavin's smile when they were within reach had her running toward him.

"We're having the ceremony in four days." He slid his hand around her waist. "I'm paying your dad extra to take care of the caterers and whatever is needed."

Hope managed a glance at her father, who gazed back with a hint of warmth. "I'm so happy for you, my daughter."

Although his words probably stemmed from however much money Gavin had agreed to give him, Hope felt content.

"Thank you." She said it more to Gavin, but her father nodded.

"Silas can come with us." Gavin gestured toward the road, seeming determined to move things as fast as possible.

"I'll send word to the neighbors." Father nodded. "Please send the money as soon as possible so I can start buying food."

Weird how Father didn't seem to doubt Gavin would come back with the promised funds. Clearly, he could see Gavin's sincerity.

When she'd called Hawi on their way to the bank to see if she was available soon, her friend's eagerness to meet Gavin had her asking them to meet with her at nine tomorrow morning. Then they made it into town before the international bank closed, and Gavin gave Silas his money. Silas thanked Gavin, shaking hands. Then he shook hands with Hope as they parted ways.

"Remember when you told me about the last time you had ice cream?" Gavin's voice brought her back to the present. His fingers laced with hers as they meandered past vendors on the crowded sidewalk. "I've had this yearning to share that experience with you. Now that we're in Nairobi, it's time to track down the city's finest ice cream."

Her heart fluttered. How was it that he recalled her casual reminiscence? Her voice was an excited whisper. "I wouldn't know where to find the best ice cream. I've never eaten in fine restaurants."

"We'll ask our driver." He guided her toward their taxi parked by the side street, then held open the rear door for her, his eyes alight with the promise of an upcoming adventure.

The driver took them to a quaint ice-cream shop that was a city favorite. As Hope took her first lick, the smooth, velvety vanilla ice cream ensconced in a crispy sugar cone awakened her senses. It felt as though she was tasting ice cream for the first time.

While the sweet creaminess evoked heartwarming memories of her mother, she whispered a heartfelt prayer to God to tell Mom everything was going to be okay after all.

But the fun didn't end with ice cream. When they exited the shop, he spotted the adjacent theater and proposed they watch a movie. "It's been a while since we've enjoyed the luxuries of civilization."

She nodded, intrigued by the idea of spending more time with him. Soon, she sank into the plush theater seat, her heart thumping. It was her first movie in a theater, and the magic of the big screen captured her, an extraordinary moment made even more special with him by her side.

His infectious laughter and the lighthearted film's comic relief helped the day's earlier hardships dissipate. She laughed alongside him as they talked about the movie on their stroll back to their taxi.

Their driver was waiting for them, probably because Gavin had promised to pay him a fair amount if he could be their driver during their days in Nairobi.

When they settled in the back seat, he rested their entwined hands on his leg and spoke to the driver. "I want to take Hope to the best restaurant for dinner. Where do you recommend?"

"I've heard lots of good words about The Gardenia." The driver wove through Nairobi's evening traffic. "If money is not a problem..."

"I..." Hope gulped. Gavin had already spent so much on her. "We can just have—"

"We're celebrating." He cut off her protests.

But the man had named the most luxurious hotel in the country! She leaned closer to Gavin and whispered, not wanting the driver to hear. "You already paid for all my mistakes." Meaning he'd paid *double* bride wealth.

His warm breath against her ear made her body tingle. Then his words resonated with sweet promise against her heart. "You're worth more than anything money can pay for."

She studied him to gauge his sincerity, then swallowed at the tenderness and love aglow in his gaze. He'd asked her hand in marriage, but had he meant it? He'd been unwavering as he spoke to her father. His confidence indicated he meant every word.

"I've fallen in love with your daughter...."

As his words whispered through her heart anew, she nudged his arm with her shoulder, trying to sound nonchalant, but needing to understand. "What are we celebrating?"

He bumped her shoulder back with his arm. "We're going to be engaged in four days. And based on your dad's presumption earlier..." His face was playful, his voice low. "We'll literally be married after the engagement ceremony."

His conviction made her spine weak. She sank back against the seat, but she couldn't let him feel trapped with her either. While some couples started their life together after the traditional marriage, others had a church ceremony in addition to the traditional. "We won't let my culture define how you do your things."

He shrugged, not letting her in on what was going on in his head. So, she'd have to assume he'd bought her freedom for the reasons he said—doing so out of love for someone he'd come to care for.

He led her into the hotel, and the server showed them to their seats. While everything was delicious and presented in the most luxurious style—from the fancy porcelain plates and ornate silverware to an attentive server—Hope couldn't fully enjoy it. She felt too guilty for not paying for anything. But how could she afford a dinner that cost a month's rent in her country?

When Gavin asked the server if the hotel had two vacant rooms for the night, she couldn't even imagine how expensive they'd be. He must have more streams of income than just helping people sell their homes. He had investments, but again, she had no idea how much anyone in investment property made. He'd even extended an invitation to their driver to join them for supper, but the man had declined. Paying for a stranger's dinner at the fancy restaurant would mean you were either rich or way too generous.

The server returned and announced plenty of rooms were available. Gavin thanked the server and slipped the golden card into the leather booklet.

Then Hope grabbed his arm. "Let's flip a coin for this. Do you have the coin you carry in your pocket to win arguments?" Perhaps she'd win this coin toss, so they could stay somewhere less expensive.

"No coin toss this time." He took her hands, his grip warm, the cozy lights illuminating his handsome face.

"But this is so expensive." Her heart thudded at a horror she couldn't suppress. Yet determination glinted in his eyes, and temptation niggled her. While she wasn't used to such luxury, what would it be like to experience a five-star hotel for *one* night?

"You're more precious, and you deserve this." He looked around at the dim string lights and the bouquets wafting a fresh fragrance on their table. "If we're going for memories, why not go the extra mile?"

In a surge of gratitude for his kindness, she squeezed his hands and spoke around the emotion closing her throat. "Thank you so much, Gavin."

"Thank *you*." His thumbs rubbed the backs of her hands, but she had no idea why he was thanking her.

Going the extra mile meant she wasn't going to let her stepmother plan her dowry payment celebration. She had four days to transform her childhood home into a warm and memorable place for a party she and Gavin would never forget.

As she gazed into his kind eyes, she realized how much she trusted and cared for him. He was her rock, and despite the adversity she'd faced, hope bloomed in her body, expanding through her chest with new possibilities and happiness.

She wasn't sure what the future held, but what if Gavin was a part of it somehow? At that moment, she couldn't imagine any other future.

CHAPTER 19

Gavin hadn't expected the ceremony would involve a game where he'd have to identify Hope from six other veiled women. The weight of the crowd's expectant gazes made him hotter as the afternoon heat seeped through his cream-colored robe. His spokesman, Hope's friend Hawi's husband, spoke into the microphone.

"All right, Gavin, there comes another bride." He spoke in English, then addressed the rest of the lavishly attired crowd in Swahili.

Gavin faced the tent entrance as three women emerged into the aisle decorated with heart-shaped orange bush lilies wrapped with soft rustling ribbons on the chairs closest to the aisle. The woman in the middle was being guided by two women on each side draping red fabric over her head and around her body, as they guided her toward him.

A strange blend of excitement and nervousness left him anxious to see Hope. He hadn't seen her since she'd left The Gardenia Hotel two days ago and returned to her childhood home to organize the ceremony with Hawi's help. No doubt Hope had handmade the heart-shaped hanging decorations and flower garlands strung throughout the tent.

"Is this your true love?" his spokesman asked.

The rule was not to examine the covered woman too closely or even touch her unless you were sure she was yours.

With the air thick with tension, the crowd fell silent. Kids climbed onto their parents' laps, and others stood on the empty chairs for a better view, while elders exchanged knowing glances. They all reveled in the drama, all but Gavin who struggled with the heart-thumping trial, each passing second a test of his connection with Hope.

He moved closer, and without having to touch the woman or uncover her, he sensed it wasn't Hope. "No."

The people in the tent, locals' kids and adults from Hope's community, cheered, humming in Swahili when they uncovered the woman and she wasn't Hope.

He did this with two more sets of relatives before another accompanied woman approached, and he felt an inexplicable rush, a surge of anticipation. Somehow, he seemed to have a sixth sense where Hope was concerned. This time, as he neared the woman covered in red fabric, his heart danced to a rhythm only it knew, and an undeniable familiarity, a pull he couldn't ignore, drew him closer.

"Do you think this is your true love?" his spokesman asked, his voice echoing amid the expectant hush.

A soft, floral fragrance wafted to Gavin, one he knew so well. "Yes." He spoke with the conviction he felt in his bones. As he unveiled her, his heart swelled, confirming what he already knew. There she was, Hope.

The crowd was louder, some women squealing and men clapping.

Beneath the elegant hair band woven through it, Hope's hair fell in waves over her dress. The African dress—a vibrant, tribal-patterned concoction of yellows, golds, and bronzes so suited to the sunshine that she was—fit snugly to her lithe body before ruffling out below her knees. Radiant and oh-so-beautiful, she nearly blinded him, and he had to remember to breathe.

The corners of her eyes crinkled, betraying her joy before her lips ever could. "Gavin!" She spoke as breathlessly as he felt.

"She's my bride." His chest rising and falling, he tugged at the massive rose-shaped bow on her hip where she'd tied off the wide yellow sash overlaying her dress before the fabric became part of her billowing skirt. Using it, he drew her in his arms. Their lips met, and he kissed her softly. "I missed you."

"And I you," she replied, her voice shaking.

Taking a moment to truly see her, he marveled at her beauty. A pixie or an angel, she seemed unsuited for the world. If one were to judge on looks or sweetness, they'd never deem him worthy to stand at her side. "You're"—he struggled to catch his breath—"breathtaking."

No other word could fit.

The sunny glints in her eyes shone. She smoothed the linen fabric of the collarless cream robe he'd donned, a traditional outfit. "You clean up pretty well yourself."

As a thrill carried through her voice, he was glad they'd done the ceremony. He could see her dad smiling, his chest puffing from the main table where he sat with village leaders and other men, perhaps relatives. Around them, the tent reverberated. The joy wasn't just about them. It was a union the whole community celebrated.

With the mood under the tent electric in shared anticipation, the vibrant colors, the exotic melodies, and the exuberant crowd created a festivity he'd only dreamed of. In such a setting, his subsequent gesture might have seemed out of place. Yet, it felt fitting to honor both their shared journey and their individual histories.

The weight of the ring box in his pants pocket beneath the robe grounded him despite his whirlwind emotions. Their teasing banter from their shopping trip with Hawi three days ago renewed his smile. Following Hope's laughter and her luminous eyes as she tried on one ring after another, he'd returned the next day, certain of his selection.

Drawing the velvet box from his pocket, he paused. The music surrounded them, the beat infectious, urging the crowd into a dance. But amid the melody and movement, time seemed to slow. The world faded as he lowered onto one knee and presented the shimmering diamond to her.

Her eyes widened, and her hand flew to her mouth. Murmurs and gasps echoed around them. Over the cacophony, his voice rang clear. "Hope." The music, the chatter, the energy—none of it mattered. "Make me the happiest man in the world—"

Cheers and squeals erupted, the already lively atmosphere even more spirited. He barely managed to finish.

"Please marry me."

Everything quieted—or perhaps he only imagined it so as his whole being attuned to her. Then her emotional nod and whispered yes pierced through the jubilation. Elated, he slid the ring onto her finger, sealing their promise when he stood and kissed her.

As they pulled apart, the crowd ushered them forward. Hand in hand, they danced in rhythm with the beats that mirrored their pulsating hearts.

When the song ended, the spokesman called the preacher to pray for Gavin and Hope and for the food before they dismissed people to enjoy the awaiting feast outside.

Gavin and Hope stayed in the tent and sat with her family and friends on three long tables put side by side. With a spread of way more food for a feast than Gavin had ever seen, the servers had to clear the heart-shaped roses from tables.

Hope's dad spoke endlessly, and his eyes sparkled. "Hope has always had good chances and blessings." As her dad spoke, Hope smiled, clearly grateful for his assurance. "I'm very sure those same blessings will be with you both."

The men, including her brothers whom Gavin had met earlier, and the women, including her sisters, lifted their juices in cheers.

Whether her family was genuinely happy for her or not, the ceremony presented a unifying moment, and Hope beamed as she addressed anyone talking to her, making him glad he'd paid her dowry. He didn't want her to feel obligated to marry him, but the experience instilled a desire to marry her for real. He couldn't picture a future without her in it. How would he ever forget this day?

During breakfast the next morning, still energized from the party, Gavin suggested she apply for a visa while they were in her homeland.

She winced, pausing between bites of a scone. "I don't have a passport."

"Then let's get you started today."

"That's a great plan." Her eyes shone in the restaurant's ambient lights. So they stayed in Nairobi for more than two weeks, taking time to explore the best beaches in Mombasa, embark on a safari in one of the national forests, and make a video call with Ruth and Brady to meet their baby virtually. She was the cutest thing with a full head of dark curls. Gavin's heart squeezed, while Hope cried tears of joy. "We'll come and visit as soon as we leave here." Hope had said, and Gavin couldn't agree more. They didn't leave for Uganda until they'd submitted the paperwork to the embassy, leaving Brady and Ruth's address in Entebbe as the return address for when the embassy was ready to get back to them. Then they headed back to the village.

UNDER THE SETTING SUN'S warm, golden glow, Gavin stood with Hope in a lush cornfield. The earthy scent of soil characterized the air, and the whisper of corn husks in the gentle breeze accompanied the birds greeting the day and the cattle mooing in the distance.

The corn husks scraped against his palm as he broke out the corn. Lately, his hands were callused and bruised from all the work without gloves. He gazed at her ahead on the next row. With her sleeves rolled up, she harvested the ripe corn with an ease that spoke of familiarity.

Sensing his gaze, she paused and shook a finger at him. "You're supposed to be working."

Her laughter floated across the field, pure and infectious, causing a smile to tug at the corners of his mouth. He was struck, not for the first time, by her resilience and grace. Here, in her element, she was radiant and untamed, and he couldn't imagine a life without her in it. She'd been the light in an unknown territory, a great support.

When malaria struck most people in the village after their vacation, he'd contracted it too. Hope had spent two sleepless nights at his bedside to ensure he took his medicine, had enough fluids, and applied a wet washcloth on his face. In roughly six months, she'd made him forget his heartbreak. He'd spent more time with her than he had with Lucky in the years they'd dated.

"Hurry up, slowpoke!" Hope called him back from his stupor. Her eyes sparkled, and her long ponytail danced over her blue shirt. She was beautiful in her simplicity.

"Well." He chuckled, quickening to catch up. "Someone has to admire the expert at work."

Who could believe this was the corn they'd planted in March, and it was already the end of July? Harvest time.

They'd gone to Entebbe after Brady and Ruth's daughter was born. Then, since their return from Kenya, Gavin and Hope continued assisting the medical team and other villagers and Komo with whatever she needed. For fun, Gavin had enrolled Hope's help to build Ali a tree house.

"A house for me?" Ali had grinned, jumping up and down when they'd finished erecting it in the tree Gavin and Hope once climbed on Komo's property.

Gavin had also built a boardwalk from Komo's house to the temporary clinic, just to have a clear path. He hadn't encountered any snakes, besides hearing Hope squeal when she saw one while they were harvesting yucca root.

They continued plucking corn, working side by side, reminiscing about their memories since they got to the village. But a thrill still infused Hope's voice whenever they talked about their visit to her hometown.

"Because of you, Father thinks differently of me." She glanced at her ring and the diamond glittering in the afternoon light. "It was so nice to talk to him as an adult."

"Your father loves you," he assured her as he'd been trying ever since he met her family. "He just focuses on his ambitions, but how could he not love a daughter so kind and hardworking?"

Her going to prepare for the ceremony had helped her bond with her family. They weren't close, but it was manageable.

"So, have you thought more about forgiving your stepmom?"

She winced. "I'm working on it. I don't want anyone, not even Shani, to have that kind of power over me."

Man, she really was something! "I'm so proud of you, Hope. Trying to let go of the past and working toward forgiving is something else."

"Thank you." She tossed the corn on the pile ahead of them.

Everybody handled pain differently, but she seemed to handle it with grace.

"I'm glad you didn't marry Silas." He fumbled with the ear of corn he'd plucked, his fingers gliding over the silky husk. "Now, I get to be in this garden with you."

"The feeling is mutual." Her gaze searched for him, tender and warm, making him warmer. "Sometimes, I don't believe you'd want someone like me."

There was that doubt again, a feeling he understood so well because he had his own doubts. He spoke the assurance he needed to hear her say sometimes. "You've captured my heart, and God's given me 'hope' through you."

He couldn't even remember the last time he thought of Lucky, not even in a vengeful way.

The sun had begun to dip below the horizon, painting the sky in orange and pink, and he stopped his task, pulling Hope close to him. He tucked loose hairs from her ponytail behind her ear before cupping her face. Her luminous eyes met his, a soft seriousness replacing her playful demeanor.

"It's getting late."

Confusion flickered on her face.

They didn't need to carry the corn out of the field until they plucked all of it, which would take another two weeks.

"You mean you want to race me out of the cornfield?" she challenged, her eyes twinkling. Without waiting, she darted off, her laughter a delightful melody.

Grinning, he just watched her, her joy infectious. How he adored her spirited side! Then he took off in pursuit. "You're on, Hope!"

The rustling of the cornstalks accompanied their playful chase, their laughter echoing between the rows. The world beyond seemed to fade. It was just them, their laughter, and this chase.

Despite her head start, he was closing in. She glanced over her shoulder and squealed when she saw him nearing her.

Within mere breaths, he caught up and wrapped his arms around her waist from behind. His momentum spun them around, and still laughing, they collapsed into the soft soil. He cushioned her fall, propping himself up on an elbow to look down at her, his stomach fluttered, and his heart felt so full. Had he ever imagined being so carefree and in love? Lucky had been another kind of love. This with Hope felt different, magical. He'd never imagined feeling this way before.

Their lips were a breath apart. Her rapid breaths fanned his skin, and he whispered against her lips. "Caught you."

Then his lips met hers, tender and yielding to his. The world beyond their little cornfield ceased to exist as their lips tangled in a gentle kiss, a silent promise of his commitment.

The laughter, the chase, the kiss—it all felt so right, so natural. As he pulled away, his fingers feathered a loose strand of hair from her face, his gaze never leaving hers. "You know, Hope." He pushed the words from where he'd locked them in his chest. "I need you to know something."

Her brow lifted, her eyes questioning, her voice a whisper. "What is it?"

His thumb traced her cheekbone, his words coming from deep within. "I cherish every moment I spend with you." Including their time in the cornfield. "Every minute spent with you is special." A memory that would never fade.

"Oh, Gavin." Her eyes glistened. She touched his cheek. "You're the best thing that happened to me."

The confession in her cracked voice reflected the genuineness in her eyes, and her words seeped into him with a sincerity that left no room for any doubts. The feelings were mutual.

He stood, taking her hand in his.

As they walked hand in hand, their boots crunching through the tall grass, he knew for sure. He wasn't leaving the country without her. Perhaps Africa was growing on him, but he was in no hurry to get back to America.

ONE MORNING ALMOST a week later, Gavin had just finished helping Hope and Akiki clean the dishes after breakfast when Dongo arrived.

"I woke up early today." Dongo took a seat on the table and slapped a large manila envelope down. "Had to deliver these."

Hope hovered near the table. "Is Ruth's baby okay?"

"Brady and Ruth doing well?" Gavin asked. "Last I spoke to Brady, right after Rayna was born, he and Ruth were so sleep deprived."

"They are very much in love with the little one." Dongo's eyes lit up, causing Gavin to feel a desire to start his own family. "They wanted me to get your embassy papers right away."

Akiki appeared from the kitchen with a tray of diced plantains with meat and collard greens and juice. Whenever any guests showed up, Akiki didn't ask if they needed food or not. Instead, she always had extra that she brought them. Just as it was whenever they went to all the homes. These people fought so hard for their food that acquiring it became their daily focus, yet they were so generous in sharing what they reaped.

"I'm so hungry." Dongo patted his stomach, wrinkling up his pink button-down.

"The embassy responded." Hope gripped the envelope in both hands. It appeared heavy with several contents. "My..." Her voice quivered, and her eyes widened.

"Are you going to open it?" Gavin moved behind her. She seemed frozen in place continuing to study the sender's embassy address in Nairobi.

"What if they said no?" Her hands shook.

"They wouldn't have bothered to send you the papers in the mail." He rubbed the back of her shoulders up and down to encourage her. "It'll be okay. The worst that could happen is you'd have to reapply, and I'll be there with you."

Dongo licked the plantain sauce from his fingers, then held one up. "Going to America when you've never been on an airplane can be scary."

"I have never gone on an airplane." Hope pressed her lips together, her luminous eyes dimming. "But my worry is the response in this envelope."

Gavin understood her fears and her belief that she wasn't lucky. But he nudged her until she opened the envelope and removed a stack of papers.

In the minutes that followed, she silently read the interview invitation letter for her visa. Then she squealed out, "Ooh! Listen to this: 'We are pleased to inform you that your application for a visa to the United States has been reviewed and forwarded to the next stage of processing.' How fantastic!" The corners of her mouth curled as her head remained dipped over the letter. " 'As part of the application process, we are inviting you for an interview in the US Embassy in Nairobi.' " She read the time and date, then looked up. "They say your presence is required if you're in the country at the time."

He glanced at the calendar on the wall. The last week in August was three weeks away. "That's a Monday."

She then read further the details of what to bring to her interview.

"Passport." Her shoulders slumped. "Proof of your relationship..."

Her voice was shaking as she read the final requirements. Stepping closer, he draped his arm over her shoulders and kissed her hair, inhaling her shampoo's soft fragrance. At this point, he knew her well enough to distinguish the kinds of tears she shed. These were happy tears.

"Congratulations!" Dongo said over a mouthful.

"Thank you, Dongo. I can't believe it." Hope let out a sigh, turning to Gavin and tilting her head, resting it on his shoulder.

He cradled her against him. "We're one step in the right direction."

"Now, we have to pray I can pass the interview."

"One step at a time." She'd pass the interview. He sifted through the stack of documents. Each page held significance, various forms requiring completion, locations for medical tests, and results to be gathered. With all of this taking place in Nairobi, they were due for another trip to Kenya.

"It looks like we're heading back to Nairobi." He addressed Dongo. "Care to join us?"

Dongo swallowed, then rested his sauce-dipped hand on the now-empty plate. "It's a tempting offer, but Brady and Ruth have a whole routine for me this month. Maybe someday I can visit you in America instead."

"Deal." Gavin then turned to Hope as she voiced the appointments and locations in Kenya.

"They need evidence of our relationship," she murmured, her brows furrowing. "We should have taken more pictures together during this whole trip."

"Not to worry." He lowered his arm from her shoulders to her slender waist. "We have the most important photos from our traditional marriage."

Dongo's eyes widened, and his jaw slackened. "You did the bride wealth ceremony?"

"We did." Hope's voice carried a smile, and her contentment warmed Gavin.

"You know you're now committed to each other, right? You're married now."

"In Gavin's culture, we're not—"

"We're engaged," Gavin interrupted, "and if it's considered marriage, then lucky me." He pressed his lips to Hope's cheek and searched for any sign of flinching at his comment, but she was genuine, radiating only happiness.

He could trust her not to be like Lucky and run away. But now that he'd be fine marrying, was Hope ready? He didn't want her to feel obligated because he'd paid her dowry. She had to be free to make her own choices.

"I'm happy for you." Dongo rubbed his hands with a bar of soap and rinsed them in a plastic bowl Akiki had set on the floor. "Ruth and Brady had a similar journey. At least, you'll have someone to answer any complicated questions."

"Yes, but Brady had to leave Ruth behind for some time." Gavin's heart ached at the prospect. "I'm staying until things work out for Hope."

Should she make the trip to America, he'd worked out a viable living arrangement. She could stay in the guest room at his childhood home, and he'd move back home himself to ensure she wasn't left alone with his parents. He needed to discuss this plan with his mom, presenting Hope as the woman he intended to bring home.

While he had his own place, cohabitating with Hope, even with separate rooms, could lead to unintended implications. He'd rather avoid any potential complications and unnecessary temptations. But with Hope new to the country and everything foreign to her, he was uncomfortable leaving her alone in a hotel or even at his own place if he stayed elsewhere. So he'd bring her home to his parents' house where there was plenty of space and he could stay as well to ensure she was supported.

The solution now crystallizing in his mind was the prospect of marrying her earlier than anticipated. The idea of them starting a family together was becoming more appealing. He'd have to bring up the topic.

CHAPTER 20

Awaiting the interview three weeks later, Gavin sat beside Hope in the embassy lobby. Her ring scraped against his palm, her palms damp. In the last weeks, they'd prayed enough prayers to last his entire life.

Hope had insisted they call Brady and Ruth to pray with them, and the couple had prayed with their infant fussing in the background. Ruth assured them God was in control. "If it's in His will, it will all work out."

Not what Gavin wanted to hear. He wanted things to work out as fast as possible. It hadn't been hard for him to get a visa for Uganda. Why should it be hard for her to get a visa to America?

People slid out of the wooden benches as they got called to different windows. At each window, hopefuls were answering questions. Some stayed longer than others. Perhaps those who left within minutes were the ones without the right paperwork.

"I can tell that person was denied." Hope's voice was warm against his ear, and he followed her gaze to the woman whose shoulders sagged as she walked, her heels clicking on the lobby tile.

Gavin didn't know whether to give Hope false hope or not, but he squeezed her hand, praying he'd not lose his mind should they get denied. Prayer had been something he was getting acquainted with, thanks to Brady's faith talk, the Jesus film, and the gospel pamphlets the kids had made him read. He still had a lot to learn about God, but he was grasping that he was created and loved by God.

"You'd better pray you don't get that man in the blue shirt." The man on the other side of Hope spoke in a hushed voice. "He has a temper, and he's so mean."

There were six windows, four staffed with women and two with men. Five of the interviewers were Caucasian.

"You've been here before?" Hope turned to the man.

Gavin bounced his knee. Not wanting to entertain negative comments, he tried to pretend he hadn't heard the man's comment.

"Been coming for the last six months. Five times, I've had to redo the process due to the required paperwork. They just don't understand how complicated some of those papers are to acquire."

"Gavin Kress and Hope Njeri."

"That's us," Gavin cut through Hope's conversation. And she reached for her shoulder bag with their documents. Gavin's heartbeat stuttered as he realized who was ushering them forward.

"Oh no. It's *that* man," the man mumbled on the bench. "You'll need all the luck."

"Good morning, Gavin, Hope." The man's friendly tanned face was a contrast to what they'd expected. "I'm Ronnie."

"I've never been to an embassy before." Gavin relaxed to match the man's warmth.

"It looks nice here," Hope said to his side, and he squeezed her hand, trying to say they were off to a good start.

"Looks like you two are escaping Africa, right?"

"Not exactly." Gavin shook his head. "We've made so many friends in the village in Uganda."

Ronnie rubbed his beard as he skimmed some papers on his desk. Perhaps he'd printed some of the application questions she'd submitted. He then looked between Hope and Gavin. "You two met about nine months ago?"

It felt less than that, but Gavin hadn't kept track.

"Just over seven, sir." Hope then explained, her confidence in place as her brown eyes radiated warmth. "It was the end of January, and I was working at the resort where Gavin was staying when he got me fired."

"I convinced her to come to the village with me." Gavin continued where Hope left off. "She's very knowledgeable about the outdoors and has great survival skills. I wouldn't have survived without her there."

That venomous snake attack... Hope nursing him back to health when he had malaria. Emotion welled in his throat as he relayed their fond memories of the village.

Hope talked about their birthing of the cow. Maybe they were talking too much. When they stopped, Ronnie was silent, tapping a pen on his bearded chin. Gavin swallowed, waiting for the big no.

"You two have made the interview so easy." Ronnie's grin eased the tension in Gavin's shoulders. "Do you have some paperwork for me?"

"Oh yes." Hope lifted the bag and pulled out the paperwork, including both their passports that Gavin slid to the man.

"Nice ring." Ronnie nodded to the diamond sparkling beneath the lights before she tipped it away from the glass and admired it. It warmed Gavin that the ring meant something to her rather than just her freedom from her household. "Thank you."

Ronnie rummaged through the photos. "I see you performed the traditional marriage, huh?" He smiled at Gavin. "What did you think of that?"

He was glad he'd experienced her culture and allowed himself to dream of a lasting future with her. "It was a great experience."

"When do you want to leave for the US?"

"As soon as we get Hope's visa," Gavin answered, although aware they needed to stay in Uganda and work alongside the volunteers arriving in early September. "I didn't want to get plane tickets until she had the visa."

He'd bought a one-way ticket to Uganda, holding off on committing to a date for his return to America since he'd wanted to make a difference in people's lives while he recovered from his breakup.

They'd talked about their future, and she was excited to move to America. And if she ended up not liking it, he was willing to keep his heart flexible on moving back to Uganda. They could travel back and forth if they had to.

"I'll try to have your paperwork processed soon," Ronnie said. "Are you staying with Hope's family here in Kenya?"

"We came from Uganda as soon as we got the letter. My family has limited space, so we're staying in a hotel."

Ronnie didn't ask more about her family. Although things had moved from tense to civil to the point of forgiving her stepmom, Hope didn't feel comfortable around Shani. They'd only stopped by to say hello one morning during their last weeks of processing paperwork.

Gavin intended to encourage her to go and say goodbye should they get the visa. And it looked like she was going to get it.

Papers rustled as Ronnie stacked them before sliding their passports and photos back. "I'll give these back to you."

"Thank you," Hope and Gavin responded.

"Come back on Wednesday—for your visa."

Hope looked at Gavin, her brow rising before she smiled at Ronnie.

"We'll see you on Wednesday," Gavin confirmed his statement, then reached to shake Ronnie's hand, but stopped when he realized how small the section below the glass was. He waved instead. "Thank you."

"Did I get the visa?" Hope asked, looking between them.

"You did." Ronnie smiled. "You had all the paperwork I needed and proof that you two belong together."

"Thank you." She sucked in a breath, seeming to hold in a squeal as she waved to Ronnie.

Gavin gathered her into an embrace and squeezed her in a tight hug. While she hugged him back, he breathed in her hair, the smell of vanilla filling in his senses. "Congratulations, angel."

Ronnie cleared his throat, so they tore apart. His gray eyes gleamed as he waved at them. "See you on Wednesday."

That was probably his way of telling them he had more people to interview.

"Thanks again." Hope and Gavin spoke at the same time, Hope sounding giddy as she slid her fingers into his. They fit in so perfectly. He carried her shoulder bag with their paperwork as they walked through the lobby. They waved at the man who'd warned them about Ronnie.

He smiled and gave them a curt nod.

"We'll say a prayer for him," Gavin said as they left through the metal security gates. Perhaps prayer made the impossible happen at times.

"Good idea." Hope slid her arm from around his waist to clasp his hand.

Their taxi came into view still parked in the distance. They'd used the driver who'd driven them the last time they were in Kenya. Gavin had kept his number in his cell phone.

"I can't believe we got the visa!" She let herself squeal now.

He couldn't believe it either. "Wasn't that the man who's supposed to be very mean?"

"We prayed God would soften everyone who is going to talk to us today." She swung their joined hands. "We prayed for every person we were going to encounter, and God answered that prayer."

If they hadn't been praying daily for the interview since they heard from the embassy, he may have doubted it had anything to do with God's intervention. But they'd prayed, and God had answered.

If God could soften Ronnie for one day for their sake, then surely, there was a God in charge of every person on earth.

CHAPTER 21

In November, they landed in New York, then flew to Pleasant View, Gavin's hometown. On the drive from the airport, Hope peered through the window in search of golden streets. But she hadn't seen any. Even after Gavin assured her there was no such thing, she'd assumed she'd see one.

Rumors about the golden streets in America were wrong, given that the geography she'd learned hadn't indicated gold streets but man-made infrastructure.

She still found the roads fascinating. She'd never before seen highways as he'd called them before he'd fallen asleep. She pressed her face to the window of the fancy car. His jeans brushed against her black pants, and his labored breaths mingled with a harmonized song accompanied by a guitar on the radio.

Gavin was fighting jet lag, but while exhausted too, she didn't want to miss anything as they drove through a winding road with a mountain view. These mountains were closer and bigger than the hills she was used to. Homes nestled in between leafless and evergreen trees were spread apart from each other. One huge home after another, nothing like the huts and small brick homes in the villages.

Soon, the car turned onto a paved street, and her heart started racing when she saw the humongous house ahead. No. This couldn't be Gavin's childhood home.

Her heartbeat jittered. He'd been living in the village without complaining after he'd grown up *here*?

The tires bounced on the paved stone until the driver parked in the expansive driveway. The majestic mansion stood in a grand testament of wealth as towering windows reflected the waning evening sun. Although some shrubs didn't have leaves, they were trimmed, and she caught glimpses of a garden where green plants nestled beneath the dry ones. Gavin had explained how, in the winter, some plants became dormant.

She glanced at him. His head leaned back. His firm jaw had more beard than when she'd met him. The necklace bead peeped over his sweater, the same necklace she'd made. With his hair rumpled, she was tempted to run her hand through it to wake him, but she hated to interfere with his sleep.

Once the car engine turned off, he jolted, looking through the window, then to her. He stretched his arms, the muscles beneath his sweater tautening. "We're here?"

The driver craned his neck to look at them. "I'll get the luggage in the house."

"Thank you so much for driving us." Hope thanked the middle-aged man Gavin had introduced as his mom's driver.

"Don't worry about the luggage," Gavin responded. "Hope and I will get it."

The man gave Gavin a pleading look. "I'm not sure your mother would understand you're capable of carrying your luggage."

Gavin waved him off. "My mother can't fire you. She hates driving."

"It's my pleasure to carry your bags," the man insisted. "It makes me feel useful."

So Gavin nodded, then stepped out, and moved to open her door.

With her shoulder bag hoisted over her chest, she felt the chill air seeping through her turtleneck sweater. Good thing Ruth and Gavin insisted she shop for warmer clothes before they left Uganda. Hope stifled a yawn, jet lag catching up.

"I'll get you situated so you can take a nap." He led her to a path between green shrubs and some bare-branched ones that she imagined once had flowers.

Hope had seen homes like this in glossy magazines, but being on the precipice of one was entirely different, a surreal experience. She felt as if her eyes would pop out as she took in the grandeur. A knot twisted in her stomach, the sprawling mansion contrasting her humble beginnings. Beside her, Gavin seemed to sense her unease. His hand found hers and squeezed it with a silent message that did little to quell her anxiety.

At the door, Gavin lifted his hand to the small square camera, but the door swung open, revealing a woman dressed in dark pants and a flowy long-sleeved shirt. She bore a familiarity to the photos he'd shown Hope, and she had Gavin's blue eyes. Except while his were warm, this woman's were sharp, more so icy as she glanced at their entwined hands.

Hope pulled hers out of Gavin's.

"Mom?" Gavin said, and the woman plastered a smile.

"Look at you, sweetheart." She moved to him, touching his cheek, before embracing him. "Welcome home. I'm so glad you get to stay with us for a while."

"This is Hope." Gavin broke from the hug. He took her hand and pressed his lips to the back of her fingertips with a tenderness that felt too intimate for the audience.

Heat crept up her neck, warming her body. His display of affection, although simple and sweet, felt magnified under his mother's watchful gaze. Hope cleared her throat, gripping her worn shoulder bag with her other hand and feeling small under the woman's faltering smile.

The woman's graying hair was perfectly coiffed, not a single strand daring to break the meticulous order of her stylish bob. Her lips were tinted a perfect shade of rose, but not curled into a genuine smile. Her eyes, cool and penetrating, seemed to assess Hope's worth.

"Welcome, Hope." She put out her hand, and Hope hesitated to shake it. "I'm Sara." The handshake was as brief as the greeting. "Come in, you two."

Her voice deceptively smooth, she stepped aside for them to enter. Having been around people who didn't want her around, Hope knew enough to recognize one.

"I was starting to wonder if you'd ever let us in," Gavin teased, his hand sliding around Hope's waist as he led them to a hallway.

"I'll take off my shoes," she whispered to him, not wanting to stain the polished white tile.

But when she tried to crouch to take off her shoes, he tugged her forward. "You're fine." He kept walking with her, leaving no room for her to slide off her shoes.

With Sara's heels clicking on the tile behind them, Hope could almost feel the woman's measuring gaze. The house smelled clean, scented with something citrus. But as stiff as she was, Hope couldn't even look at the walls to see what kind of art adorned it. The rooms felt much colder than the outside as she continued to sense Sara's reception.

"You'll need some serious grooming after your wild trip in the jungle." Sara's comment confirmed Hope's thought.

"We've been showering every day, you know." Gavin spoke lightly as if used to handling his mother.

A chill crept through Hope. She should've worn her usual dresses and skirts rather than pants. Perhaps, in a dress, she'd have appeared more presentable.

They walked to the kitchen where a man with skin not much darker than Hope's was slicing something. As the knife hit the board, the smell of onions and something delicious tinged the air. While big windows with drapes drawn aside admitted natural light, the lighting above was fancy.

"What have you been up to, Morgan?" Gavin greeted the man.

The man's smile was warm as he set the knife on the slicing board and assessed Gavin. "You look different—you have a glow of happiness." The man walked around the counter, his white chef coat on. Then he slid off the gloves and hugged Gavin, slapping his back energetically.

When Gavin drew back, he motioned to her. "This is my girlfriend, Hope."

"Morgan." The man reached out, and she shook his hand.

"Nice to meet you." Nice to see a friendly face. But she kept that comment to herself.

"I spent most of Gavin's teen years fixing his favorite meals." Morgan grinned as he spoke about Gavin with fatherly fondness. "But, as hard as I tried, he still decided to grow up and leave us."

"He'll be here for a while now." Sara's voice sounded as she stepped beside them. "How long before dinner is ready?" The woman meant business, and Hope longed to be curled up back in Ruth and Brady's house in the village.

"In less than an hour, ma'am," Morgan responded, his voice professional now.

"We already ate. Sleep is our priority," Gavin said, making Hope glad they'd eaten at the airport. They'd both been so hungry, and he'd taken her to a Chinese restaurant. She'd never eaten Chinese food before, but they served rice, which was familiar.

"Nonsense." Sara waved a manicured hand. "Let's have some drinks." Her commanding tone allowed no argument. "By the time we're done with drinks, you'll be hungry for dinner."

"If we get sick, it'll be your fault," Gavin teased.

And Hope had no doubt she'd never get to that level of comfort with Sara. That was if Sara ever let her marry her son.

"I pay Jolene to clean," Sara said. "She can handle cleaning up in case you get sick."

Sara moved with the grace of a queen traversing her court, her heels clicking authoritatively. With each word, step and gesture, she made it clear she was in charge in this house.

They sat at a small table with four comfy chairs, near a sofa in the sprawling sitting room adjoining the kitchen. "Hope will take the guest room downstairs. I've already texted Gomez to take your luggage to your respective rooms."

"Hope can sleep in my room, and I'll sleep downstairs." Gavin placed his hand atop Hope's. "It's a bit lonely down there."

"I'll be fine." Hope tucked her shoulder bag safely out of sight at her feet, eager to be safely secluded far away from Sara.

"Of course, you'll be fine." Sara glanced at her pink nails, her expression bored. "There's a TV and anything you need to kill your boredom."

A woman in her twenties delivered a tray of fancy glasses.

"Hope and I will have soda," Gavin said as the woman set the tray on the table and picked up a wine bottle.

"We have Sprite and ginger ale," the woman said.

Hope tucked her hands in her lap. "Anything is fine."

"We'd love ginger ale," Gavin said.

The mountain backdrop teased her from one of the windows. If she wasn't anxious, she'd love to explore the property and take an extra look at the mountains.

While they had their drinks, Sara gave a gentle shake of the glass, the dark red liquid dancing in it. "How was your trip? Tell me everything."

"Meeting Hope was the highlight." Gavin's hand found hers under the table. "We had more adventures than I've ever had my whole life." He told his mom about wrapping wounds and giving immunization shots and working in the fields and the village. "Hope taught me how to give haircuts using a plain razor."

"I'm sure she did." Sara's fingertips clicked against the delicate glass, and her eyes raked over Hope in careful assessment, causing Hope's heart to lodge in her throat. "You mean to tell me you've been with Hope this entire time in Uganda?"

His sincere smile offered some comfort. "From the day I arrived in Uganda." He winked at Hope, apparently clueless about his mom's attitude. "If it wasn't for her, I would've died—"

"God would have protected you," Hope interrupted, not wanting more daggers from Sara, but Gavin continued telling all the dangers he'd faced. "The snakebite and malaria—"

"What?" Sara coughed on her wine and set the glass down. "Of all the places you shouldn't have been—"

"I'm fine, Mom." He squeezed Hope's hand under the table. Maybe he, too, was nervous or he wanted to kiss her to show off to his mom. Because he was lifting her hand to his mouth.

Hope shivered as Sara's shoulders straightened and her gaze focused on Hope's hand nestled in Gavin's. The woman's eyes enlarged, fixated on the ring, and the knot tightened in Hope's stomach. Clearly, Gavin hadn't mentioned their traditional ceremony to his mother. Sara's shocked eyes confirmed it, and Hope's heart started flailing like a bird caged in her chest. Why was she sitting here, at a grand dining table set with crystal and silver? The opulence of it all screamed at her, accusing her of her humble background.

Sara's gaze darted between them both like they'd done something forbidden. Her lips quivered, parting in an involuntary sound of astonishment. "Oh my. Are you two... *engaged*?"

He squeezed Hope's hand, a secret gesture that he had her back, then responded in such a steady voice it left no room for doubt. "Yes, we are."

Silence descended. It was only a few seconds, but it felt like an eternity. Was that hurt or disappointment now dimming Sara's cold eyes? Whichever it was, a quick recovery masked it. Her smile returned, though more strained.

"Well, this is a surprise." A hint of something unreadable tainted her tone when she grasped her wine and lifted it to them in a toast. "Congratulations."

"Thank you," he replied, his voice firm.

While Sara guzzled the rest of the wine, reached for the bottle, and tilted to pour more for herself, Gavin sipped his soda. But with her mind awhirl, Hope merely stared at the fizzling bubbles in her glass. Should she say something to make things better for him? The last thing she needed was to strain his relationship with his mom.

She looked up at the chandelier and the modern art on the wall. She didn't see pictures of the family, but in a house this big, another sitting room probably displayed those photos. "You have a lovely house."

"It takes hard work," Sara snipped. "What do you do for a living, Hope?"

"I'm..." *Yeah, Hope, tell her you never graduated secondary school and you're self-taught.*

"She's a naturally talented interior designer." He nudged her foot under the table. "She might work with me if she finds me deserving."

Sara didn't say anything.

But the lightness in his voice offered Hope the slight strength she needed to realize she didn't need all of his family to like her. All she needed was Gavin.

"Weren't you making some hors d'oeuvres?" Sara called after Morgan as she refilled another glass of wine.

"Coming right up."

Gavin pressed his lips together and gave Hope an apologetic smile, squeezing her hand. He finally seemed to understand that his mom didn't want her here. Hope wanted to escape, but she was going to be stuck here, for how long? She had no idea. Her visa was for six months, with a clause for them to get married within ninety days of arriving in America.

"Where's Dad anyway?" Gavin asked, probably needing someone around as a buffer.

"He should be home for dinner."

An ugly wave of familiarity washed over Hope. Her past was nipping at her heels again. She'd always struggled to find favor with her parents, and few people ever genuinely embraced her. So why had she hoped Sara, Gavin's mother, would be any different? What made her think his family would be okay with him marrying a woman from a different culture?

This wasn't her first time facing disapproval. This pattern was all too familiar.

A yearning welled up within her, an ache to return to the simplicity of Jinja and her work for Lumbe. At least, she wasn't entangled with Lumbe. It was a professional environment. Her heart shivered at the possibility of going back. The village—she'd be fine staying with Akiki at Ruth and Brady's house and doing charity work.

Instead, she was thousands of miles away, and she and Gavin were entwined in a bond that seemed to be scrutinized at every turn.

HOPE WOKE IN THE STRANGE room to a gentle tap on her door the next morning. Light streamed through the window, and the bedside clock displayed ten thirty. She yawned, still being pulled by sleep as she took in a room as fancy as the rooms at the resort where she'd worked.

Beautiful landscape photos hung on sage-green walls, and her fingers traced the soft bedsheet, then the duvet cover. She felt like she was in a film until images flashed of her arrival last night.

Sara's cold gaze.

Her body tensed, and she gripped the bedding. Maybe she was in a bad movie.

A knock sounded again, and she dragged herself out of bed, reaching for the silk robe and throwing it over her. Even if Sara hadn't been friendly, she'd gone through the trouble of buying Hope some clothes and nightgowns and slippers.

When Hope swung open the door, Gavin grinned at her as he extended a bouquet of colorful flowers sprinkled with some roses. "Welcome to America."

Even as her heart warmed, she self-consciously patted her hair. The hardness of the braids reminded her she'd had her hair braided before they left Uganda.

"You're beautiful."

She accepted his flowers, hugged the glass vase to her chest, and dipped her nose to the blooms, inhaling a fragrance as soft as the petals when she traced her finger over a rose. "Thank you. These are so beautiful." Her gaze rose to meet his, and his fresh scent mingled with the flowers. "You're already dressed and cleaned up."

"It will take you longer to adjust to the time change than I did." He jammed his hands into the pockets of his faded jeans, the motion stretching out his black T-shirt. "Ready for breakfast?"

She stiffened her spine to hold back a shiver as she dreaded eating with his mom after last night's intolerable dinner. His dad had been friendlier, or maybe it only seemed so because the man spoke so little. His silence and unreadable expression had been better than Sara's critical questions.

As if reading her mind, Gavin touched her shoulder. "It's just you and me. My parents already ate."

Relief flooded her, and she blew out a breath. "I'll clean up first."

"I'll wait for you out here in the basement living room."

"Thank you." He didn't have to wait on her, but facing day one in the strange land and unfriendly house, she'd let herself cling to him.

"Sorry about my mom." He'd already apologized last night when he'd walked with her downstairs. "At times, it takes her longer to warm up to people."

At least, he'd noticed his mom's unfriendliness.

"It's not your fault. I'm okay, really." After all, Sara wasn't the first person to disapprove of her.

"No matter what, just know I'm with you, angel." He touched her cheek, tipping her gaze toward his and making her feel safe and almost secure.

When she closed her door, she could hear the TV from the sitting room as she set the flowers on the bedside table. She stepped into a bathroom bigger than most she'd seen in Uganda or Kenya. It took her several times to figure out how to turn on the shower. She almost stepped out to fetch Gavin. Then a miracle happened, and she twisted one of the many attachments to the handle. The water shot at her, cold at first, then too hot. It made for a fast shower, so she'd have to have him walk her through how it worked before she showered again.

After she'd showered and they'd eaten, he drove her to his house. The charming two-story structure with whitewashed walls and large French windows hinted at the cozy living space within.

The midafternoon was brisk as they walked side by side on the cobblestone. She thrust her hands into the pockets of the cozy winter coat he bought her in New York. Having a six-hour layover, he'd taken her shopping for warmer clothes than she'd bought in Uganda. He'd also insisted on getting her a phone in case she needed to call home. When she suggested they flip the coin to decide on that, she lost. But she liked the idea of having a phone. She'd texted Ruth last night to let her know they'd arrived, but she'd spared her Sara's cold welcome.

"This." He swept an arm toward the house. "If you like it, maybe we can live here when we get married."

When, not if. He still wanted her to be a part of his life. She didn't care where she lived as long as she was with him.

"It's beautiful, Gavin." The sweeping view of the mountains and outdoor space captured her imagination, and for a moment, she allowed herself to envision their kids with amber skin tones running around the open space, their happy echoes filling the air. "I love it."

He smiled sheepishly, tugged her to his side, and wrapped his arm around her waist. "I don't mind building a different house. I'd love for you to have a say in what we live in."

"If you like it, I like it as much." She rested her head on his shoulder. That he wanted her to give her opinion meant a lot. Standing there in his arms, she took in the house and the area close to the front with stones designed to protect a garden. "Is that a garden?"

"I didn't plant it myself. I had a landscape company design it. The flowers are all dead now, but in the spring, you can plant any you want."

She imagined the blossoms springing to life during the sunny days, and a smile curled her lips.

"Let's go check out the inside." He released her, and she slid her arm into the crook of his. The garage door opened with him tapping on his phone. They made their way through the garage and into the house, and a burst of afternoon sun streamed in, illuminating the interior.

As they crossed the threshold, the charm hinted at by the house's exterior came to life in an array of inviting details. Spaces flowed seamlessly into one another, and she spun around, appreciating the open floor plan with the sleek, modern kitchen giving way to the inviting living area. She moved to the kitchen and traced her fingers along the cold marble counters. "I love this."

"I'd offer you something to eat or drink." Crossing his arms over his chest, he leaned against one of the counters. "But I've been gone for almost a year and haven't bought anything for the house."

"We just had breakfast."

"Lunch," he corrected, then tipped his head, encouraging her to move to the sitting room. "I bought black furniture, but we can always change it to whatever you want."

"I like the unique furniture." It was as if pieces were selected with an eye for elegance yet remained unpretentious and comforting. Design, light, space, and furnishings went hand in hand, complementing each other. "I'd just add some African art and a favorite blanket and pillows in my favorite colors to make it personable."

The cozy fireplace promised warmth and companionship on chillier days. She could see herself nestled with him on the sofa watching a favorite film on the TV.

She lowered herself to sit and patted the soft leather for him to join her. "Is this where you watch sports?"

He'd talked about watching sports more often than he watched films.

He nodded, the sofa dipping when he sat. "But we can watch other things too." He winked at her, and her heart melted. It wasn't the first time he winked at her, but even his smallest reactions always warmed her.

She couldn't help thinking his house was one of those in the magazines. It was different from his parents' all-white plain-and-fancy look, simpler, warmer, with fascinating features. The grand windows, unadorned by heavy drapes, invited natural light to dance across the spaces. The sunlight painted its warm cleansing glow on every surface.

"Hope." Gavin's voice was soft as he took her hand in his. "I want us to fill this home with love, laughter, and memories of our life together."

As her heart swelled, she struggled to breathe against the emotion lodging in her throat. His sincerity, so evident in his eyes, and the depth of his feelings for her was palpable. Despite her initial anxiety, she felt a sense of calm. She was home. No matter where they were, as long as she was with him, she was home.

"Gavin, I love it. I love the thought of us building a life here together."

He snugged her into his arms and pressed a tender kiss to her forehead. "And I can't wait to start that life with you."

Several minutes later, he led her back to the garage.

"I'll show you one of the homes where you can temporarily live once the tenants leave in two days."

They walked past two parked cars. The one he'd driven and parked in the driveway was from his teens, a car he kept at his parents' house.

He then asked what she wanted to do for a living. "If you don't want to work, that's okay too. I can take care of you."

"I want to be an interior designer." Just looking at his house filled her with inspiration. "You already told your mom, I'm one, so I might as well fulfill it."

"You don't have to be an interior designer just because—"

"I want to. I've wanted to since you told me what interior designers did."

"We can check out a school for you to learn more about designing and interior decorating." He opened the passenger door for her but blocked the way for her to sit as he told her the variety of options she could approach to her education, starting with a GED since she never graduated high school. "You can do that online without leaving the house."

"Really?" Her heart thudded. Did they offer such an alternative to graduate in the comfort of one's home? "How much does that cost?" She'd need to get a job to pay for school.

He stepped aside and guided her to sit. "How about I pay for your school and maybe you work for me to pay me back?"

"Really?" Joy filled her to the extreme. That sounded better than him handing her the money for free. "I can do any job."

He beamed. "I have no doubt you can do anything. You may not even want to work for me."

"I think we make a great team."

He stooped to kiss the top of her head. "That we do."

She settled back while he shut her door and sprinted around to the driver's seat. She was so used to being around him, and she loved how he'd bounced ideas off her, genuinely asking for her opinion when he built a cupboard or a structure for one of the villagers.

As he started the car, he suggested they go to a movie, not telling her what it was.

The surprise was when they were the only two people in the theater as he held a big pail of popcorn that scented a room dimly lit by the screen playing movie advertisements. Her drink was in the pocket of her chair, and he had his soda on his side too.

"What time does the movie start?" she asked. Maybe everyone would come later. Or maybe their small town didn't have a big audience of moviegoers.

"Soon." He scooped a handful of popcorn from the bucket, and she did the same, their hands brushing against each other, shooting tingles through her arm.

Then the film started playing, and she saw the title. She clamped her hand to her mouth, gasping. "*Gone with the Wind*?"

"It was high time you watched the movie." He squeezed her shoulder.

"Isn't this an old film?" She'd known there was a film about the book, but that was years ago.

He shrugged. "The theater's owner is a friend."

Ah, that explained why they could have the luxury of being in the theater just the two of them.

Gavin had gone out of his way to do this for her? Wanting to be as close to him as possible, she took the popcorn pail from him and set it on the carpeted floor. Turning to him, she snaked her hand to the back of his neck and leaned in. "Thank you."

Before he could respond, her mouth was on his, and she was kissing him with all she was worth like a teenager who'd lost control.

Maybe he, too, had lost control because his hands slid around her neck as he thrust his fingers into her hair. Tangling up her braids, he kissed her with tenderness, a long, sweet kiss that erased all the doubts she'd gained in Sara's presence.

As they resumed watching the movie, she was confident this excitement would last, even if her life was filled with strife. That realization was something she clung to that evening when they returned to Gavin's childhood home and Lucky was the guest of honor at dinner.

CHAPTER 22

Mom's cold welcome to Hope had caught Gavin off guard, shocked him even. She'd never been anything but gracious and welcoming to his friends, but then he'd never gone out with anyone other than the dates his mom initiated. Perhaps Mom was no different from Bryce's mom. Both too snobby for their own good.

Gavin had worried Hope would be terrified and want to leave right away, but she was all smiles and chatty as they discussed *Gone with the Wind* on the ride home.

"You're my Rhett." She placed her gentle hand on his leg as he drove, and he savored the warmth of her palm seeping through his jeans.

"You are my Scarlett." He gave her a sideways glance, his chest expanding at the sight of her happiness. The garage doors opened, sensing his car approach.

"You really made my day. I can't believe you managed to get the theater to show us that movie, but I still like the book better."

Gavin had to agree. He'd read the book during their time in the village. When they landed in New York, he'd texted the theater owner and offered him a lump-sum amount if he could find the movie and reserve the theater for them. It had worked out perfectly since they'd watched the movie before the theater's regular opening hours.

After he parked in the garage, they walked hand in hand as she hummed one of the songs from the movie, her voice a lullaby while they stepped into the house.

Laughter carrying through the kitchen cut into his happy elation. He tightened his hand around hers and halted. She stopped singing, perhaps noticing the change in atmosphere.

The sizzle of whatever Morgan was cooking and the smells of spices all faded in the background. Morgan might have said something, too, because Mom turned and so did the other woman. Maybe his eyesight was failing him.

"Hey." Dad lifted his glass with amber liquid in greeting, his white polo shirt an indication he'd come from playing tennis. As a former CEO of a successful multinational energy corporation, he'd retired early to enjoy doing things he loved.

"Lucky?" Unable to concentrate on Dad, Gavin's gaze flitted to his ex, and his low voice blended in with the knife hitting the cutting board. Man, it felt like the knife was cutting through his heart as annoyance tore him apart.

Mom had a knowing grin. Dad shrugged as if he had no control over the situation.

"You're in time for dinner." Mom ushered them forward, and the dampness of Hope's hand slicked his palm.

Gavin walked closer to the island where his parents sat with the woman who should be a stranger to him by now but was a big part of his past. Anger, pain, regret, and even empathy and other emotions crashed down.

Lucky met his gaze before she looked away and reached for her wine.

"Lucky has been trying to reach you for almost a year, but you wouldn't respond." Mom spoke with the certainty that she was doing the right thing. "It was only fair that I invited her to dinner."

"You had to invite her *tonight*?" While she knew very well Gavin was dating Hope? Well, technically, she was his fiancée, and in her culture, they were considered married.

"When else was I supposed to get you two together?"

Hope's grip tightened on his hand. He took a deep breath, turning to her to make introductions. "This is Lucky." The words left a bitter taste.

"Nice to meet you... Lucky." Hope's voice wavered, loaded with doubt.

Lucky's penciled eyebrows lifted as she took in Hope. What a snob, just like Mom. Maybe he'd been a snob, too, if he'd never noticed the way Lucky acted.

"Nice to meet you too," she drawled out as if bored. Her gaze then flickered to him, taking him in from head to toe. "Gavin, you look great." A soft smile, once familiar, now seemed foreign. "Even Africa couldn't get you to look any different."

She rose from her seat, and he took two steps back, afraid to be embraced by her.

Lucky must've gotten the memo because she didn't come closer.

"Glad to have you home." Uncanny sweetness coated her voice. In a sleek red dress, she looked as striking as ever, her blonde curls cascading over her shoulders. But her presence in his parents' home, the same property where they'd stood to get married and she jilted him, felt like a punch in the gut.

Mom cleared her throat. "Lucky happened to be in town, Gavin. It would've been rude not to invite her."

"But—"

"Let's go have dinner." Mom cut him off, her lips set in the thin line that warned he wasn't going to win this conversation. Taking charge, she led everyone to the dining room, a room resplendent in its formal décor. The chandelier light shone over the mahogany table and polished silverware folded in white napkins. Empty plates and water goblets set with ice meticulously waited at five of the six places.

Gavin clung to Hope's hand, afraid she'd flee the moment he let her go. She seemed to be taking in the scene, but he could only imagine what she was thinking. He gave her hand a reassuring squeeze and pulled out a chair for her, taking the place next to her.

When she excused herself to use the bathroom, he did the same. He hadn't been prepared for an ambush. He needed to wash his hands and compose himself, but he returned to the table before she did, fearing to leave her alone with unfriendly strangers.

"Well..." He drew out the word, awkward and avoiding looking at Lucky at the end of the table. "This is a surprise."

"It shouldn't be." She reached to touch his hand, but he jerked it away and tucked it in under the table. "I wish you'd told me you got engaged."

Mom must've filled her in on the details. Raising his chin, he faced her. "I don't have to tell you anything." In case she'd forgotten... "You lost that right when you left me standing at the altar."

Hope slid into the chair, and he placed his hand on her jean-clad leg.

"Darling," Mom addressed him, smiling as if all this should be a normal situation. "You dated for three years, and you've known Lucky since you two were in diapers. You both deserve to hear what she has to say."

His gaze flitted to Lucky, and the familiar softness in her eyes touched him. Maybe he should listen to her, then move on with Hope without the lingering rejection and hurt.

But she'd humiliated him. Why give her his time?

"So, Dad, how was tennis today?" Gavin sipped from his glass, diverting the subject.

"We're going to try a league in the spring." Dad's eyes lit up as he talked about his tennis friends. He then talked about golf and the upcoming Scottsdale tournament.

Morgan rolled in a cart filled with various dishes he centered on the table. The pungent aromas of garlic, onions, and fine meats infused the room, and Gavin's mouth watered. He'd missed American food, and Morgan was a great cook.

"Thanks, Morgan," Hope said, reminding Gavin of his manners.

"You're the best." He addressed Morgan when he placed the last serving plate of meat on the table.

"I have to fatten you up." Morgan winked with his usual playful tone. Too bad, he couldn't join them at the table. They sure could use the buffer.

Soon, the housekeeper brought more wine, refilling Lucky's and Mom's glasses. Dad asked for a beer, which the server brought him minutes later.

While the food was passed across the table, Gavin squeezed Hope's hand with a silent prayer so as not to attract any attention. Seeming to understand his intention of saying grace, she squeezed his hand in return. This dinner was about to become more complicated than he'd anticipated. And all he could do was brace himself and pray it didn't end in disaster.

He then reached for the serving bowl with chicken, one of the dishes Hope was more likely to eat, as she wasn't yet familiar with American food. He still wanted to add an option for her to choose, though. "Would you like some chicken or steak?"

"Chicken is fine, thank you."

He forked a chicken breast and set it on her plate, then one on his plate. While he wanted a steak, no way would he enjoy it served with such unmistakable tension.

Hands crossed at the table as everyone filled their plates.

"Can you pass the asparagus, please?" Dad asked, and Gavin passed the plate, then asked Hope if she'd care to have some roasted potatoes. Morgan had likely prepared them with Hope in mind since Gavin had suggested familiar dishes for her. After being in Africa so long, Gavin almost called them "Irish potatoes" the way they did to differentiate from sweet potatoes.

"Yes, please." She shifted in her seat, her shoulders stiff as if she were sitting on a thorny briar, not a cushioned chair.

When she reached for the broccoli and offered it to him, he thanked her, even if he didn't feel like broccoli. But she was trying to make herself comfortable.

"Guess what movie Hope and I saw today?" He attempted a conversation as he sliced through his chicken breast.

"What did you see?" Dad cut a bite of his steak.

"*Gone with the Wind*. It's Hope's favorite."

Lucky sneered. "Since when are you into classics?"

Since Hope. "I've been missing out. High time I expanded my entertainment preferences."

Another silence followed before Lucky spoke again.

"Remember when we went to New York for the premiere of *The Reverie*?"

Gavin shrugged, not wanting to make a big deal of his excitement when he'd been thrilled to propose to her and had gotten tickets to the final installment of her favorite trilogy.

Mom raised her glass in a toast, her eyes gleaming. "Do you remember what happened that summer before you went to New York?"

He rolled his eyes, dreading where this conversation was headed. Then he let out a breath and pretended not to remember anything good that happened with him and Lucky. "I've had too much going on lately to remember the past."

"I'm sure you still remember when you broke your arm climbing the old oak tree at the back of the cabin."

He stiffened as Lucky's curls bounced when she laughed and leaned forward.

"That was something else." She lifted her fork, her voice bright and resonating with a shared history he didn't want to revisit. "He thought he was invincible. I held his arm until the doctor arrived."

She seemed to be showing off, and Mom wasn't helping when she continued with one recollection after another of him and Lucky. The three-legged race they'd won during a family picnic, their crowning as prom king and queen.

"What does prom king and queen mean?" Hope asked, taking an interest in the conversation.

"It means they were always the perfect couple for each other." Mom smirked and eyed Lucky who brushed her hair to the side, flirtatiously.

"We broke up after high school." He spoke up, needing to say something to end this.

"But you ended up back together after college," Mom reminded. "Each time you two broke up, you always found your way back to each other."

He felt a prick of unease, a tightening in his chest as though the room was becoming smaller. Mom seemed to be hinting the same would happen now. He stabbed a piece of chicken and chewed on it furiously. Through the corner of his eye, he could see Hope eating faster than she should, clearly uncomfortable too. His hand covered hers under the table, and his thumb drew circles over her skin to show her he wasn't interested in revisiting a past love life.

He had some good memories with Lucky, but he was with Hope now.

Desperate to steer the conversation away from his past with Lucky, he asked Hope. "Do you remember the time we got lost on our hiking trip?"

"I remember." Her voice was for his ears alone, and her gaze only at him.

"We discovered that hidden waterfall."

She mustered a small smile at the memory, one that was theirs and theirs alone. "Yes, I remember. The water was freezing."

They stared at each other, lost in their own world, and perhaps that was what they needed. They needed to turn in for the night.

"You're ready to call it a day?"

She nodded, her chest rising as he breathed out his relief. He pushed back his chair, taking her hand. She offered to clear the dishes, but Mom lifted her hand to stop her.

"You forget we have a server to take care of that sort of work. Plus, we haven't had dessert yet."

But Gavin was ready for an escape. He'd gone almost an entire year without dessert in Uganda, so he wasn't even craving it.

"We're still dealing with jet lag." He squeezed Hope's hand. "It was a long day."

"Thank you, so much for dinner, Mr. and Mrs. Kress." Hope managed politely.

And Dad responded, "Glad you could join us."

A line was drawn between Mom's penciled eyebrows, her gaze on Gavin. "As soon as you escort Hope, you need to come back and talk to Lucky."

"I can see myself to my room." Hope tried to free her hand, but he kept his hold firm, bothered by Mom's tone as if she was commanding a child.

"I'd forgotten I'm a grown man. But thanks, Mother, for reminding me of my age."

"Don't be ridiculous." She waved him off, flashing her perfectly painted pink nails.

Hope was walking faster, gripping her shoulder bag, the one he'd given her when they'd just met. She seemed to favor it more than the others. She yanked her hand out of his as soon as they turned around to the stairs. With her taking two stairs at a time, he had to do the same to keep up.

She was upset, and he didn't blame her. Mom and Dad seemed to have forgotten everything that happened at Gavin and Lucky's supposed wedding over a year ago.

As they stepped into the living room downstairs, Gavin turned on the light and gathered Hope in his arms. He could feel her hesitancy through her stiffened shoulders.

"Hey." He buried his face in her hair and breathed in the soft fragrance of the spray she used in her braids. "I didn't know Lucky was going to be here."

Hope struggled out of his embrace, and he shifted a step back to look at her. She'd ducked her head and was rubbing her temples. Her braids quivered, and her chest rose and fell as she breathed out. "Lucky and your parents are probably waiting for you."

"Hope, what's wrong?"

She swiveled to meet him, her eyes flaring. "It's obvious, don't you think?"

His brows squeezed closer. He hadn't indicated any interest in Lucky for Hope to be mad at him. "What do you mean?"

Hope huffed. "Well, it's obvious Lucky still loves you. And your mom is shoving her at you." She pressed her lips together as if holding back on whatever else she wanted to say.

His parents, particularly Mom, had a soft spot for Lucky. "I told you how Mom likes to control everything, and I used to care about what she thought. Now, I don't." Especially after Lucky jilted him. After that, they could never go back to what they'd been.

Hope crossed her arms, her skepticism keeping her stiff. "You and Lucky have a history, and I feel like an intruder."

"Lucky is the intruder." He stepped closer and cupped her chin until her gaze met his. His thumb traced the dainty point on her pixie face. "You're not the only one who has an imperfect family, angel. My family is right there along with yours. They just have different imperfections, enough to complicate our lives."

Her eyes softened as she gave a gentle nod, closed the gap between them, and wrapped her arms around his waist.

"You are the one I want." He drew her close, the steady rhythm of his heart beating against hers. With a gentle kiss to her forehead, he whispered,"Lucky is a part of my past—nothing can change that. But you? You are my new beginning and my future—that's set in stone."

She melted into him, her lithe form so dear, so precious, so fragile. "I'll try not to let your mom get to me."

"I'll talk to Mom. She needs to know how important you are to me." He'd never let anything hurt her, though holding her tender heart left him fearful of that precious responsibility. "And I'll set things straight with Lucky."

Hope melted into his embrace, but his nagging worry lingered. With Lucky now around, Mom's persistence could test his relationship with Hope. Surely, nothing Lucky would say could ruin what he and Hope had built over the last months together.

"I love you so much," she whispered, her breath warm through his T-shirt, her voice shaking as she squeezed him tight as if she feared to let go. Yet he could sense her slipping away somehow.

"I love you too." The words tumbled from his lips, raw and honest. He leaned in, capturing her lips in a kiss that tasted of desperation and longing. His arms clung to her, part of him terrified she might disappear into the night.

"Good night, Gavin." She eased back, her voice a delicate brush against his heart. As she pulled away, she pressed a soft kiss to his cheek, and the featherlight touch sent shivers down his spine.

His heart stuttered when the living room's recessed light caught the sheen of tears on her cheeks. He watched, helpless, as she wiped them away and retreated with a brisk turn. The soft click of her door echoed in the silent room, a resounding finale to their conversation.

The air hung heavy with a threatening undercurrent. A storm was brewing, its eye fixed on the delicate ties binding him and Hope. Pushing away the gnawing worry, he chose to ignore his mother's insistence on him talking to Lucky tonight. His focus remained on the woman behind that closed door, and his mind swirled with the echo of their shared declaration.

GAVIN STAYED IN THE downstairs living room and sat on the sofa, contemplating remaining downstairs and hiding until Lucky left, but the laughter echoing upstairs between Lucky and Mom indicated she might even stay the night. She'd stayed in the guest room before, but if he hid downstairs and left things to Mom's persistence, Lucky might be staying in one of the spare bedrooms on the third or fourth floor. The last thing he needed was her joining them for breakfast.

He didn't want to talk to discuss their past, but when he returned upstairs, Mom and Lucky were still there, laughing and sipping wine like best friends now that Dad had already left.

Mom wagged a finger at Gavin, pointing to the chair Dad had vacated. "You need to sit and talk."

He stifled a yawn. "I'm tired. Hope and I have a long day tomorrow." He needed to remind Mom and Lucky the days where he'd yield and take back Lucky after she'd messed with his heart were over.

In less than a week, the tenants were leaving one of his rentals. Since his parents were making things harder for Hope, rather than helping her feel welcome in a new country, he now planned to move Hope to the vacant house and move back to his house. She'd be more comfortable alone than in his family home.

"Please, Gavin." Lucky searched his eyes with a sadness that hinted at an apology and made him feel unreasonable.

"Please can you let me move on?" he asked, his resolve wavering. Was he being too harsh not to talk to her?

"I'll leave you two to talk." The chair scraped the tiles as Mom pushed back to stand.

"No." *I hate to break it to you, Mom. But Hope is my fiancée, I'm going to marry her, and nothing you can do will change that.* He swallowed the words. He'd have to have that conversation with her—and soon. But not in front of Lucky. For now, he lifted a hand to stop Mom from leaving. Then he spun around and strode toward the winding staircase.

"Gavin Paul Kress, come right back here." Mom's command bounced off his back. And that alone made him care less about giving his time to Lucky.

"It's okay, Sara." Lucky's voice trembled as if she was already crying.

His heart ached. With each step he took forward, he felt Lucky's sad eyes on his back. Not giving her an audience grated, feeling wrong, especially while Hope probably lay awake worrying that he was meeting with Lucky.

In his room, he collapsed on his childhood bed and clasped his hands behind his head in the dark. It had always been big, but now, he fit right into the queen-size bed.

Not wanting to think of all the reasons he should find closure with Lucky, he reached for his phone from his nightstand to text Hope. She needed to know he wasn't up late talking to his ex.

Gavin: Are you asleep?

The response came right away.

Hope: Aren't you supposed to be talking to Lucky?

Gavin: It didn't feel right. I'm in my bed.

Hope: Are we okay?

Gavin: Are we?

Hope: Don't you think you should talk to Lucky? You might need some answers.

Gavin: Do you want me to talk to her?

Hope: I don't want you to, but it's necessary.

Gavin: Let's talk more tomorrow. Get some rest. I love you.

Hope: I love you more.

He thought of Hope's words as he lay back after turning off his phone. A battle raged in his mind.

"What can I do, God? Why does life have to be complicated?" Was this what praying was like? He assumed so since Brady and Ruth said prayer was like talking to God as a friend, a father figure. In the days following his wedding that wasn't, Eric and Bryce had taken him four-wheeling. They'd ended up praying over Gavin, praying God would strengthen him to recover from the unexpected events. At the time, he hadn't embraced prayer to grasp what it meant, but then he'd understood when he witnessed it in the village—witnessed it through people who, having nothing, remained hopeful in their faith in God.

While he could talk to Dad about this, Gavin knew who was in charge of this house. Dad may have all the money and pay the bills, but Mom ran the show.

"If I don't talk to Lucky, I may always have the sting of rejection and fear that Hope will do the same thing." He might even end up with cold feet on their wedding day and be the one jilting her.

He shivered at the possibility of hurting Hope.

Maybe Lucky had a good reason, something she'd not told him that day. He flung an arm over his closed eyes. The pressure over what to do increased early the next morning when Lucky's text woke him.

Lucky: It was nice to see you last night. I owe you an explanation on why I didn't follow through at the altar. It had nothing to do with you.

Gavin read and reread the text, his finger hovering as he wondered how to respond.

Then he typed.

Gavin: Okay.

Lucky: Can we meet at the Pleasant Grind? Any day or time. I'm flexible.

Gavin: I'll talk to Hope first and get back to you.

Lucky: Thank you so much.

She seemed to think it was obvious they were meeting already, but he still had no idea if it was right. God hadn't given him a clear response last night. However, Lucky's text seemed to have no hidden motives. Plus, Gavin hadn't felt the attraction and desire last night he'd once had for her. Maybe he needed final closure so that chapter could end.

CHAPTER 23

As the sun descended, painting the sky in twilight hues, the first snowflakes of the evening twirled and spun with grace. Gavin guided his car through this winter wonderland, steering it toward Eric and Joy's residence. Hope sat beside him, her face tipped to the window to catch the snow's dance.

"You'll love it when we get our biggest snowfall of the season," he said, even though his mind whirled with chaos over Lucky and the impending meeting.

"I can't wait to see more snow." Hope glanced at him with a smile that didn't quite reach her eyes.

Despite spending the entire day with her, teaching her to bowl and introducing her to new experiences, he'd found himself struggling to share Lucky's text message from that morning.

"It's been a good day today." Hope reached to touch his shoulder. "But something's bothering you."

Surprised she could sense his internal struggle, he swallowed hard. He pulled up to the black gate, which opened automatically. Giving a quick wave to the familiar gatekeeper, he saw an opportunity to unburden himself before they arrived at Eric's.

"Lucky texted me this morning. She wants to talk." Man, it felt good to have that off his chest.

"You should talk to her." Hope seemed sincere, even though a tremor quavered in her voice. "You both need it."

He placed a hand on her thigh, her warmth radiating through her blue denims. "I need to understand why she did what she did." He tried to explain his reasoning. "I don't want to be scared you might do the same to me or I might panic and leave you standing at the altar someday."

"I'd never stand you up." She spoke with conviction, leaving no room for him to doubt she was all in on their relationship.

"Lucky is aware I'm with you, and I intend to make that very clear to her." Lucky wouldn't sabotage his newfound happiness, not when she didn't want him.

Placing her hand atop his, Hope threaded her fingers through his, her smile soft and tentative. "We'll be okay," she said as he parked beside the house. "When are you meeting her?"

"Would midmorning tomorrow be okay?" He needed to get this done before he returned to work next week.

She nodded. "Maybe you could drop me at the library during that time."

Since he'd told her their town had a great library with a variety of books, she'd been thrilled to visit. They'd stopped by earlier before they went bowling today, but she'd been eager to touch and open every book on the shelf.

However, he understood her coded request. She didn't want to be left alone with his mom. "I've got a plan." He assured her, intending to drop her off at a shopping area on the library's street. He undid his seat belt. "For now, let's go meet Eric and his family."

She fiddled with her seat belt, making no move to exit the car as she'd learned he liked her to wait until he got her door. "Should we bring the bag with the souvenirs?"

"I'll come back and get them later." He stepped out of his seat and moved around to get to her side. They were yet to give his parents the souvenirs they'd brought them. Only Morgan and the house employees deserved the souvenirs since Mom would undermine the woven basket the moment she learned Hope had anything to do with buying it.

But Hope's time in the Stone residence would be much better than at his parents'. Perhaps meeting Joy, someone else with African roots, would ease Hope's transition into the new country.

He extended his hand, and Hope took it, her grip warm and comforting as they navigated the snowy sidewalk. She stilled and held out her other hand to catch the snowflakes. Her coat swaddled his petite pixie, and he found himself smiling before brushing the flakes from her braided hair.

"You look beautiful." He adjusted her scarf to cover her neck against the chill.

"You always look handsome." She patted his dress sweater.

This sight of her, with her boots peeking from under her jeans and her winter coat swallowing her, was a whole new look after how she'd dressed in Africa. But she looked stunning either way, and he'd never tire of looking at her.

The front door opened, and a joyful outburst greeted them. "Gavin!" Eric's wife's warm voice flowed from the hallway before her affectionate hug enveloped him. Their children's lively chatter echoed beyond the hall, laughter making the home even more welcoming.

Joy released him and turned her attention to Hope. "You must be Hope."

"Yes, madam." Hope smiled.

Joy's skin was two shades lighter than Hope's, and she was probably three to four years older than Hope, but not noticeable. "None of that madam stuff now that you're here." Joy shook a finger at Hope, her voice light as she wrapped Hope in an embrace.

And his heart lightened as Hope's genuine smile reemerged, a sight he hadn't seen much in his parents' presence.

"How are you finding America so far? Still shaking off the jet lag?" Joy peppered Hope with questions, leading them further into the house, her warm welcome such a contrast to what Hope received in his home. He should have asked Eric and Joy to host Hope. "I can't wait to hear all about your first experiences in America."

"It's been nice so far." Hope remained polite, just as she had with her boss Lumbe. Today, however, might be a turning point for her American journey.

Joy led them into the living room's playful chaos. "Gavin, oliotya!" Eric greeted in Luganda from his place on the floor surrounded by trains and giggling toddlers. A pair of little girls were prancing around in princess dresses, their giggles infectious.

Rising to his feet, Eric shook hands with Hope. "Thank you for your dedication back in Uganda. I feel I already know you through Gavin's stories."

Hope shared a look with Gavin, her radiant smile reemerging, and his stomach flipped, excitement and happiness bubbling within. "I'm grateful Gavin took me to the village."

"The feeling is mutual." Gavin managed to whisper, his gaze lingering on her.

More children entered the room, older ones ranging from five to the eleven-year-old triplets. They greeted Gavin, shaking his hand. "Daddy said you were in Uganda," one of the boys chimed in, to which Gavin nodded.

The six-year-old girl grinned cheekily up at Hope. "Are you Ugandan like Mama? My grandma is American, but Grandpa was Ugandan. He's in heaven now."

"That's wonderful!" Hope stooped to the girl's eye level, her interest genuine.

Once the older children dispersed, Joy nudged Hope toward the kitchen. "Join me to talk more about Uganda."

"Of course." Hope waved in Gavin's direction as she and Joy left.

Gavin settled on the sofa opposite Eric. The toddlers had switched their attention to him, demanding he play with them. Despite their much wider age gap, Eric had always been a good friend through mutual connections and Eric's brothers, Brady and Bryce, Gavin's friends.

"We can take a break." Eric told the children, standing up and reminding them to greet Gavin.

The kids let go of their playtime, their attention now on Gavin. He lowered himself to pat the boy's curly hair. His sister followed suit. "You guys are getting so big."

"I'm ten thousand times bigger than you." One of the kids insisted, her little fingers trailing Gavin's face as she tried to tiptoe and touch his head. Way too precious. His chest squeezed, and he wanted to have kids sooner than he could.

Once the kids took off, Eric sat with Gavin.

"Let me guess. You're planning to go back to Uganda next year?"

Gavin had to laugh. "I loved it, don't get me wrong." He crossed one leg over the other. "But I have a job."

Their friendly chatter continued, the ladies' laughter murmured in the kitchen, and the kids' noise echoed from upstairs all accompanied by the pitter-patter of running feet, the house abuzz.

"Bryce and his family were supposed to join us, but they seem to be running late." Eric checked his smartwatch and squinted to read a message. "Bryce says we should go ahead and start dinner."

"No need to rush on mine and Hope's account." Gavin nodded toward the kitchen where the women were engrossed in conversation. They sure hit it off. "Maybe we could play a game of chess while we wait?"

Eric loved the game, which was evident when he laughed. "As long as you don't expect me to let you win like I do with the kids."

As Eric set the chessboard on the table, Gavin imagined a future where Hope and he had a home filled with the joyful echoes of their own children. Although not quite as large a family as Eric and Joy's, a bustling household would be wonderful, and already anticipation and longing surged through him.

One step at a time, though. He had to deal with his past before embracing his future.

CHAPTER 24

Hope sat in a booth with Joy and two of Joy's friends, Liberty and Tessa. She'd met Liberty at dinner last night when Liberty and her husband, Bryce, joined them at Joy's house, Bryce being one of Gavin's best friends. For the first time since her arrival, Hope felt comfortable amid new friends in the American café. All the girls were beautiful with brown skin and just as welcoming as Joy.

Gavin was Hope's first friend, but he was now driven in different directions. Probably torn between his new life with Hope and his old life with Lucky. If he took his mom's advice, Hope's chances with him were dwindling. So, when Joy extended the invitation yesterday for when Gavin would be meeting with Lucky, Hope had agreed.

"I'd expected Chad to be all excited, but the news..." Tessa's trill pulled Hope back to the present as Tessa continued to share about her pregnancy and her husband's reaction. "He panicked, and now he's terrified about whether he'll be a great dad when he never had a father while growing up."

"Once that baby comes"—Liberty's dimples deepened—"Chad's worries will be forgotten."

"He'll get over it before the week is over." Joy spoke, moving her fork through the strawberries and blueberries next to her half-eaten pancake.

"Congratulations again." Hope pretended she hadn't missed a single part of Tessa's conversation.

"Thank you." Tessa scooped a dollop of yogurt and took a bite.

Hope wiggled in her seat, grateful to be distracted from thinking about Gavin and the meeting with Lucky that could determine Hope's fate with the love of her life.

Snow drifted beyond the window, thicker now than the small snowflakes that had been swirling when they'd arrived at the café. Gavin's promise rang in her head again: *"I can't wait to take you out when we get more snow."* Was this going to turn into more snow?

She'd better stop thinking about him now that he was out of reach. She reached for her fork and picked at her stack of blueberry pancakes, hoping they'd taste better than the eggs. The eggs weren't as flavorful as the ones she ate in Kenya or Uganda, and the pancakes... Well, she had no idea what they'd taste like. But Joy had suggested them, certain Hope might enjoy them.

She loved the fried-food smell in the café and the music accompanied by guitar strings playing in the background. She didn't know the genres of songs enough to determine what music was playing, just that she enjoyed it.

She cut a piece and lifted it to her mouth. Forks and spoons hit porcelain as everyone ate their food.

"You may want to add syrup to get a better idea of the taste." Joy pointed her fork at the syrup bottle, noticing Hope's plain pancake.

While she enjoyed the syrup's sweetness, the pancake itself reminded her of mandazi without sugar.

"What do you think?" the girls asked simultaneously.

They weren't as scrumptious as she'd expected, but with all their expectant eyes focused on her, she nodded.

"They are good." It would take some time to acquire the taste.

Gavin had been so excited to see her reaction to all the foods she tried. She reached for her phone in her purse to check the time, hoping he sent her a text.

There was no text, but it was 11:25. An hour since he'd dropped her off. He'd been kind enough to show her where he would be meeting with Lucky, although Hope wouldn't interfere with their meeting. It was her fault. *She'd* encouraged him to meet with his ex, but she sensed he needed answers. She'd have wanted answers if she were in his position.

"You should at least have some eggs." Joy, the only one in the group Hope had confided in about Gavin's meeting today, had concern on her face. "Are you feeling okay?"

"Oh." Hope blinked, looking at her barely touched pancakes and the squashed eggs on a separate plate. She was far from okay as her bad luck caught up to her. "I don't think I'm that hungry."

"Gavin will be here soon to get you." Joy tried to keep a positive note.

Not wanting to drown under all the attention, Hope glanced at the ladies. "What do you do during the snow season?"

"Life just keeps going." Joy scooped blueberries onto her fork. "With eight kids, there's no window to stop."

"You came to the US at the right season." Liberty gave a firm nod and lifted both hands. "There's nothing like the twinkling lights on Main Street."

"The lights are there all year long." Tessa chimed in. "But you have to check out the Christmas Market."

"Yes! That's a must!" Liberty squealed. "They do ice sculpting at the park, and there's the tree lighting ceremony at the beginning of December with vendors serving endless hot chocolate and snacks and offering handmade gifts while groups sing Christmas carols."

Hope found herself smiling and anticipating Christmastime. In her village in Kenya, it was a one-day event. Yes, they played Christmas carols, but it wasn't a whole month's worth of celebration.

"If you're here next year, my husband and I have a soldier ministry. We package up gifts for soldiers, a care ministry I started through my church—kinda how I met him. Now, it's gotten so much bigger than I ever imagined! But we have to send packages by the end of September so they get there by Christmas. If you ever need a job, the ministry needs a part-time receptionist since I have another job as a trainer and need help running things." She paused and brought a hand to her tummy, rubbing her soft white sweater. "I won't be doing much training once I get too far into the pregnancy."

Joy, too, had plenty of job opportunities for the charities she and her husband ran in town and around the world. Apparently, Joy's husband was a self-made billionaire with various investments and had founded the financial company where Gavin's brother worked.

"I know you'll need a work permit first. But my art studio needs a curator if you want to work there temporarily—that is, if art's something that interests you? If you decide to stay, just know you have friends and places to hang out if needed."

If she stayed. Was Joy as doubtful of that as Hope currently was? Hope swallowed hard and pushed out a dry response. "That would be nice." But oh, how she dreaded going home without Gavin. Where was home anyway?

She'd known Gavin for less than a year, yet she couldn't think of anyone she'd rather spend her life with.

The conversation shifted to church, and Hope asked if she could join them tomorrow.

"Of course." Joy stirred her citrusy tea, something bright and yellowy—turmeric? "Eric and I take our family to a different church from Liberty and Tessa's. But we can go to theirs tomorrow so you have more familiar faces supporting you."

Hope nodded. Would Gavin go with her? They were still new to faith in God. But while she was a foreigner, she'd have to cling to God more than anything, especially if Sara was going to be her mother-in-law.

The server returned and took their plates, asking if they needed any more drinks. Everyone seemed content with what they had. Hope barely drank her tea, which had no spices like she was used to. So, no, it would be a long time before she tried tea again, though Joy's looked more interesting.

As the women shared events and secrets and laughed together, Hope gradually relaxed, thankful to feel embraced in a new country, by new friends. Through their lighthearted chat and shared laughter, her worries eased. For the first time since Lucky joined them at dinner, Hope allowed herself to believe everything would be okay.

By the time Gavin picked her up, she hadn't checked her phone again for his messages or kept track of how long he'd been gone. Having sat so long, she almost stumbled over her seat when she rose on stiff legs as he approached their table.

"Gavin!" She kept her gaze on him. His broad chest stretched out his checkered button-down shirt, and he still wore the necklace she'd made him, unlike her who'd safely tucked away the necklace he'd given her since she'd been wearing turtlenecks.

He smiled, but something clouded his smile as he met her halfway with open arms. He kissed her on the cheek. "Did you have fun?"

"I did."

"Thanks for letting Hope join us today."

At Joy's voice, Hope stepped out of the embrace and returned to the table to pay for her breakfast.

"We've got this covered." Joy waved her off. "You lovebirds go on. You'll have plenty of time to pay for us since we do this once a month."

"Your visa is for six months, right?" Tessa asked.

"I'm hoping to convince her to stay longer." Gavin retrieved his credit card from his wallet and handed it to the approaching server.

"What do you think you're doing?" Liberty asked.

"This is for the ladies' breakfast," he told the server, ignoring Liberty.

After they said goodbye to the girls, Hope reached for her coat from the spare seat, and he helped her slide her arms in. His fingers traced along her neck, and like all the other times her body came in contact with his, tingles shot through her.

"I'll text you the church address." Joy rose to hug Hope. "If you need a ride to church tomorrow, you have my number."

"Thanks." Hope pulled her gloves and hat from her shoulder bag.

"You want to go to church tomorrow?" he asked as they stepped onto the sidewalk. The snow had accumulated on the grassy areas around it while large salt crystals seemed to keep it melting off the cement.

Tugging on her gloves, she tipped her face to the gloomy sky, then peeked at him. "Would you like to come with me?"

"Of course." He slid his arm around her waist.

"You need a coat," she said. As eager as she was to know how the meeting had gone, she stalled in asking. If she asked too fast, would she be acting like a jealous girlfriend?

"I left it in the car." He snugged her in closer, and his warm breath teased her neck. "But you're keeping me plenty warm."

Not ready to go home just yet, she asked if he wanted to check out Main Street. "The ladies said it looks so nice."

"That sounds fantastic." He gave her an extra squeeze, seeming excited about the idea, and pressed a kiss to her braids just below the hat she'd donned. "I wanted to take you there soon."

After they got in his car, he drove into the quaint town. Then they strolled down the cobblestone streets, both bundled in their winter gear. She spun around several times, taking in the glittering lights strung across the streets.

"We should come back here at night. It's beautiful." He clasped her gloved hand.

"There's so many shops." Her gaze skimmed the displays in glass windows, an array of holiday decorations, intricate designs, and twinkling lights. People strolled in and out with bulging bags. "And the lights..."

They were amazing. She sighed, her wistful breath fogging before her.

He chuckled and tightened his grip on her hand. "Well, I did grow up here. But seeing it through your eyes makes it more magical."

As they walked, he shared childhood memories associated with the quaint storefronts. He showed her his favorite bookstore where he used to lose himself for hours, the candy shop that "sold the best brownies in the world" according to ten-year-old Gavin, and the old theater where he had his first job as a popcorn vendor. "It's sad to see it as a fitness center now. The two things just don't match up in my mind—lounging around eating goodies and watching cinema versus working out. It's kinda fitting though, one being appropriate for childhood and the other for adulthood."

She tried to nod along, though it all seemed so strange. The idea of "working out" as he called it, working for no purpose, still baffled her, and she'd never been around so many sweets her whole life. Here, she encountered them with each meal. They hadn't appealed to her much.

Not like his stories. She was hungry for more of them, fascinated with everything Gavin, taking in each vivid detail, all new to her. At one point, they paused, and he pulled her closer, pointing to an old stone building and urging her forward. "And that"—his warm breath kissed her cold cheek—"has the best hot chocolate in town."

They were at the shop in a matter of moments, and he ordered them two cups of hot chocolate. "Snowball fights usually happened as we stood in line waiting for hot chocolate."

Hope giggled, giddy at the thought of a young Gavin wreaking snowball havoc. "I can just imagine you leading the charge."

"Well, I've always been a bit of a leader." He grinned down at her before sipping his drink.

She lifted the cup to her mouth and tested a cautious sip, then another and another. Oh! This one was bliss. "I like this drink."

"We'll get plenty more, then." He assured her.

They meandered down the snow-dusted street, the silence between them thickening with unspoken words. Gavin remained tight-lipped about his meeting with Lucky, but Hope's curiosity bubbled over. She needed the conversation resolved, no matter how much she wished to avoid it.

"How was your time with, um..." What was she supposed to call his "date" with his ex, anyway?

"Lucky." His voice emerged quiet and measured. "Complicated."

A pause hung between them, only interrupted by their boots crunching against the fresh snow. She stole a glance at her feet, appreciating the warmth and comfort her boots offered in contrast to the icy conversation. As she exhaled, her breath lingered like smoke in the frigid air, and her dreams... Were they about to "go up in smoke" as she'd heard said? "Did she, um, tell you why she left you at the altar?"

"She apologized." His grip on her hand tightened, an alarming reaction she hadn't expected. He kept his gaze fixed ahead as if the distant streetlights could provide the solace he so desperately sought. "Apparently, she was scared she'd lose her freedom if she married."

The words jabbed at Hope like spears, each thrusting deeper as she detected the tinge of regret lacing his voice. Like a window into his past, the sentence revealed fragments of a memory he had diligently buried. The frigid air seemed to carry his words away, leaving an emotional chill that cut deeper than the winter's cold.

And at that moment, a cold seed of uncertainty nestled into the recesses of her heart. Each echo of Gavin's words from his past made her question her place in his life. How could she, an unlucky woman from a different world entirely, compete with an American woman who had been woven into his life since childhood? A woman even named Lucky as if to mock Hope's fears? He had to be dealing with an internal battle, despite his efforts to hide it.

Fear threatened to choke her, but she clung to the thrill of the present. Needing to shake off the distressing thoughts, she proposed a change in their surroundings. Somehow, she managed a smile. "How about we play in the snow?"

"Guess what?" he asked, his excited voice bringing an infectious energy to the otherwise melancholy atmosphere. "On Tuesday, your house will be ready for you to move in."

His response, so unexpected yet heartening, carried the promise of a new beginning, and that reality washed over her like a balm. Then he nudged her. "For now, I have just the place to take you."

There was a shift in his demeanor as they climbed back into the car. His broad shoulders relaxed, and the tension in his face eased. He drove them to a secluded road fringed with rolling hills, and their shared present and future silenced the echoes of his past as they sculpted a snowman, his gloved hands guiding hers. Then he introduced her to the thrill of snowball fights, their breaths hitching in the crisp winter air. She squealed and ducked, playfully tossing snow while his teasing urged her on. Their spirited fun stole her worries away, her heart fluttering like a child on a playground.

As they stopped their snow fight, both panting, he caught her hands. His gaze delved hers, seeming to see straight into her soul. "Time to prove you're my angel." He walked her into the meadow to a patch where the snow lay undisturbed from their play.

Her heart fluttered as he gripped her hands and helped her lay flat on her back, the world around her a sparkle.

"Now, spread your arms and legs, back and forth, back and forth." Kneeling nearby, he guided her in a movement like a dance. Then he caught her forearms again and scooped her up, lifting her away from the imprint she'd left. Holding her arms, he nodded to the "angel" on the snow. "There she is, Hope. The reflection of how I see you, my angel."

What a delightful afternoon! One forever etched into the canvas of her memories like the angel now etched the meadow.

Much later as the day ended, they shared a meal before heading back to his parents' home, and a cozy joy wrapped her like a warm blanket. She was grateful not to have dinner with his family.

As Gavin walked her to her door, he leaned in, their lips meeting in a tender, lingering kiss. The taste of him was like a sweet promise. His promise of attending church together the next day reassured her, calming the creeping doubts in her heart.

Regardless of what he and Lucky had discussed, as Hope stood on the threshold of her door, kissed by the man she loved, she didn't need to know anything else. All that mattered was that he was there, with her, in the now. And she was his, as he was hers.

Her happy elation lasted for an hour, before a lingering discomfort seeped into her veins like an icy draft. She should've gone to bed after she showered. Instead, she was thirsty and headed upstairs to get some water. In the dimly lit kitchen, she bumped into Lucky, a stark silhouette of intimidating beauty. Her glossy hair cascaded over her slim shoulders, her hourglass form accentuated by her tight pajama shorts and silk shirt.

"Lucky." The word bled out of Hope's mouth. She had to act polite. But Lucky was a threat, and they both knew it. "Hi."

"Holly, right?" Lucky glanced over, her smooth voice lacking warmth. She continued prying the cupboards open with the familiarity of one who lived there—who'd grown up there.

Faced with this confrontation, Hope didn't bother to correct her name. Instead, she swallowed the anxiety in her throat, then maneuvered around Lucky to retrieve a glass from the cupboard and fill it with water from the fridge dispenser, now that she knew how it worked. The cool liquid seemed like an antidote to the tension.

When Hope rinsed the glass to put it in the dishwasher, Lucky paused from whatever she'd been doing and leaned against the counter with her arms crossed. Her next words froze Hope in her tracks. "You're not the only one engaged to Gavin." The glint of her ring caught the kitchen lights, stabbing Hope's with insecurity.

In that instant, her fear transformed into a fierce determination. She was tired of being overshadowed, of being trampled over. Clicking the dishwasher closed, she released the words building in her throat. "I'm glad to know polygamy is practiced in America too." After a lifetime of running away, of surrendering all she had, this was her chance to stand up for herself, for what was rightfully hers. "I know you have a history with Gavin, but he's with me now."

"Gavin is a nice man." Lucky's penciled eyebrows lifted, her lips parting. "But do you think he's going to stick with you forever?"

"Is that why you're moving in, because he's nice and forgiving? You already wrecked your chance with him." Hope's defiance surprised her. But she was Gavin's angel now. It didn't matter if she'd been unlucky her whole life, things had changed, and she'd not let Lucky tarnish her newfound happiness.

Lucky blew out a breath. "I just want you to know he won't have the nerve to tell you that whatever you two had was just a fling for him to get over his temporary—"

"You mean after you left him at the altar?" Her veins heating, Hope fought to keep her composure. "If you think Gavin loves me out of pity, why are you wasting your time talking to me now when you could've addressed these issues during your lunch?"

The silence between them stretched, something thick and tangible threading through the air as the quiet war of words reverberated in Hope's head. This confrontation wasn't something she anticipated or appreciated, but she had a right to stand up for herself.

But she was no match for Lucky. "You and Gavin…" Lucky waved her hand in the air, her smirk slicing Hope like a sharpened knife. "You're not his type."

The dig stung, piercing the protective bubble of happiness that had cocooned Hope throughout the day. But, as much as it hurt, she wouldn't let Lucky see her crumble. Gathering her every shred of courage, Hope fired back. "I could say the same about you." Then, with all her remaining dignity, she turned on her heel and left Lucky alone in the kitchen.

Despite her bravado, a gnawing fear nipped at Hope. Had Sara orchestrated this confrontation too? Gavin was far too kindhearted ever to act in such a cruel way, but his absence during this confrontation added to her mounting fears. *Of course, he's asleep and has no idea Lucky is here.* He'd texted his mom that he and Hope wouldn't join them for dinner that night.

She found herself back in her room, her heart heavy. Did Lucky occupy a room near Gavin's? The heaviness in her heart thudded to her stomach. If so, Lucky would find some excuse to worm her way into Gavin's space, playing the innocent while harboring hidden intentions.

Swallowing the rising tide of unease, Hope burrowed into her bed where the bitter truth blasted her—their financial differences were so glaringly evident.

But did that truly matter? Did people in America divide along social lines? What about Eric and Joy's lavish mansion? The couple had never made Hope feel inferior despite her humble background.

Perhaps she should inform Gavin about Lucky's presence. Or was he already aware Lucky was staying for the night? Maybe he had chosen not to tell Hope?

The taunts echoed in her mind, steady as a whisper in the dark.

"Whatever you two had was just a fling!"

"You're not his type!"

She buried her head under her pillow to block the unwanted thoughts. She shut her eyes and huddled under her blanket as she fervently recited Bible verses.

" 'The battle belongs to the Lord,' " she whispered, then added, " 'God has not given us a spirit of fear.' "

Her voice was a barely audible murmur, as though each word was a charm to ward off the penetrating gloom. The fight against her fears seemed overwhelming, but she clung to the belief that God was on her side. Even as despair threatened to pull her under, she had to cling to God.

CHAPTER 25

Gavin churned in his sheets, his mind a turbulent beast that refused to be tamed. His fingers interlocked behind his head, and his unseeing vision focused on the ceiling above him where moonlight cast elongated shadows of the grillwork from the French doors to his balcony. Lucky's confession, marked by fear, longing, and regret, rang in his memory. *"I was so emotional that day, and having my period hit me that day didn't help."*

That didn't explain why she didn't follow through, and he'd told her so, his words firm but not unkind. He wanted answers, clarity amid their murky past.

"Think of all the times we've been together," she'd pleaded. "I miss you."

Her words hung in his head now, an incense clouding his judgment, even after he'd pressed her further.

"I panicked. My mom and dad fought so much, and I feared that maybe..."

When she couldn't finish her sentence, her fear evident in the quiver of her voice, he'd empathized. His past was tainted with his mother's failures and the subsequent destruction of his father's dreams. Yet, he'd learned to differentiate between his past and his future.

"I don't assume the woman I marry will be like Mom, and you shouldn't assume your marriage is going to turn out like your parents' marriage." He'd spoken decisively, aiming to let her know she wasn't the only one with fears.

Tree shadows flickered across those moonbeams, the wind hurrying their dance, even as shadows flickered in his thoughts and his heartbeat quickened.

He wasn't mad at her since he understood now, but he was with Hope.

Wasn't he?

He tossed aside the tangled sheets and flung his arm over his eyes. But the doubts remained wrapped around him, and he could still see the questions before his vision.

Was he making the right decision to end a relationship with the only woman he'd dated long-term? He was serious with Hope, but they'd known each other for a short time in comparison. He scratched the stubble on his jaw and pushed himself to sit back against his headboard where the shelves still contained his childhood trophies.

Recollections of Lucky abandoning him multiple times—for a beauty pageant, a modeling gig, and then a short-lived stint in a reality TV show—came rushing back. The roller coaster of breakups and makeups had left a gaping void in his heart, a wound only Hope's love seemed to heal.

Lucky's litany of reasons why she loved him, her tear-streaked face, and the surge of memories were bittersweet reminders of the past. But her reminiscing only highlighted the stark difference in his relationship with Hope.

Hope was a beacon of kindness and selflessness. Her luminous eyes, so warm and compassionate, flooded his vision as did their adventures, their muddy treks, and their intimate moments under the frigid waterfall. A smile pulled at his lips over his time in Africa.

Hope's resilience inspired him. And her love, so pure and unwavering, warmed him in a way Lucky never had. Hope's compassionate reaction to his snakebite and malaria bout surpassed any tender care he'd ever received, and their traditional marriage ceremony had mended the cracks in their relationship. The trust in Hope's eyes was a testament to their commitment.

He needed to propose to her again under different circumstances, ones she could believe he meant with no obligation or expectations. But cultural ties had already bound him to her, his angel, his Hope, his future.

In stark contrast, pain tinged his memories of Lucky. Unnecessary arguments and ceaseless drama all led to her ultimate betrayal. The ghost of that disappointment haunted him, a wound Hope had bandaged. If he chose Lucky again, the past would forever loom over their relationship, threatening to shatter his peace. And he'd lose his Hope. Who could go on without that?

Hope, however, brought serenity and assurance. The opposite of his mom, she was a harbor in the storm, a sanctuary that assured him unwavering support. He was cherished and protected in her company, and she would stand by him through the highs and lows of life. She thought she was unlucky, but even if he did believe in luck, he'd still give up both luck and Lucky to share Hope's love and life. After all, who needed luck, if they had Hope?

Gavin inhaled deeply, each breath carrying a memory of Hope. He yearned for a future unburdened by the past. Lucky was a symbol of his youthful whims, but Hope embodied his mature understanding of love. His realization was a gentle tide washing over him, clearing the haze of confusion. Love was about mutual respect, shared dreams, and unconditional understanding.

Hope embodied all of those and more.

His heart belonged to her. She was his present, his future, and his eternal love. His turmoil subsided, replaced by the comforting certainty. He chose love. And Hope.

A smile lifted his lips, and he let himself drift off to sleep, waking up to a chime on his phone.

It was seven o'clock. And Hope was texting.

Hope: Still okay going to church?

Gavin: What time does it start?

Hope: 10.

Gavin: I can be ready in 30 minutes. We can go out and eat breakfast.

Hope: Sounds wonderful.

Gavin: Meet me in the kitchen at 8?

Hope: Can't wait to see you.

Gavin: I'll be there at 7:50 then. :)

Hope: Love you.

Gavin: Love you too.

His heart light, he showered fast, anticipating a wonderful day. His parents usually slept in on Sundays, and Morgan fixed a brunch rather than breakfast.

He'd texted Mom last night to let her know he and Hope weren't making it home for dinner. She responded by texting that she hoped his meeting with Lucky would change a few things. Whatever that had meant, he hadn't cared to ask or find out.

Yesterday, he hadn't told Hope everything Lucky shared. Today, he would, his mind made up and his doubts gone. And for that, he'd thank God at church.

Showered and dressed, he stepped out of his room at 7:48, taking two stairs at a time. He shoved his phone into the pocket of his chino pants. Then he walked into the kitchen, and his exhilaration vanished.

The woman at the kitchen island sipping coffee as if she lived here was the last person he wanted to see. "Lucky?"

"Morning." Her chirpy voice grated. Undeterred, she rose from the barstool and nudged her cup aside.

He kept his distance, his brows tightening to the point of giving him a headache. Maybe he was sleepwalking.

Or not.

Lucky flipped her wavy hair over one shoulder, smiling coyly. Dressed in dark leggings and a clingy neon-green exercise top, she would probably hit the gym in the house since she liked working out. But, with her hair falling in waves over her top, he doubted she'd come from a workout.

He swallowed, his heart pounding. "Did you stay the night at our house?"

"Your mom invited me for dinner." She shrugged, taking a step forward and stopping. "I was disappointed you didn't join us, but I didn't want to drive home in the snow."

"Couldn't your driver pick you up?" Like Mom, Lucky preferred to be chauffeured. He opened his mouth to explain why she couldn't just make herself comfortable in his house, but then he shut it. After all, their families spent a lot of time together.

"You look handsome."

An alarm blared in his mind, but he didn't respond. Hope should be arriving any moment. His gaze darted toward the hallway and the stairs where she'd be emerging. He'd go fetch her if she didn't appear soon.

Lucky touched his shoulder, causing his shoulders and neck to tense.

"Have you had time to think more about what we discussed?" she murmured, her voice low and persuasive.

He cleared his throat, taken aback by her blatant disregard for his engagement. "Our discussion ended there. I made my stance clear." He detached her hand from his shoulder, discomfort rippling through him at the touch he once craved. "I'm engaged to Hope now."

Lucky shook her head. Her expression defiant, she pulled something from her pocket. As she held it up, the morning light streaming through the windows caught on a diamond ring, causing it to glitter.

"We were engaged too, remember?"

"That engagement ended the moment you left me at the altar."

Footsteps sounded on the stairs. Relief washed over him as he spun, but not quickly enough. It happened so fast, Lucky lunging toward him, her lips crashing against his. He pushed her away, gasping and wiping at his mouth. "What do you think you're doing?"

"Gavin?" Hope's voice, so soft and tremulous, sounded behind him.

He froze, a sick dread sinking into his stomach. Then he turned to meet her horrified eyes.

"Lucky?" Hope's voice was barely above a whisper, her gaze darting between him and Lucky, who had the audacity to wave.

Heart pounding, Gavin watched Hope spin and run down the stairs. He raced after her, calling her name, but she was too quick. She reached her room and slammed the door in his face before he could explain.

"Hope!" he called, but his pleas went unanswered. He knocked on the door, his knuckles aching from pounding the wood. "It's not what you think."

Why had he let it happen? He should've gone downstairs as soon as he saw Lucky in the kitchen. He rested his head on Hope's door, banging it until his forehead started to hurt.

"Please, Hope." He rubbed at the sore spot on his forehead, but he only heard muffled sobs. So he sank to the floor across from her door to wait for her. She'd have to emerge at some point.

Several minutes later, Hope came out, her eyes swollen, her hands gripping her luggage.

Gavin stood, stopping short of touching her when he remembered why she was crying. *He* was the reason for her tears, and that jabbed him with sharp pain.

"Where are you going?"

She wouldn't look at him as she strode to the stairs, her rolling luggage in tow.

"Let me help you carry that." Gavin followed, but she was climbing two steps at a time.

"I've got it." She jerked it away from his reach. For someone wearing a long, slim skirt, she was good at trekking. He wasn't sure where she was going until he followed her out the door where a car was waiting. Her words, when he'd asked her what she'd do when her parents were pushing her to marry Silas again, came rushing back—*"What I do best—run."*

What she did best. His chest hollowed. Hope was running again. This time from him.

He slowed his steps, intending to study the plates so she wasn't abducted. But Joy Stone was behind the wheel and rushed to her, taking her luggage and hoisting it to the back before wrapping her arms around her.

Then she helped Hope into the car, and beyond the windshield, Hope wiped her face. Something cold gripped his heart, the scene too painful to watch. He'd hoped she would hear him out.

Joy waved at Gavin, her lips pressed together with sadness as she backed out of the driveway.

Don't go, Hope! Don't run from me! The words shouted in his mind and tried to claw free from his throat, but there was no use.

The weight of his mistakes crushed him. He shouldn't have met with Lucky yesterday. He should've run the opposite way when he saw Lucky in the kitchen.

When he walked back inside, the anger churning within roiled like a volcano ready to explode. Good thing, he didn't encounter Lucky on his way back to his room. Otherwise, he'd likely say something—something he wouldn't be able to take back.

He gathered up his items, tossed them in his luggage, and hauled it to his old car, the one he'd kept at his parents' house and had been driving Hope in. He wouldn't need to bring it back any time soon, and he didn't want to see Mom, Dad, or anyone who'd nag him about Lucky.

On the way to his house, his phone rang, and he reached for it, hoping it was Hope. But seeing Mom's contact on the screen, he tossed the phone onto the passenger seat, tempted to toss it out of the window so he didn't have to hear from her for a long time.

By the time he got to his house, Mom had called several more times. He finally answered needing to express his outrage.

"What?" He tossed his car keys on the hallstand, not caring if he was being curt.

"Lucky was really upset—"

"Seriously, Mom!" He ground his teeth and paced to the kitchen, too upset to know what to say next. Good thing he'd already purged all the photos of him and Lucky from his fridge last year and donated all their mementos.

"I get it that you're hung up on Hope, but—"

"No. You don't get it. That's just it," he snapped, gripping the phone to his ear and clenching his other hand as he marched into the living room. "It's one thing to drive me away from home, but driving away someone I love—"

"You love Lucky."

"Please, stop. I'm going to marry Hope, and you didn't even give her a chance!" In a rising burst of anger, he ended the call.

There was no sense in talking to Mom. She wasn't going to help him clean up the mess she and Lucky created. But he needed to talk to someone who'd understand. His fingers hovered over the phone screen.

Eric was probably in church. So was Bryce. Had Hope gone with them? Either way, Gavin would be the last person she wanted to hear from.

He sank onto the sofa and called Jeremy. The only thing Jeremy did on Sundays was golf in the afternoons. And since he was an early riser, despite the time difference between Colorado and San Francisco, he'd most likely be home working or whatever else he did on Sunday mornings when he wasn't in the office.

"Man!" Jeremy answered on the third ring, panting. "I almost broke my ankle jumping off the treadmill."

"You sound like you're about to pass out." Gavin relaxed as he bantered with his brother. "When was the last time you worked out?"

"The phone call jolted through my music workout."

"All right. I'll let you blame me for your clumsiness."

"Sounds fair. So..." Jeremy dragged the word out. "How are you adjusting to your first week back stateside, and how's Hope taking to the mountains and adapting to the culture?"

"I think okay." If it wasn't for Lucky.

"I'm talking about our home culture. You know with Mom—"

"Mom invited Lucky to dinner." His muscles tensed, and Gavin stood to move to the window. Icicles hung on the evergreens, and the overcast sky reflected his gloomy heart.

"Told you taking her home was a bad idea." Jeremy tsked. "Remember how Mom reacted when I was dating the carpenter's daughter in high school?"

"That didn't stop you from seeing her." Jeremy had always disregarded Mom's orders where dating was concerned, except for the one time she almost succeeded with her matchmaking.

"Too bad she was married by the time I got back from college."

"She was a nice girl." Gavin raked his fingers through his hair, his breath now fogging the glass as he stood too close to the window as if he could strain to see his way to Hope. "Don't let it get you down, bro. There's no reason to look at the past when you can't change the outcome."

Which was true enough for Jeremy, but it wasn't too late for Gavin and Hope. Was it?

He hadn't expected his mom to act so cold toward Hope. He re-capped the events. "I hadn't expected Lucky to show up."

"That's why I've decided not to come home for Thanksgiving," Jeremy said.

"Are you serious? You're not coming?" Now more than ever Gavin needed to see his brother.

"When Mom started talking about inviting Sonya..." Jeremy's breathing dragged through the phone. "I have no mental capacity for a forced reunion with my ex-fiancée right now."

Gavin couldn't blame his brother there. "She dumped you and eloped with—"

"That marriage didn't last but six months. Now, Mom thinks we should start where we ended when I come home."

"It's not like Mom is making you marry her."

"Have you already forgotten the awkwardness Mom's willing to put us through to achieve her matchmaking goals?"

Gavin nodded after his three-day whirlwind. "I was hoping you would come."

"I'll come for Christmas only because I want to meet Hope."

Would Hope even be part of his life anymore? Closing his eyes, Gavin still saw her crushed expression after Lucky's stunt, and it still paralyzed him. He drew out a breath and leaned his forehead on the cool glass window. Jeremy seemed to know what was eating Gavin up.

"Surely, Hope knows you love her."

But Hope had been rejected far too many times by people she'd trusted. She also believed she didn't deserve anything good. "I lost her trust when Lucky launched herself at me."

"If Hope has known you for almost a year, she should know you are loyal. She should also trust you when you tell her that Lucky kissed you without—"

"It doesn't sound very believable, even if she can give me a chance to explain."

"It'll all work out, bro," Jeremy soothed. "This time, you've gone against Mom's matchmaking to pursue Hope. My big brother is growing up."

"Shut up." Gavin felt his shoulders shake as he laughed and his heart warmed. "How did my baby brother get so wise?"

"After dating a woman Mom fixed me up with for years, I guess experience *is* the best teacher. Looks like we're both victims of her setups."

"Unfortunately, she thinks she's the best matchmaker in the world."

After hanging up, Gavin almost felt better until he flopped on the sofa to scroll through his phone and saw the photos he'd taken with Hope and their snowman and her snow angel yesterday.

As if he needed to torture himself, he perused more photos of them at the airport in New York, then in Pleasant View. Her smile, so innocent and sweet.

He'd brought her here, and she'd trusted him to fly across the world with him. Now, here he was in the house of his dreams, feeling emptier than he'd been when he left for Africa.

Oh how his heart ached! This house, once filled with the promise of a future with Hope, now echoed with a hollowness, so big and empty. It was only eleven thirty, and even if Eric wouldn't answer now, Gavin typed a text. He had to know if Hope was okay.

The longer he waited for her to get over the vivid scene, the more doubts would be creeping into her. So, with a deep breath, he pressed the call icon, then held that breath as he rang her number. One ring. Two. Three...

Voice mail picked up. Would Hope even know to check her messages? "Hope?" He forked his hand through his hair, unsure if she'd ever hear what he said here. "Angel, you can't do this. You always run when things get bad in life, but I'm not one of the men who hurt you. I'm not someone to run from. And even if I were, *you* have to quit running. Running can't be your answer to every problem you encounter. We have to talk things out."

After ending the call and tossing the phone on the coffee table, he buried his face in his hands and attempted a prayer, hoping he was getting the hang of it. Speaking to God like a friend. Talking aloud wasn't a problem for him, so maybe praying would be as easy.

"God? How did five minutes this morning change the outcome of my entire day if not my future? I was supposed to be at church with Hope today. Now, I'm in my house, pathetic and deflated, with a cloud hanging over my destiny."

He breathed in, then out, wondering what to say next, something spiritual that didn't involve him whining.

"I don't know how to pray, besides the Lord's Prayer." He'd memorized it with Hope after a week of them leading prayer time with the children in the village the second time the medical team came.

All he could do now was wait for the seconds to tick and assume Hope would hear him out tonight. Or maybe tomorrow if he had to test his limit with patience. But until he saw her, he couldn't return to work tomorrow as he'd planned. Hope was supposed to go with him. He'd text his manager later.

At that, he reached for his phone again, determined to find a church with a later service. It was going to be a long day at home alone. He'd rather connect in church somewhere.

CHAPTER 26

The gentle rhythm of the toddler's breathing comforted Hope as the girl slept in her arms. With each breath, she inhaled the scent of baby powder and marveled at the innocent slumber. But her arms were tiring, and she needed to pass the toddler over to Joy.

"Here, let me," Joy murmured, her voice hushed. She eased the little girl from Hope's arms and cradled her against her shoulder. "I'll be right back." Joy's skin seemed to glow in the soft living room light, and her whisper was barely audible before she disappeared up the stairs with the sleeping child.

Hope's gaze turned to the window, her mind lost in the silhouettes of evergreens now mere shadows against the darkening sky. The joyful laughter and squeals upstairs brought a welcome distraction. The house was bustling with life, a combination of cheery chaos and comforting routines. Yet, emptiness hollowed parts within her at the prospect of spending the night in this lively home without Gavin.

Ignoring his call and leaving the message unchecked had been difficult, but it left her with a bitter taste of guilt and betrayal. She wrapped her arms around herself to soothe the shivers running down her spine. So many betrayals... Lucky's flirtatious antics at the dinner a few days ago, Lucky's confidence in the kitchen last night, and now, Lucky's lips on Gavin's—*Hope's* Gavin.

She trembled at the raw memory. It had seemed like Lucky initiated the kiss, but why would she if Gavin hadn't given her the impression they had a chance together?

"Can I get you some tea?" Joy's voice made Hope jump. She'd changed into a set of long-sleeved pajamas adorned with cartoon characters. Her cotton attire looked warm, soft, and inviting, a stark contrast to the chill wrapping Hope.

"Those look so comfortable and cute."

"It's only eight." Joy waved off her compliment. "But I wanted to get comfortable, and I've left a similar pair in your room if you'd like to change."

Hope managed a weak smile. "You've made me way more comfortable than I could ever ask." Yet, despite the soft couch under her and the warm welcome, comfort felt elusive.

At his parents' house, Gavin was probably sharing a meal with Lucky again. Hope shivered, feeling like a cold hand clenched her heart. The laughter and chaos of Joy's home couldn't combat the storm of emotions brewing within her. Every sound, every smell, every sensation was a painful reminder of her loneliness.

"Everything will be all right." Joy patted Hope's back, her words a salve on Hope's raw emotions, softening the edges of her turmoil.

"Thank you, Joy." It wasn't necessary to elaborate on the events. Joy had seen her tear-streaked face when she'd picked her up from Gavin's house. "I appreciate you taking the time to pick me up this morning."

The church service, then lunch at Joy's and Eric's, and a quiet gathering with Liberty's and Tessa's families had been a welcome distraction. Yet, as the laughter and chatter faded with their departure, she'd wrestled the same troubling thoughts.

"Hope, I know Gavin loves you." Joy's hands moved from Hope's back to her knee, the shift in her position drawing Hope from her thoughts. "His mother is pulling the strings here. I'm sure of it."

"I can't shake off that scene." Hope fought a fresh wave of tears. The memory was too vivid, too raw.

"I know." Joy's tone was sympathetic as she squeezed Hope's knee. "Liberty has a similar story with Bryce. You should ask her about it."

Liberty and Bryce had the same story?

Nodding, Joy elaborated. "Bryce's mother, Wendy, didn't think Liberty was a suitable match for her son. Even after their marriage, she tried to set him up with other women."

Hope scooted closer, now curious and eager to talk to Liberty. Liberty's mother-in-law couldn't be as cold as Sara. "How did Liberty deal with that?"

"Through prayer, of course," Joy replied with a soft chuckle. "But mainly by holding on to her love for Bryce. They went through tough times, but they were so crazy about each other that their love eventually saw them through."

Hope drew parallels between Liberty's story and her own, her heart aching. But Joy's words gave her hope.

"You said Lucky initiated the kiss. Do you think Gavin kissed her back?"

The question—the one Hope had been trying to answer all day—hung in the air. Everything happened too fast. Long after she'd left, she'd begun to replay the scene and imagine Lucky's personality.

She was cunning enough to have enticed Gavin or initiated the kiss. Hope had been too terrified to listen to him, afraid he'd confess he'd kissed Lucky.

"Did Gavin push her away?" Joy kept her gaze steady on Hope.

"Yes, he did," Hope admitted, and his horrified expression seared into her mind. That, too, had given her the impression Lucky was to blame. But no way would Hope go back to Sara's house. No way!

"Then do you believe Gavin loves you?" The soft question packed a punch.

"Yes, I do." Gavin had treated her with nothing but kindness and respect. He'd made her laugh, made sacrifices for her, and shown her a love she'd never known before.

"Then why not listen to him? Why not let him explain?"

Hope rubbed her aching chest. Confused and broken, she'd pushed Gavin away when he'd knocked at her door, pleading to talk to her before she'd texted Joy and taken off. With a soft sigh, Hope wiped away a stray tear. "You're right. I should've given him a chance to explain. I just... I was scared."

With the admission heavy in the air, she waited for Joy's response, hoping it would guide her through.

"Hope? Gavin's here." Joy's words seemed to reverberate through the room, scattering Hope's thoughts.

She blinked, sitting up, her heart pounding. Gavin. Here? She looked toward the kitchen, trying to understand.

"He's in the driveway. He's been texting Eric all day. We didn't know if you wanted to talk to him yet, but he said he couldn't let the day end without talking to you."

Each word, so calm and steady, stood as a counterpoint to the chaotic rhythm of Hope's heartbeat. Her breath hitched as she wiped her eyes, ensuring no residual tears betrayed her earlier emotions. "What should I do?"

"Listen to him." Joy gripped Hope's hands, grounding her, understanding glimmering in her eyes. "If you don't, you'll go to bed wondering, and you won't be able to sleep. At least then, you'll know the truth."

Deep down, Hope knew Gavin didn't initiate the kiss. She nodded, then shook her head, the whirling vortex of her emotions threatening to overwhelm her. Confusion had woven itself into the fabric of her existence.

"So, I go outside?" She made to rise, her movements unsteady.

"No need for that. It's too cold. I'll text him, and he'll come in. Even if the car heater is running, you'll be more comfortable inside." Joy moved to the kitchen, the tap-tap of her fingers on her phone a comforting noise.

"I'll show you to the study so you guys can have some privacy." With a wave of her hand, she beckoned Hope down a hallway to a large room lined with brimming bookshelves and modern art Joy must have painted.

"This is where Eric and I escape to relax. It's a no-kid zone." Joy gestured to a cozy corner equipped with a table, two chairs, and a mini-fridge. "There's water and soda in the fridge if you need anything."

"I'm fine. Thank you."

"May God be with you." Joy patted Hope's shoulder, then left.

Alone in the quiet, Hope focused on the air cool against her skin and the soft rug beneath her feet as she paced. Despite her sweater, her palms were clammy.

Minutes later, she knew he was there. His presence filled the room without him having to utter a word.

"Hope," he called, his voice a whisper in the quiet. When she turned, the sight of him tore her heart. His hair was disheveled, his face twisted.

"Gavin." Her voice mirrored his.

"Can we talk?"

She nodded, and he moved closer, retrieving something from his hoodie's front pouch.

It was her wisdom book. He flipped it open to display the pressed flower she'd saved from the resort. He handed her the book. "I thought you might want this."

Was he here to end things and give her back anything that reminded him of her? Her hand shook as she stared at the flower, the beginning of her journey with him. He'd borrowed her book and was returning it after three months, but why now? "Why... are you giving this back to me?"

"For the memories."

"Oh." She covered the book, afraid to look at him.

"I don't need tangible reminders of flowers and pictures to know you and I belong together." His statement had her letting out a shaky breath. "I'm in love with you, and I know you feel the same way about me—even if you don't know it."

"I do." She lifted her gaze to meet his in the ambient lighting. They needed to talk about Lucky. She needed to know Gavin's ex wasn't always going to weave in and out of their lives.

Before she could say anything, he reached out, his touch featherlight on her cheek, forcing her to swallow a breath. "Your eyes." He winced, his voice a soothing melody amid her tumultuous emotions. "You've been crying."

His concern ignited a fresh wave of pain. Tears welled up, but she forced herself to hold his gaze. Crossing her arms over her aching heart, she swallowed past a grief she'd never known. She'd only been separated from him for one day, and she'd fallen apart.

"Hey." His thumb traced a path on her cheek as he wiped away her tears. "I didn't kiss Lucky. I wouldn't betray you like that. And if you think about it, no one would when they knew you were about to join us. I didn't even know Lucky was at our house until I showed up in the kitchen."

As his words confirmed what she'd known, some of the fog vanished from her clouded mind. With his heartfelt statement resonating, she stepped into his arms, her arms finding their way around his body, and the book slipped from her hand to the rug.

Gavin's arms enveloped her, creating a cocoon of warmth and understanding. Her head found its place on his shoulder, nestled in the curve. As they held each other in silence, she breathed in the familiar scent of him, and a reassuring comprehension settled within her.

Pulling back, her eyes still blinded with tears, she spoke in a trembling voice. "I'm not used to things working out. Or having something that's truly mine. It was hard for me to see past the kiss." Past her doubts.

He traced soothing patterns on her back, a comforting presence. "I wouldn't have reacted well if I found another man kissing you either."

A shaky chuckle escaped her lips, her eyes meeting his. "That will never happen." She was certain. "You're the only one for me."

His hand moved to tuck a braid behind her ear. "Like your name"—his sincerity set his eyes aglow—"you brought hope into my life when I was at my lowest. Losing you would feel like losing myself."

"I would lose myself without you too, Gavin." She tangled her fingers in the soft hair at his nape. "I'm sorry about my reaction. It's become such a part of my nature that running always feels the safest. But it isn't. I do know that now, and I won't ever run from you again. I'll try not to run from anything, but to confront issues instead."

"The house will be ready for you by Tuesday. I don't want to rush you, though. You now have Joy as a good friend. If you'd rather stay here longer, I understand."

She might need some time to herself. But that was a decision for later. She snuggled in again, unwilling to let him go for a moment. "Can I come to work with you tomorrow?"

"I took tomorrow off, not knowing how tonight would go." He squeezed her tighter. "I thought I might need to find ways to convince you of my love."

"You've shown me enough for me to know how much you love me." Oh how her heart soared, feeling lighter! This was Gavin, not the men in her past, including her father, who had betrayed her. She needed to trust him and see him as him, not as the others.

"Tomorrow, let's focus on your future. We can look into your online schooling and work out the visa applications."

"You mean a green card?"

"Something along those lines."

Once again, she felt like she was in a film. This wasn't normal in her life. Gavin, the man she loved with all her heart, was here with her, his warm arms wrapped around her. He wanted to make things right, pursuing her and apologizing—all things she'd never experienced before in a relationship. No words could express how monumental he was in her life, but she had to try.

She cleared her throat to speak past the lump. "Before you, I felt abandoned. But you... you made me feel special. You made me feel like I belonged somewhere." Her throat tightened, and she sighed to free the pressure, overwhelmed by the reality of how he made her feel—accepted, desired, loved, safe. That was more than enough.

His eyes, shining with understanding, met hers, and his fingers traced along her lower lip until she trembled with desire.

"I love you, Hope."

"I love you..."

The rest of her words vanished when his lips captured hers, and he was kissing her with firm determination. His left hand snaked into her braids until he molded his palm to the back of her head. A spool of yearning unraveled inside her as he kissed her without any hesitation.

This kiss was like the grand finale, topping all the other times they'd kissed. It was loaded with certainty, comfort, hope, and stability.

As she kissed him, making up for lost time, emotion swept over her. Every challenge they'd faced together seemed to melt away, strengthening their bond, and her heart swelled with newfound freedom, the dark shadows of her past receding. The warmth of his embrace made her heartbeat resonate with his, their combined rhythms singing a hopeful tune.

Right now, she knew they stood on the threshold of a new journey—their love as their compass, trust as their guide, and an unspoken pledge to stand by each other through the unpredictable paths of life. Side by side. Together. Forever.

EPILOGUE

Hope adjusted her soft scarf to ensure no gap lurked between it and her jacket. The fresh scent of recent snowfall tinged the crisp night air, and the stars shone overhead. The crunch of their boots on the snow-covered sidewalk punctuated the evening's quiet, their breaths visible in the frosty air.

"I always thought snow would feel like ice." Hope confessed to the girls as she strolled alongside Joy, Liberty, and Tessa. In fascination, she waved toward the shop rooftops blanketed in a layer of snow.

"Now that it's stopped snowing, the snow will probably freeze overnight." Liberty's face caught the glow of the twinkling shop lights.

"Didn't Gavin say something about taking you skiing this weekend?" Joy adjusted her vibrant yellow snow hat over her ears against the chill.

"Last time Chad and I went skiing, I slid on an icy patch right by our cabin. I waddled around like a duck for days!" Tessa's animated retelling of her misadventure displayed such a gleeful spirit that she had Hope suppressing laughter. When all three women broke into laughter, their warm and infectious merriment resounded in the serene winter night.

Joy then added her memories of her first snow experience, explaining how she'd always had a special fondness for building snowmen.

Listening to her new friends, Hope felt her heart swell. Forming new friendships hadn't come easily to her, so this rapid acceptance and bonding was nothing short of a blessing.

After reconciling with Gavin nearly two weeks prior, Hope had accepted Joy's invitation to remain at their house for another week. The thought of living alone was still daunting. Consequently, she and Gavin had celebrated Thanksgiving with Eric and Joy's family instead. Gavin had chosen not to visit his mother's house after the incident, although he still kept in touch with her.

When Hope confessed that she felt guilty about driving a wedge between him and his mother, he had reassured her that he just needed to establish some boundaries, but it didn't mean they wouldn't visit.

Hope was somewhat relieved by this arrangement, as she wouldn't have to face Sara every day like she had while living in his childhood home.

Over the last fortnight, she'd spent nearly every day with him. He had taken her to several of his properties that were still under renovation. While he hired workers for different projects, he liked to be involved too. She'd assisted him by passing tools and hammering nails as he directed. It felt reminiscent of their time in Uganda, working on people's homes and Komo's farm together.

They had also browsed the United States citizenship website to understand the procedures Hope needed to undertake. Securing a green card could wait, but she'd applied to extend her visa. She had no definitive plans to leave the country unless Gavin was planning to go with her. She had also researched the application requirements for becoming an interior designer, planning to start in the spring once her visa situation was sorted. For now, she enjoyed perusing the websites Gavin had subscribed to for her to gather ideas. He still believed she'd work alongside him in the future, an idea that filled her with a sense of purpose and joy. She loved the flexibility of his job—the fact that he could work from home and had a capable team of employees who kept his business running smoothly.

Earlier that afternoon, Hope and Gavin had enjoyed a dinner outing with all the girls and their spouses. Joy's and Liberty's children had stayed home, being looked after by a nanny to ensure they had a proper bedtime.

After their meal, the ladies had visited Joy's art studio on Main Street. They'd wanted to appreciate the Christmas-themed art pieces local artists contributed.

Now, their destination was the park for the highly anticipated tree lighting ceremony where they'd meet with their significant others.

As they rounded a corner, the park came into view—a magical scene with twinkling fairy lights. A banner near the entrance proclaimed "Closed to the Public."

"Is this the park we're heading to?" Hope asked, wondering if they had much further to walk.

"That's the one," Joy confirmed.

So Hope pointed at the banner. As a noncitizen, she didn't want to get on the bad side of the law. "Aren't we the public?"

"Joy and her husband own the park," Tessa explained, touching Hope's shoulder.

"Well, they built it for the community," Liberty interjected. "But they do have some say about when it's closed to the public."

"We don't have much influence." Joy looped her arm through Hope's arm. "But today is an exception. Today, the park is decorated to welcome you to America. Tomorrow, we'll have the actual community tree ceremony."

Hope gasped as she entered the park. A web of fairy lights amplified its natural beauty. The trees, sporting a fresh layer of snow, shimmered under the warm light, casting an enchanting glow on their path.

"Oh my." Hope breathed out in a soft rush, her eyes widening as she took in the snow-dusted trees adorned with tiny, glowing orbs.

She was still processing what Joy had said. They were welcoming her to America. They'd done all of this for her?

"Isn't it breathtaking?" Liberty gushed.

Then deep voices came from beyond some of the evergreens and leafless trees scattered throughout the park. Turning toward the familiar faces, Hope watched the girls drift off to reunite with their spouses. Gavin must be somewhere nearby. Her heart pounded a rhythm of anticipation. How could she express her gratitude? Joy and Eric must have arranged this, but Gavin was undoubtedly involved as well.

Something cold struck her neck. Whirling around, she found Gavin laughing, already crafting another snowball in his gloved hands before darting further into the park.

His contagious laughter spurred her into action. "You're going to regret teaching me how to have snowball fights." The last time it had snowed, they'd built a snowman together, and he'd taught her how to form better snowballs for a friendly duel.

Another icy shock absorbed into her hat, trickling down into her braids as she gathered some snow, fashioning it into a substantial snowball. She gave chase, her laughter resonating throughout the park as she hurled the snowball toward him just as he ducked behind a tree.

She'd missed, but he was quick.

"I didn't show you all my tricks," he retorted, flinging another snowball her way when she bent to scoop up more snow.

She pursued him, running past their cheering friends. "Get him, Hope!"

The men were full of laughter.

Gavin halted and spun around in front of an arch decorated with delicate lights.

When she threw another snowball, it landed squarely on his chest. She brushed off her snowy gloves, then jammed her hands on her hips, and smirked. "You're lucky I have a terrible aim."

"I know that," he responded, the starry backdrop illuminating the twinkle in his blue eyes. Warmth emanated from the firepit near the arch. When she took a step toward him, he closed the remaining distance and enveloped her in his arms.

Snuggling in, she brushed her cheek against the wet patch on his coat, the residue of her snowball. "One of these days, I'll get better."

"That's the beauty of snow." He removed his gloves, stowed them in his pants pockets, then wiped her damp cheek. The playful light in his eyes darkened to something deeper, his gaze reflecting excitement and apprehension.

"Hope?" His voice was low, carried by the cool breeze. He drew a deep breath, his exhale fogging in the chilly air as he shifted his weight. The fairy lights cast a soft glow over his handsome features, highlighting his anxious smile. But why would he be anxious?

He reached into his jacket pocket and dropped to one knee in the fresh snow, revealing a small box. It had to be her ring. He'd asked for it so he could have it cleaned almost eight days ago. As he flipped it open, diamonds glinted in the twinkling light, and it looked like he'd had more done than cleaning. This ring seemed more substantial than her original one. "Is this—"

"Your ring. I wanted to keep the original, so I added slight upgrades."

A wave of joy surged through her, causing her heart to flutter.

Their friends fell into silence as if the world was holding its breath, the quiet only broken by the soft rustle of trees and the distant hum of passing cars.

"I was in a dark place when I came to Uganda." His voice trembled slightly. "I fell in love with you from the first day I saw you at the resort, and that love only grew as I got to know you."

A wave of heat rushed through her, her heart expanding as she listened to his sincere words. She pressed her gloved hand to her mouth, holding herself silent while he recounted how she'd become the highlight of his journey to Uganda. "You replaced my doubts with certainty and despair with joy. Through you, God brought me... hope."

"Gavin..." She managed the one word, her voice quivering. "You brought light into my life when all I knew was darkness." She'd believed in her bad luck until she met him. "You made me believe in love."

"I vow to cherish each second I'm lucky enough to spend with you. From this moment on, I vow to love you and value you. Will you marry me?"

"In my heart, I'm already married to you." She lifted her gloved hand to show her the ring, then remembered he had her ring in his hand. "You proposed to me already."

He slid off her glove and singled out her ring finger. "This time, I want to ask you without any conditions. Not for freedom from your family, not for an escape, and not for someone to run away with or run to, but just for us."

"Yes." Tears welled up in her eyes, sheer joy overwhelming her. With her nod and another tearful yes, he slid the meaningful ring onto her finger, its redesigned form exquisite. Then he stood up and pulled her into his arms, sealing their moment with a passionate kiss.

The park erupted with applause and cheers. When they broke apart, her tears blurred their friends' faces. Then another figure approached, clapping his hands and shouting his joy. The man's face broke into a wide smile that displayed a daunting familiarity as he extended his hand toward Hope. "Congratulations! I'm Jeremy, Gavin's big brother."

"Little brother," Gavin corrected, his tone playful. "Being the big brother comes with a lot of responsibilities."

"I'm the responsible one. That makes me the big brother." Jeremy's eyes twinkled as he shook Hope's hand. He resembled Gavin in a way, though his photos didn't do him justice. "It's great to meet you."

"It's a pleasure to meet you too." But she had no memory of Gavin mentioning his brother would be coming into town before Christmastime.

"Jeremy has a knack for showing up late to family events." Gavin chided his brother. "He should have been here hours ago, but he'd just arrived from the airport a few minutes before you girls got to the park. I had to stall off the proposal with a snowball fight so I'd be sure he could make it here."

So he'd flown here specifically to witness their engagement? She blinked back fresh tears. "Thanks for coming."

"I wouldn't have missed this for the world." Jeremy gestured to her ring. "I'm staying at Gavin's tonight. Would you care to join us for breakfast?"

"Jeremy will be cooking, by the way," Gavin said, and Jeremy argued, claiming Gavin had better culinary skills.

Hope smiled. Perhaps she'd show up early and cook instead. "I'm looking forward to breakfast."

"And I'm looking forward to getting to know you." Jeremy scooped her into a hug and pressed his lips to her ear. "Welcome to the family, sis."

Oh! Her heart brimming with joy, Hope squeezed him tight and whispered back her thanks.

"Congratulations, big brother." Jeremy released her and slapped Gavin's back, his voice husky.

The girls then stepped forward to hug and congratulate Hope while the guys surrounded Gavin, patting him on the back and congratulating him.

"When's the wedding?" Tessa asked.

"Probably soon." She and Gavin had discussed a spring wedding, and while she knew the date, she and Gavin hadn't discussed whether to tell anyone yet or not.

Gavin was answering the same question amid the guys' chatter. "We'll talk, but maybe sometime in the spring." Then he crossed his arms and nodded to his brother. "Jeremy, as the best man?"

"Again?" Jeremy teased.

"Yes, *again*." Gavin rolled his eyes. "Surprisingly, I still haven't gotten a better brother to replace you. So, you'll need to start setting some time aside. And maybe our wedding will be a good excuse for you to get back into dating."

With the soft glow of twinkling lights enveloping them and the melodic backdrop of their friends' laughter and chatter, Hope felt cocooned in one of those shake-up globes Gavin had bought her from Main Street. But this one sprinkled the scene in sheer joy. The overwhelming emotion pulsed within her as her gaze swept over her close-knit circle: her friends, her fiancé, and her soon-to-be brother-in-law.

While she had a journey ahead to win Gavin's parents' hearts, she was grounded in the understanding that life wasn't always picture-perfect. It was okay not to be embraced by everyone as long as she had true friends she could trust and love.

More than anything, with Gavin, she had discovered home. He'd shown her that the moments she'd considered unlucky were blessings in disguise. With this revelation, she vowed never to dwell on her "unlucky" days, lest she miss the blessings right before her, blessings like true love and true friendship that all those "unlucky" days had led her to.

-THE END-

Have you read the first book in the Caregiver Series? If not, start with The Doctor's Nanny

NEXT IS JEREMY AND Zuri's story in Yours Temporarily. A new Spin off series: The Office Heartthrobs

Read Logan and Serafina's story in The Billionaires' Reunion Logan is the CEO of Stone enterprises, and He's also featured in The Office Heartthrobs Series

Join my Insider Group and get an exclusive Novella, THE THERAPIST'S NEIGHBOR

Join Rose's Facebook group and connect with her and other readers.

ROSE (This is by far the best way to stay in touch with me! I share details about future releases, work in progress, sneak peak chapters before I mention them anywhere else.

Listen to my books for free on YOUTUBE

Stay connected with Rose Fresquez

Bookbub

Goodreads

Next in the Spin off Series!
Yours Temporarily

He needs a fake fiance; she needs business funds. Can genuine feelings emerge from their pretend relationship?

Jeremy Kress means business when it comes to his job, as COO, and his strict work ethic hasn't made him popular with his employees. But they aren't the worst of his problems. If he can't find a fake fiancée to accompany him to his brother's wedding, then his meddling mother will guilt him into another disastrous relationship.

Cooking blogger Zuri Reed just moved into town for a chance to reconnect with her brother, even if he does complain an awful lot about his boss. She's excited to meet his coworkers at a party he's hosting—until she accidentally swings a door into his disapproving boss's face.

Desperate to make amends and keep from complicating things for her brother, Zuri brings Jeremy lunch. Yet the simple gesture of apology spirals into her becoming his pretend fiancée! As sparks ignite, can they deny the growing attraction?

A NOTE FROM THE AUTHOR

Thank you for reading *The Realtor's Attendant.* The last stand-alone book in the Caregiver Series. Come back and visit some of your favorite characters in the spin-off series. The Billionaires' Reunion and The Office Heartthrob Series.

It's always a blessing to meet new readers. And to those who have read all my stories, thanks for giving me another chance and for your reviews and notes of encouragement.

I can never forget to thank God who enables me to create these stories. Thank you Lord!

You can connect with Rose on Facebook, website rosefresquezbooks.com or email her at rjfresquez@gmail.com

ABOUT THE AUTHOR

Rose Fresquez is the author of the Buchanan -Firefighter series, Romance in the Rockies, The caregiver series, The Billionaires' Re-union Series and The Office Heartthrob series, Two short stories and two family devotionals. I'm always adding new series, so connect with me so you don't miss any updates.

Rose is married and a proud mother of four amazing kids. She loves to sing praises to God. When she's not busy taking care of her family, she's writing.